Tuck's Landing

Black Dress Trilogy Volume 2

by

Kenneth James Taylor

TELEMACHUS PRESS

TUCK'S LANDING: BLACK DRESS TRILOGY VOLUME TWO

Cover Designed by Telemachus Press, LLC

Cover Art:
Copyright © iStockphoto/602068
Copyright © iStockphoto/23964277

Published by Telemachus Press, LLC
http://www.telemachuspress.com

Visit the author website:
http://www.kennethjamestaylor.com

ISBN: 978-1-939337-80-1 (eBook)
ISBN: 978-1-939927-40-8 (Paperback)

Version 2013.06.18

Printed in the United States of America

10 9 8 7 6 5 4 3 2 1

Black Dress Trilogy contains no obscenity or foul language. However, it does contain violence as might have occurred during the 1836 Texas Revolution. The trilogy is presented in the following three volumes:

Volume 1: Runaway Fever

Molly McCracken's husband does not return from the war. She flees unprepared with her beloved sister from the onslaught of the 1836 invasion of Texas. Along the boggy road to safety her friends and neighbors bury their loved ones where they fall. Attempting to save her niece, she risks it all and fails. Her life spins out of control and her survival becomes uncertain until a Ranger tries to help.

Volume 2: Tuck's Landing

Molly McCracken rebuilds her life and meets a colorful new friend who sooths the agony of her loss. Determined to find her niece she struggles to keep from falling in love with the man who saved her life during the war. She knows she must learn to fight. Then an altercation lands her in the most dangerous town in Texas where she cleverly improves the lives of the innocent children she encounters.

Volume 3: Call of the Grackle

Molly McCracken confronts a corrupt madam, outsmarts a crooked store owner, and pursues a gang of infamous smugglers to free those in bondage. Then a mysterious bit of information sweeps her into the wilderness and plunges her into a conflict that binds her to her soul mate. Will she follow her heart and betroth herself to the man she loves or will she continue to search for her missing husband?

TUCK'S LANDING SYNOPSIS

Molly McCracken has nothing to return to after the Texas Revolution. Whisked off to a place of safety called Tuck's Landing she meets a colorful new friend who helps heal the pain of loss the war has left in her agonized soul. She begins to rebuild her life. Determined to locate and rescue her lost niece she struggles against the temptation to fall in love with the man who saved her. Contrary to her deepest instincts she knows she must learn to fight. As she acquires the skills she needs she discovers her destiny. Then an unexpected altercation puts her to the test and launches her on a campaign to find her niece. Drawn into a fray of corruption, debauchery, and slavery, the weight of judgment is cast upon her shoulders and the power of life and death is placed in her hands. Landing in the most dangerous town in Texas, she finds that her clever interventions and unyielding kindness will change forever the lives of the innocent children she encounters.

Table of Contents

MAP OF THE BLACK DRESS TRILOGY

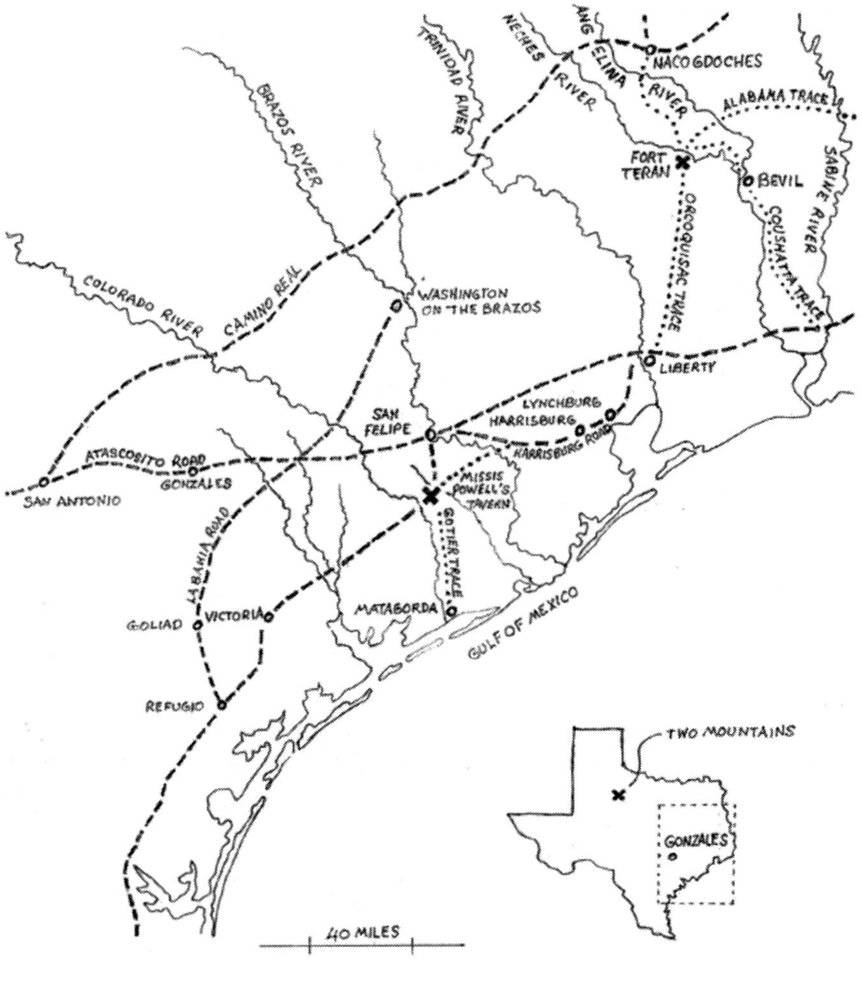

TRILOGY CHARACTERS

Adama: fictitious middle-aged former slave woman

Alsey: fictitious Texas Ranger serving under Captain Boots Williams

Arnwine: fictitious doctor in San Antonio who attends Texas Rangers wounded in skirmishes

Banish: fictitious owner of a mercantile in Nacogdoches, and a competitor of Hoxie's General Mercantile

Benson, Maria and five boys: fictitious secondary character, flees with Molly and other refugees from Santa Anna and re-emerges in the story while returning to Gonzales

Biladeau, Christiana: fictitious representative of Bildad from the *Book of Job*, encounters Molly at Missis Powell's Tavern

Buffalo Head: fictitious secondary character of Mexican-Indian decent, trader, smuggler, ally of Santa Anna, known by Texas settlers as a land pirate, outlaw or bandit

Carrigan, Emily, husband Innis, and daughter Amy: fictitious character, Emily is Molly's sister, and flees with her and other refugees from the invading army of Santa Anna

Casey, Colonel Martin: fictitious Indian agent for the Republic of Texas

Córdova, Vicente: District Prosecutor for District of Nacogdoches

Doyle: fictitious Texas Ranger serving under Captain Boots Williams

Fannin, Commander: defeated by the Garza rancheros in the area of Goliad, he was again defeated by General Urrea at Coleto Creek, and was executed with the remainder of his forces at the presidio in Goliad on Palm Sunday

Folkvar, Klaus: fictitious ferryboat operator for Aunt Ruthie at Tuck's Landing

Garza rancheros: allied with Santa Anna, they banded together against Commander Fannin and his forces in the area of Goliad

Hamadi: former slave, husband to Adama, and is captured by John A. Murrell

Hodge, Arlan: fictitious Texas Ranger assigned to Fort Casey near Nacogdoches, formerly rode with Captain Boots Williams

Hort, Henry: fictitious neighbor to Molly, flees with her and other refugees from Santa Anna, and re-emerges in the story while returning to Gonzales

Houston, General Samuel: leads Texan army against the invading army of Santa Anna, and orders Gonzales burned

Hoxie, Dugan, Mrs. Hoxie, and son Jeffery: fictitious owners and operators of Hoxie's General Mercantile in Nacogdoches

Justin: fictitious farmhand for Aunt Ruthie at Tuck's Landing

Karnes, Colonel: stationed in San Antonio, commands the Texas Rangers in the southwest territories, and is Captain Boots Williams' superior officer

King Ghezo of Dahomey: deposes Adama's royal family in Africa and sells her into slavery

LaMonte, Herman, and Madam Fredericka: fictitious plantation owners in Louisiana where Molly's sister, Emily, worked as a seamstress

Manuel: farmhand for Aunt Ruthie at Tuck's Landing

McClellan, Asa: Texas Ranger serving under Captain Boots Williams

McCracken, Emmet: husband of Molly McCracken

McCracken, Molly: main character and diary writer who flees with other refugees from the invading army of Santa Anna

Milliken: fictitious plantation from which Adama and Hadami obtain freedom

Mora, Juan: Judge for the District of Nacogdoches

Murrell, John A.: historic criminal and slave smuggler

Noah: fictitious Texas Ranger serving under Captain Boots Williams

Nomusha: fictitious adolescent slave and victim of slave theft

Owen, Margaret, children Callie and Toby: fictitious characters dispossessed by war, Margaret is forced into prostitution, and her children are abandoned

Pallet, Sam: fictitious de facto owner of Fort Teran

Phipps, Pastor Eli: fictitious circuit preacher representative of Eliphaz from the *Book of Job*, encounters Molly in San Felipe

Powell, Missis: owns tavern serving travelers at a southern Texas crossroad, assists Molly and her family when they are in distress

Santa Anna: President of Mexico, attempts to drive American settlers out of Texas by leading invasion

Sarah: fictitious housemaid serving the LaMonte plantation

Santo Muerte: Saint of Death worshiped in parts of Texas

Schauble, Titus and Annie: fictitious elderly owners of mercantile in Gonzales before it is burned, they flee with Molly and other refugees from Santa Anna

Susser, Elli-Lou, and husband Franklin: fictitious representative of Elihu from the *Book of Job*, neighbor and close friend of Molly, flees with her and other refugees from Santa Anna, and re-emerges in story while returning to Gonzales

Thaxton, Zacharias: fictitious Texas Ranger serving under Captain Boots Williams

Timble, R.C.: Chief Surveyor, Bexar District, San Antonio

Travis, Colonel: writes letter asking for help to defend the Alamo

Tuck, Aunt Ruthie, and deceased husband Foster: fictitious owner and manager of Tuck's Landing, a boarding house and ferryboat crossing at the Trinidad River near Liberty, Texas, she is the aunt of Captain Boots Williams

Uncle Elmer: fictitious relative of Elli-Lou Susser

Uriel: canonical Archangel prior to exclusion from veneration in AD 745, formerly considered one of the Archangels of the four winds including Gabriel, Michael, and Raphael

Urrea, General: served Santa Anna, invaded southern Texas and the coast

Williams, Avery and Elizabeth: fictitious father and mother of Captain Boots Williams, both deceased, Elizabeth was sister of Aunt Ruthie Tuck

Williams, Captain Boots: fictitious main character, born Francis Jacob Williams, Surveyor, Texas Ranger, and Aunt Ruthie's nephew

Xavier: fictitious old man and neighbor of Molly, flees from Santa Anna with his Anglo American daughter-in-law, Maudie, toddler grandson, and other refugees, and then re-emerges in the story when he returns to Gonzales

Zsohar, Padre: fictitious representation of Zophar from the *Book of Job*, encounters Molly in Matagorda

TRILOGY PLACES

Alabama Trace: no longer exists, located in southeast Texas, it was a native trail west-east connecting Fort Teran to Louisiana

Atascosito: west-east bound road connecting San Antonio, San Felipe, Liberty and Louisiana, roughly the route of present day Highway 10

Bevil: Texan settlement south of Fort Teran and located at the mouth of the Angelina River, presently submerged as a result of water conservation

Camino Real: southwest-northeast bound road connecting Mexico to Laredo, San Antonio, Nacogdoches, and Louisiana

Coushatta Trace: exists only in part today, originally located in southeast Texas, a native trail used by the Coushatta Indians to trade with Mexico, north-south bound, it connected the Sabine River to Bevil, Fort Teran, and Nacogdoches, then extended westward to become the La Bahia Road

Fort Casey: fictitious center of Indian Affairs located near Nacogdoches

Fort Teran: no longer exists, originally established to stop slave smugglers, built by General Terán from Mexico during his inspection of Texas in 1828, located along the Kisatchie Wold on the Neches River; it is also the shallow rock bottom fording place for the Orcoquisac Trace, Coushatta Trace, and the Alabama Trace, and was frequently used by Native Americans, traders, and smugglers

Gotier Trace: (Gōćhər Trace) trail north-south, connecting San Felipe with Matagorda

Harrisburg: destroyed by Santa Anna and becomes present day site of Houston Texas

Harrisburg Road: east-west bound road connecting San Felipe, Harrisburg, Lynchburg, and Liberty

Kisatchie Wold: ridge extending from the Mississippi floodplain to the Rio Grande valley and running roughly east and west and parallel to the Gulf of Mexico, it slopes gradually northward up to 400-450 feet above sea level and then drops off sharply, deflecting rivers, including the Neches River, eastward along its northern edge

La Bahia: road connecting Mexico north-south to Victoria, Goliad, then crossing the Atascosito Road and connecting to Washington-on-the-Brazos, Cole's Settlement, and then northeast to Nacogdoches

La Calle del Norte: road north out of Nacogdoches

La Casa Piedra: commercial building built in 1779 of quarried iron ore stone, including a two-story covered porch, and two stone chimneys, located in Nacogdoches

Neches River: east Texas river which flows generally south to the Gulf of Mexico, deflected east at Kisatchie Wold, which becomes the location of Fort Teran, especially the fording place where multiple native trails merge together, used by smugglers during the 1800s

Orcoquisac Trace: no longer exists, formerly a native trail north-south connecting Liberty to Fort Teran

Trinidad River: renamed Trinity River

Tuck's Landing: fictitious ferryboat crossing along the Atascosito Road at the Trinidad (Trinity) River

Two Mountains: fictitious Comanche village located on the Brazos River in northwest Texas, present day location is called Double Mountain

TRILOGY WORDS AND PHRASES

alcalde: the mayor of a community (Spanish)

acetate of lead: also called sugar lead, causes lead poisoning, a neurotoxin formerly used in the 1700s and 1800s as a sweetener, a fixative for dye, and as a treatment for cholera

bear oil: rendered from bear fat, preferred by Texas settlers in the 1800s as a shortening, binder, or additive in the preparation of breads and pastries

bismuth: since the late 1700s this brittle elemental metal, 86% dense as lead and resembling arsenic, but with low toxicity, is commonly used in colloidal subsalicylate form to treat nausea, heartburn, indigestion, upset stomach, and diarrhea

Brown Bess: surplus Napoleonic muzzle-loading rifle used by the Mexican army during the invasion of Texas by Santa Anna

buckboard: four-wheeled carriage with one or more seats and plank floor-boards for cargo

calomel: mercurous chloride, a cathartic used widely from the 1700s until the 1900s, and commonly believed to expel infection from the body by inducing diarrhea

carryall: 1800s slang for a simple carriage, lightweight, four-seats with or without a top, and capable of being drawn by a single horse

catarrh: inflammation of the nose and throat

cholera: plague-like outbreaks of this disease occurred world-wide until 1855 when a bacterium was isolated and discovered to be transmitted through contaminated water, infecting the small intestine, causing profuse diarrhea and vomiting of fishy smelling fluid frequently referred to as rice water, causing rapid loss of bodily fluid, severe dehydration, wrinkled bluish-gray skin, and usually but not always resulting in death

collywobbles: intestinal disorder, bellyache, also 1800s slang for cholera

coneflower: Echinacea

dogtrot: unique Texas building design joining together two cabins in close proximity with a common roof, porch and breezeway

dyspepsia: indigestion

escopeta: muzzle-loading shotgun (Spanish)

exfluncticate: 1800s slang which means to utterly destroy

freebooter: 1800s slang referring to a smuggler

grippe: influenza

hames: part of a harness, a two piece device which encircles a horse's neck for the attachment of reins

laudanum: tincture of opium used as 1800s treatment for various ailments

Mystic Clan: historic criminal organization founded by John A. Murrell

Paterson: first mass produced revolving pistol produced by Samuel Colt in Paterson New Jersey 1836

poultice: cataplasm made of heated cloth and saturated with various types and mixtures of medication and applied to inflamed area of body

pull foot: 1800s slang to leave in a hurry

repeater: see Paterson

rice water: see cholera

root hog or die: 1800s slang meaning to run for your life

sarsaparilla: popular, 1800s beverage similar to root beer, made from the root of the Sassafras albidum

sin-ta-Crockett: 1800s slang, which means behavior causing shame to Davy Crockett

sockdolager: 1800s slang for a sluggard or brawler

sugar lead: see acetate of lead

tasso: dried meat without salt, preservatives, or flavor

Vesuvian: early version of a common stick match

Wapato: edible aquatic plant, Sagittaria, also called Arrowhead

whooping cough: also called pertussis, typically occurring with infants and toddlers; the first stage is mild coughing; the catarrhal stage includes coughing fits followed by a high-pitch sound, vomiting, subconjunctival hemorrhage, fractured ribs, hernia, vertebral artery dissection, and unconsciousness; the paroxysmal stage includes spasms and seizures; usually not fatal when proper care and treatment is administered

TRILOGY ACKNOWLEDGEMENTS

To my lovely wife, Marilyn, I couldn't ask for a better partner. You are the love of my youth, the love of my life, my soul mate, and my best friend. I don't think anyone could write a story about a soul mate, unless they actually have one. While I poured through mountains of treatises, historical writings, diaries, and letters to gather information for the story, you were the only one who believed I could do it. You never stopped encouraging me. But that wasn't all, you also sat patiently for hours, listening to me read and re-read my rough manuscript to you. Your comments and insights helped bring my characters to life, and helped me find my voice. I couldn't have done it without you.

To my favorite daughter-in-law, Deborah, (my only daughter-in-law) I never would have known how much I needed your help if you hadn't come over to listen to my long, long, reading sessions. I wouldn't have gotten any of those Spanish phrases right, and I would have flubbed some of the most important elements in the story. Your inner beauty has spilled over onto my pages. My readers and I are enriched because of it. Your input has been invaluable.

To my father, I solemnly declare to you my dependence. It is my deepest desire to live at the center of your will, doing that which you've laid before me, and fulfilling your purpose. You've provided for the needs of my family, and have kept us safe. Thank You. You've inspired words which please you. I've never been so thrilled to go to work, as I have since you've given me the honor of working in collaboration with you. I will love you and serve you with all my heart and with all my soul, all the days of my life, and then I will be satisfied.

To the Romance Writers of America, thanks, it's been almost twenty years, and I wasn't a member for very long, but the skills you gave me influence my writing today. Not only did I learn how to create mystery, and hook the reader, but I also gained an understanding of romance. Simply stated, romance is life. The story of everyone's life includes romance, more or less. Without it there is usually no story to tell, at least, no meaningful story that folks want to read. So, thanks again, Romance Writers of American. You brought my historical fiction to life by teaching me how to wrap it around an intriguing romance.

This work is lovingly dedicated to my children Matthew and Angela, and their families.

FORWARD TO THE BLACK DRESS TRILOGY

The ***Runaway and Scrapes*** occurred during the Texas Revolution in 1836. The Runaway represents the flight of Texan refugees from Santa Anna and his advancing army to the safety of the United States. The Scrapes represent military skirmishes, which occurred during the war. The Runaway might be the most dramatic, and the most overlooked disaster in American history. To put the event into perspective, imagine that an army invaded America today, and that army had the same proportion to our modern population as Santa Anna had to Texas in 1836. The army in this scenario would number about 70 million. We wouldn't have much of a chance, would we? Those are the odds the Texans faced.

Add genocide to my scenario. If an army of 70 million experienced, high tech soldiers swept across America today, killing everyone, men and women, young and old, destroying every city, and burning every home, we would be wiped off the face of the earth, even if we made a stand against them. The world would be appalled. Is it any wonder that the settlers in 1836 Texas ran for their lives? Shouldn't we be appalled? This tragedy could be the worst disaster ever seen on American soil. That is why I am telling the story of the Runaway.

The loss of life during the Runaway dwarfed the combined losses at the Alamo and Goliad, but the full extent will never be known. While General Houston and the fledgling Republic of Texas were keeping records of their skirmishes (Scrapes) with Santa Anna and his troops, the settlers in the Runaway were not keeping records, except for a few letters and diary entries, which exist today. The refugees were mostly women, children, and the infirm. Taken by surprise, they fled with little or no provisions for the cold, wet, and unsanitary conditions they would face. Criminals found them to be easy prey. As a result, many refugees died along the way to Louisiana. They were buried where they fell, beside the roads they had been traveling on. Using the stories written by those who survived, I've tried to portray what it was like to be a settler, running for their life. From these meager beginnings arose some of the fiercest fighters the world has ever seen, the Texas Rangers.

The Rangers began to emerge before Santa Anna invaded Texas. He'd withdrawn his support from the frontier. Outposts, which were designed to protect the frontier from incursion and depredation, were abandoned. Mexican troops were called away, and the frontier was left defenseless. This was the first sign Santa Anna gave that he wanted Americans to leave Texas. For their own protection the settlers were forced to band together, and from those first defenders emerged the Texas Rangers. The conclusion of the revolution established a need for a standing army to defend the Republic, and like state policemen on steroids, the Rangers filled that need. To this very day they continue to protect Texas. Their story cannot be told without including the story of the first mass produced revolver.

The balance of power had to change or the Republic of Texas would not be able to stand on its own. Fearing that the United States intended to annex Texas, Santa Anna had attempted to drive all the American settlers out. Mexican traders and landowners in Texas aligned themselves with him, and supported his military ambition. Native American tribes viewed Santa Anna's invasion as an opportunity to claim territory from the settlers for themselves. Their interest in Texas can be seen in negotiations they had with Mexico as early as the 1820s. At best the balance of power was about equal between three main struggling forces, American settlers, Mexicans, and natives. Throw in the freebooters and boarder ruffians, who sought refuge from the reach of United States law, include the depredations committed by raiding parties, and the sovereignty of the Republic became precarious. That is, until Samuel Colt invented a five shot repeating pistol called the Paterson.

One of the difficulties with defending the Republic was the weapons they used. A muzzle-loading rifle could not be fired from horseback because of its large size and weight. Prior to the introduction of the Paterson revolver, the Rangers responded to depredations by first pursuing their enemies, and then dismounting to fire their muzzle-loaders. They only had one shot, and it took too long to reload. A mounted Native American could shoot up to twelve arrows point-blank into a Ranger before he could reload his rifle. If the Ranger's enemies were numerous, his chances of success were greatly diminished. When the Paterson revolvers were introduced, the Rangers could ride into a skirmish with two revolvers each, firing ten shots while mounted atop their horses, and they could reload without dismounting. The balance of power changed at that point in favor of the Republic, and that is the point where Molly McCracken's story begins.

Early writings have revealed that many Native Americans coexisted with Texan settlers before the revolution. Only a few tribes were aggressive, and those were also the largest tribes. What I've seen in those writings was not the stereotypical Native American, as seen on television or in the movies. I've attempted to express this truth in my writing. Granted, their attire and their behavior differed from that of the settlers, but that's what makes the story colorful and interesting. I will show things about Native American life, which the reader has never seen in word before. Molly McCracken's trouble is caused by the life and times of 1836 Texas, rather than Native American depredations. Her troubles grieve her, and like Job, her troubles arouse within her an age old question.

Volumes have been written about Job. I've read some of them, and I've read the *Book of Job* several times. It explores life's most difficult questions. Those who survived the Runaway were probably asking themselves those same questions. When I noticed the similarity between Job and Molly McCracken, I decided to winnow the book down to its essence, and include the essence in Molly's story.

First, I searched for period names, which sounded like the names of Job's accusers. Eliphaz became Pastor Eli Phipps, Bildad became Christiana Biladeau, Zophar became Padre Zsohar, and Elihu became Elli-Lou Susser.

Pastor Phipps quotes Eliphaz to condemn Molly and the refugees traveling with her. He believes they are wicked and have been punished and driven out of their homes due to their wickedness. He tells them that if they confess their wickedness they will be restored.

Christiana Biladeau is more interested in her views about suffering than she is in the actual suffering of those around her. She accuses Molly of complaining, believing that she should rather be examining her relationship with her Creator.

Padre Zsohar's opinions not only condemn Molly, but they express the general feelings of period Hispanics toward the Americano. Suggesting that God will extract restitution from all Americanos, he implies that restitution will also be extracted from Molly. She will have to pay for her wickedness. Since Catholicism was the official religion of Mexico at that time, and was imposed on Texas, I've portrayed Molly as a Catholic.

Elli-Lou Susser accuses Molly of questioning the character of the Almighty. She believes that Molly should accept her trouble, and search for what the Almighty wants her to learn from it.

Elli-Lou's husband, Franklin, offers a dissertation on why the innocent suffer, based on his battlefield experience when he was visited by the archangel Uriel.

Angelology isn't included in literature much anymore, and a story about Catholicism in Texas probably shouldn't exclude Angelology. It's part of the biblical canon. The archangels of the four winds were Gabriel, Michael, Raphael, and Uriel. The reader might not have heard of Uriel. That's because a tendency to worship angels caused Uriel to be removed from the Church's veneration in AD 745. Some have portrayed Uriel as the angel of death. I found this portrayal particularly intriguing, because in south Texas there exists among some Catholics a tradition of venerating a being they call Santo Muerte, the Saint of Death. It is rumored that Santo Muerte is actually worshiped in some places. Is it possible that Santo Muerte is Uriel? Molly McCracken's story explores this possibility.

PREFACE TO THE BLACK DRESS TRILOGY

Black Dress is historical fiction, which is a contrived story set in historical fact. Though I've identified this story as fiction, the reader needs to understand that it connects together all the bits of truth and historical reality I could weave in. There is no other way to tell the story of the Runaway. Not enough is known. I've tried to make it an interesting read, and as accurate as possible, but I expect to get comments about the story not being right or not happening a certain way. That's why I've identified it as fiction. Others might complain about the way I write dialogue, because folks didn't talk in 1836 south Texas the way I wrote dialogue. I've read period lingua franca, and most readers wouldn't tolerate it.

Molly McCracken is a fictitious character. Her story is inspired by accounts of depredations, which occurred prior and during the invasion of Texas by Santa Anna. She flees from Gonzales before it is burned in 1836. The town folks, their farms, and the mercantile are also fictitious. Their names and hers are not intended to imply or resemble any historical persons.

The scouts, soldiers, and General Houston's arrival at Molly McCracken's camp is fictitious. Though we know that something similar actually occurred, the explanation Houston offers to the town folks concerning his abandonment of the Alamo and retreat from Gonzales is also fictitious. Though I've tried to create a scene as historically accurate as possible, the exact events and words spoken will never be known. Based on my studies of Houston's character and accomplishments, I've written what I thought he might have said, and how I thought the town folks would have responded.

Molly's flight from Santa Anna is based on my own inspection of the approximate route taken during the Runaway. Conditions and incidents along the way are taken directly from the accounts of those who survived, and are embellished to fit her story.

Molly arrives in San Felipe before it is burned. I've attempted to describe period building construction as accurately as possible, but I've embellished the layout of the settlement to fit the story.

Molly visits Missis Powell's Tavern before it is burned by General Urrea. I don't know what the establishment looked like, and little is known about Missis Powell. I created buildings which fit the period. In this story Missis Powell is a fictitious character. She is real in name only. I gave her an appearance, personality, and words, which fit both history and the story.

The next settlement Molly visits is Matagorda. I created what I thought a small, industrial seaport would look like in 1836. The characters who occur there, and those from there, are fictitious, and are not intended to resemble anyone.

Buffalo Head and his gang of Comancheros are fictitious, but their crimes are based on actual historical accounts.

The thicket along Gotier Trace is fictitious, and is inspired by my own experience in the Big Thicket.

The cabin on Gotier Trace and the Rangers using it are fictitious, but created for the story to be similar to historical accounts. Captain Boots Williams is a combination of several noteworthy Texas Rangers, and is not intended to resemble anyone in particular.

Tuck's Landing is fictitious. Though it reflects period construction, it is not intended to resemble anything in history. The characters at Tuck's Landing are fictitious. The owner, the owner's family and all relatives are fictitious. Their names are not intended to resemble anyone from that or any period.

The settlement of Liberty is real, but my description is fictitious. The festival, the town folks, and the businesses are also fictitious.

Fort Teran was real, no longer exists, and is embellished to fit the story. Sam Pallet is fictitious. His appearance, the things he says, and any implications the reader might derive concerning him are fictitious. His character was created to fit the story.

John Murrell was a real criminal, and the Mystic Clan was a real criminal organization. I've tried to incorporate historical facts concerning him and his clan into the story. His appearance is derived from historical accounts. Nomusha, Hamadi, and Adama are fictitious victims of the mystic clan. Their story is inspired by crimes, which Murrell actually committed.

The appearance and behavior of Native American tribes residing in Texas in 1836 are derived from period descriptions, and embellished to fit the story. Incidents involving Native Americans, which occur in the story, are also taken directly from those same descriptions and embellished.

The reader should find Nacogdoches an interesting place to visit in word. My book club liked Nacogdoches so much they wanted the main characters to return and make it their home. The businesses and business owners, as described, are fictitious. Their names are not intended to resemble anyone. La Casa Piedra is real, and I've tried to include it accurately in the story. Vicente Córdova and Juan Mora are real historical characters in name only. Their physical description, mannerisms, and the words they say are fictitious, but are intended to reflect what I think they might have said and done.

The Owen farm and characters are fictitious, and are not intended to resemble anyone or anything.

Fort Casey, Colonel Martin Casey, and the Rangers at Fort Casey are fictitious and are not intended to resemble anyplace or anyone, but are inspired by period events.

The Cherokee village and the Comanche village are fictitious villages set in real places. I've tried to depict living conditions, behavior, and attire as accurately as possible based on period accounts.

The depictions of the hostel and infirmary in San Antonio are fictitious. Doctor Arnwine is fictitious. Colonel Karnes and R. C. Timble are real historical characters, but their role in the story is fictitious. The things they are supposed to have said were created to fit the story.

The infirmary in Lynchburg is fictitious.

Plantations owned by Milliken, and owned by LaMonte are fictitious. Their names are not intended to resemble anyone.

TUCK'S LANDING

Black Dress Trilogy Volume 2

PROLOGUE: SUNDAY

MOM CALLED ME after church and told me she was ready to go back to Grandma's bungalow in Gonzales and finish packing her belongings. Her voice sounded more cheerful than yesterday, so I assumed that she was adjusting to her mother's passing. Grandma had been ninety-five. Climbing into the moving van, my wife and I drove over to pick her up and take her out for dinner before driving all the way to Gonzales from San Antonio. We took her to the SOUPER!SALAD! Mom's favorite.

Once inside I asked Mom how church was, and she implied that it was the same as usual. Jokingly I said, "Too bad Pastor Eli Phipps isn't around to light a fire under your congregation."

Mom asked, "You mean the one that accused Molly and all those other refugees in San Felipe of being wicked, and said that's why Santa Anna drove them off and burned their farms? His kind is a thing of the past."

"There's still a few like him around," I continued. "And how about Padre Zsohar? He could get everyone fired up, couldn't he?"

Mom asked, "Wasn't he the one in Matagorda who accused Molly of inhumanity and exploitation? I think he'd get a fire going all right, and then folks would grab him by his cassock and toss him right into it."

"Mom!" my wife gasped. "That doesn't sound like you!"

"Well, I'm not Catholic," Mom added.

Mom was feisty for her seventies. I'll give her that. Folding my arms I said, "You'd be surprised how much you have in common with the

Catholics. Remember Christiana Biladeau? Do you know anyone like her in your church? The one who said Molly was dysfunctional."

Mom raised her thin gray eyebrows, lowered her chin and admitted, "Unfortunately I do. But I can't condemn her for it. I'd be just like her if I did a thing like that. We're all more or less dysfunctional in different ways you know." Mom looked up at me, shook her head and asked, "Do you think Padre Zsohar knew he was being used as a diversion by that alcalde in Matagorda?"

"His brother?" I wondered.

"Yes, I guess he was his brother wasn't he?" Mom countered.

Pursing my lips, I thought about it for a moment and then said, "We know the alcalde lied about the ship in Matagorda Bay. It was a Mexican warship and not the Independence. He must have known that the laborers at the loading dock were Comancheros, and they were smuggling supplies to General Urrea. But I don't think Padre Zsohar knew he was being used as a diversion. I didn't care for what he said to Molly either, but he seemed pretty genuine other than that."

"It made me so sad," Mom hung her head as she swished a forkful of salad in a puddle of ranch dressing. "I was still thinking about it when I woke up this morning … Son," Mom said, "when I read that Innis was killed in that ambush, I didn't want to read the diary anymore. I felt bad for Molly, because she lost her beloved sister, Emily, to cholera, practically dying in her arms, and then her brother-in-law was killed in that ambush. It was too much for me."

"Molly was lucky to be alive," I added. "It's a wonder anyone survived the runaway when Santa Anna tried to drive everyone out of Texas."

My wife added, "After Molly was captured by the Comancheros she found her niece, Amy. That was a good thing."

Nodding, Mom noted, "But then Amy was traded to the Kiowa for nothing more than a couple of horses."

"But she's still alive," my wife contended.

"Yes," Mom continued. "We know she's alive, but where and for how long?"

"Remember that bizarre nightmare Molly had?" my wife asked. "First she was a slave on a slave ship. Then she faced a Comanchero in a boudoir. Then she had to crawl through a thicket and found the beautiful woman in white holding a chalice in one hand and Amy under her other arm. And right after that Molly escaped from the Comancheros by crawling through a real thicket. I think she had a premonition about the thicket, and I think she had a premonition about Amy. I think she will find her and rescue her. I just don't know how it's going to happen. When Molly crawled through all those tunnels in the thicket I expected her to find the beautiful woman again, but she didn't find her. I wonder who that woman was anyway."

"She can't be real," I protested. "You're talking like she's real or something, that beautiful woman in white. Things like that don't really happen. They can't be real. It was just a dream. Molly had a bad dream. She wrote about it in her diary, and then we read about it. That's all."

"Don't be such a spoilsport." My wife jabbed at me with her fork. "We're having fun here. It's a girl thing. So, don't spoil it!"

"Suit yourself," I said, and shoved a spoonful of cream of broccoli soup into my mouth to keep it from saying anything else.

Again she turned to my mom, and said, "I think Molly likes Mister Boots."

At this my mom produced her second smile of the day and replied, "I think Mister Boots likes Molly, too. And he would be a good catch for her. He's educated, a surveyor, and a Texas Ranger."

"But she's married to Emmet," my wife admonished Mom.

"Emmet's dead," Mom speculated. "Everyone knows it and now she has Boots, and he's a handsome, eligible man."

"A tall and handsome Texas Ranger," my wife added.

"Hey!" I tried to mumble at her, but it came out all gurgly with cream of broccoli soup. Swallowing, I wasn't feeling very fond of the idea that my wife was goggling over another man, even though she was in her late fifties, even though we had been married for thirty-five years, and even if the man had lived two hundred years ago.

"Well, he was," she argued. "He bumped his head on the roof beams of that cabin, so he had to be tall. And he had wavy sandy hair down to his shirt collar, and he had ghost-blue eyes, so I think he's a doll, just like Bon Jovi."

"Oh, come on," I groused, and set my spoon down. "What's Bon Jovi got to do with this? Molly's not ugly herself you know. She's tall, has almond-shaped hazel eyes, curly auburn hair and high cheekbones like a princess. I think she probably looks like Audrey Hepburn."

My wife squeaked, "Audrey Hepburn! She was small not tall. Do you mean Kathryn Hepburn?"

"Well, Molly's a babe," I persisted. "How do you like that? And I think maybe she looks like Julia Roberts." I had to stop and think for a moment, sipped another spoonful of soup and then asked, "Does Julia Roberts have hazel eyes?"

My wife laughed and jabbed me with her fork again, and asked, "Would you like to go with Julia Roberts?"

"Would you like to go with Bon Jovi?" I asked in return.

"If he knocked on my door," she replied.

"At least Captain Williams rescued Molly," Mom reminded us. "And he's taking her someplace safe."

"If he doesn't drown in the Brazos River," my wife added.

"That's right!" Mom's mouth dropped open, and she said, "They were swimming across the river, weren't they? And they were tied together with a rope. Boots was hanging on to his horse, and Molly was hanging on to a raft. Then a tree or something washed down in front of them and pulled Boots and his horse under water."

My bowl was empty. Clinking down my spoon into it, I looked over at Mom and asked, "Do you still have the diary with you?"

"It's right here." She pulled it out of her handbag and held it up to me.

"Read some more and let's find out what happened."

"Right here in the restaurant?"

"Why not?" I asked. "It's well past noon and the place is thinning out anyway. No one will mind. I'll get us some tea. Then you can read."

When I returned with three tall sweet teas, Mom carefully opened the brittle diary and began to read that last paragraph again, saying, "'I kicked my feet as hard and fast as I could, and tried to catch up with him to warn him of the danger of the approaching tree. I screamed with all my might, but alas I could only watch as the tree caught up with him and rolled him and his horse under the Brazos.'"

TUCK'S LANDING

THE TREE PULLED the rope tight and jerked it hard, pulling the nose of the raft below the surface. Molly realized that she would have to let go of the sinking raft and swim for her life. As she swam away, something tugged at her waist. She realized that she was still lashed to the rope, and it was pulling her down. There was never a knot she couldn't untie, never until now. Water and tension had pulled the knot into a clench of slippery hemp that wouldn't let loose. Struggling against the knot with all her might, she screamed and stabbed at it with her fingers. The raft jerked hard down into the depths, submerging completely. Pieces of it began to pop up out of the water around her. Then the sea-chest popped up.

She couldn't see Boots or his horse, only the bushy tree ahead. At the next bend, the tree caught in a massive, tangled jam of logs and debris and rolled beneath it with the violent current. Pieces of the raft and the sea-chest floated with her toward the logjam as the rope continued pulling her down. She strained with the knotted strands, screaming, and finally, sucking in her last breath, she went under.

Down into cold, watery darkness she was drawn, as the current surged around her. She could see nothing. Limbs and roots brushed against her legs and her arms, catching her clothing, spinning her around and then letting go. Her lungs burned and her head felt like it would explode, but she held her breath.

This was the end.

Everything she'd survived until now came to this. She would drown in the murky blackness of the Brazos River. Wanting to cry out, she instead held her burning breath, and a peculiar calm swept over her. Maybe this wasn't so bad after all. She was ready to cross over and be with Emily again, but she didn't want to leave Amy behind. Slowly she let the burning air escape from her burning lungs and prepared to suck in the cold blackness, which would end it all. She was at peace, and noticed a muted glow had surrounded her with eldritch resplendence.

Before her appeared a strange distant tunnel. In it she could see a bright light, and in the light she could see the form of a person walking toward her, a woman illuminated in the depths of the Brazos with her. The woman wore a radiant white gown, and Molly recognized the beautiful woman in white from the bizarre nightmare she had after the Comancheros captured her. In the beautiful woman's hand she held a golden chalice, and in her arms she held a child wrapped in a brilliant white blanket. Molly knew that the child she held was Amy.

Around Molly the wind began to blow, whipping the beautiful woman's white gown and long, black hair into a fountain of flowing ripples behind her.

With a voice like the rushing wind the beautiful woman said, "Don't be afraid. It is I."

"Who are you?" Molly asked.

The woman did not answer.

"Are you the Holy Mother?"

The woman remained silent.

"Are you an angel?"

The beautiful woman in white opened her mouth and began to speak saying, "I am the Archangel of the four winds. So it has been since the beginning. With fiery sword I have guarded the Gates of Eden, and in my hands I am given the key to the pit. Over thunder and terror I am appointed the watcher. My name is Usiel and I have been called Uriel, the destroyer of the hosts of Sennacherib, the flame of the Almighty, and the angel of death, escorting souls from this life to the next. Some have called me Santo Muerte."

Molly fell on her face before her saying, "Then I am dead, for I have seen the face of Santo Muerte, the Saint of Death."

"Please rise. You must not worship me, for I am a servant of the Almighty. He alone is worthy. You are not dead," the woman assured Molly. "You are chosen."

Molly rose before the beautiful woman, and beheld her resplendence. To Molly she held out the chalice and said, "Take this cup and drink."

With nothing to lose, Molly took the chalice in her hands.

The woman lifted her eyes to heaven and said, "The wrath of the Almighty is in your hands. You must drink all of it."

Molly raised the chalice to her lips and drank the dark red liquid. In her mouth it tasted sweet like wine mixed with honey, but in her stomach it became sour.

"You and the wrath of the Almighty are now as one," the beautiful woman declared. "Listen to the small voice, which is inside you, and obey it. Do not turn to the right. Do not turn to the left. But follow only the path before you. Look and you will see. Seek and you will find, for the Almighty has placed his hand upon you." From Molly she took the empty cup and then held out to her the child, saying, "Take this child."

As Molly's hands touched Amy, the woman became scintillant, too bright for Molly's eyes, brighter than the sun. She shielded her eyes and a stunning peace came over her, unlike anything she'd ever known. Then upon her shoulder she felt a hand gently lifting her, raising her up to a distant bright light.

Above the surface of the Brazos her head broke into the glare of the morning sun. She gasped, sucking in as much air as she could pull into her lungs, blowing it out and again sucking it in, several times. In front of her the tree was drifting. The rope was fastened yet around her waist, but no longer taut, and the child, who had been in her arms, was gone. Behind her the logjam receded from view. Her gasps began to slow, becoming a rapid pant, and behind her she heard rhythmic splashing.

"Missis McCracken!" someone was yelling.

She could see Boots swimming vigorously to catch up with her. Upon reaching her, he sliced off the rope with his Bowie, and then swam her limp and exhausted body to shallow water. From there he carried her to shore, and sat her on dry ground.

"Are you going to be okay?" he asked.

She nodded.

Stripping off his jacket and pulling off his boots, he waded again into the river, and swam into the current. She watched it sweep him downstream and away from her sight. Eventually, her respiration slowed, and against the grassy riverbank she reclined, nauseated, as she waited for the sky to stop spinning.

She waited and dozed, awoke and dozed again. Waking again, she became fearful, for Boots had not yet returned. He had been gone quite awhile. The sun had risen about halfway to noon when she heard a sloshing sound downstream. Sitting up, she watched, as Boots waded slowly up the edge of the river, carrying her sea-chest by its end handles.

He sat it down before her, slumped into the grass next to her, and raked his hair back with his fingers. His hat was missing. Everything was missing except him and the sea-chest. As he caught his breath, he explained, "We're lucky I was able to get your sea-chest. I saw it floating in the current and went after it before it was lost. My horse is gone though, and my saddle, saddlebags, rifle, and all my other belongings. My horse got tangled up in that tree. I wanted to dive in and cut him free, but that tree would have taken me down with him."

Molly reached over to touch his arm and said, "Thanks for pulling me out from under that logjam, Mister Williams."

"You say you went under that log jam?" he asked. "I was trying to catch up with you but I couldn't. You were going too fast."

"I felt you grab my shoulder," she insisted, "and you pulled me out."

"I didn't see you go under, Missis McCracken. I wasn't anywhere near you, or I would have seen you go under."

"I felt your hand on me as surely as I'm talking to you now."

"It wasn't me but I'm glad you got out."

With amazement she gazed at him, pondering her circumstances under the logjam, and what she thought she had seen. She wanted to tell him, but he would probably think she was crazy. "What do you want to do from here?" she asked.

"Let's rest awhile, and get dried out. Then we'll have to walk the rest of the way."

"How far is it, do you think?"

"Hundred miles, probably."

"You're going to carry that sea-chest a hundred miles?"

The corners of his mouth twisted up, as he replied, "It's your sea-chest. I thought you should carry it."

"What?" she asked. "It has your things in it, too."

"Then I'll take my things out." His mouth broadened into a mischievous smile.

"I can't carry that heavy thing a hundred miles," she protested.

"How about this, you carry it halfway, and then I'll carry it halfway?"

Dropping her chin to her chest she mumbled, "Guess I'll have to take what I need and leave the rest behind."

Laughingly, he gave her a pat on her shoulder and said, "How about I whittle us a travois? We'll drag that sea-chest a hundred miles. I know what it means to you. It means something to me, too. It saved my repeaters and my shooting supplies. We can drag it together. That won't be so bad, will it?"

"No," she admitted, and she also had to admit that his playfulness had lifted her spirits a little.

For the remainder of the morning they walked with one travois pole hoisted over Boots's shoulder and the other over Molly's shoulder. He'd fastened the sea-chest low on the sled-like vehicle to give them leverage and reduce the load. When she became weary, he bore the weight of both poles.

The second day they turned north. On the fifth day they intersected the Harrisburg road to Lynchburg. As they walked, they encountered jubilant riders traveling in both directions, and declaring victory over Santa Anna. They also learned that Santa Anna had burned Harrisburg to the ground.

Walking on over to Lynchburg, Boots hoped to obtain fresh horses and gear. Among the soldiers who were there, he found two of his Rangers, Alsey and Asa, and brought Molly to them.

"Missis McCracken, you remember Alsey Arnette and Asa McClellan, don't you?"

"Yes, and it's nice to see you again. I'm happy to see that you are safe and well. I hear there was a battle nearby. Were y'all there with General Houston?"

"Yes, ma'am, we were, in fact," Asa explained, and then flashed her the same attractive smile, which she remembered from the cabin on Gotier Trace. "Twas, most likely, the proudest moment of my life."

"Folks have been telling me that Santa Anna made a big mistake by coming here. So, what happened?" Molly asked.

"Yes, ma'am, he made a big mistake, for sure. He took his army across the San Jacinto River down yonder on Vince's Bridge and bivouacked on the bayou. We figure he thought he was in control of the coast by doing that. What he didn't figure is there weren't no other way out, except for that bridge.

"Me and Alsey was assigned to Sidney Sherman's regiment. We engaged Santa Anna's infantry in a vigorous skirmish up here on the Harrisburg road and forced them to retreat back across Vince's Bridge to that bayou. That's when General Houston figured he had them cornered.

"Then we learned that one of Santa Anna's generals had joined up with him, and his troops were reinforced up to about twelve hundred in all. Well, that was about how many of us General Houston had to face him with. So, the general took a thousand of us down on that bayou and he had us burn the bridge so there weren't no way out. While Santa Anna and his troops were engaging in a siesta, General Houston had us strike them. Can you imagine them boys taking a nap while we were breathing down their necks?"

Boots shook his head and smiled. "No I can't, Asa. No I can't."

"Me and Alsey was charging in with Sherman on the left. Burleson's regiment had the center, and on the right Hockley and them twin sisters was belching fire and brimstone all over Santa Anna and his troops. It was a sight to behold, Captain Williams. You would have thought the devil had caught their britches on fire. They was jumping and running for the swamp to get away from us. We took after them, screaming, 'Remember the Alamo,' and we chased them into the swamp. We shot a few of them, but most of them we beat to death with the butts of our muskets, about six hundred of them, and that's where we ended the fight, right there in the swamp. We avenged them boys that were defending the Alamo, and the ones that was butchered in Goliad. Then we drug their bodies out of the swamp and stacked them up like a big pile of cordwood. We also took over seven hundred prisoners, and all their cannon, cattle, and supplies, too. And, we caught Santa Anna his-self, trying to pass his-self off as an infantryman."

Boots slapped both men on the back and said, "I couldn't be more proud of you boys. Sure wish I could have been there with you."

"Don't pay it no mind, Captain Williams," Asa admonished him. "You were saving Missis McCracken here from falling into the hands of General Urrea. Me and the boys would have taken it real bad if something like that would of happened to her. You did the right thing, Captain."

"I appreciate that, Asa."

"So, Captain, how many casualties do y'all think General Houston had down there at San Jacinto, when it was all done and over?"

"Hard to say."

"Nine. We only lost nine of us to their muskets the whole time."

Boots raised his eyebrows, and said, "Amazing."

Molly added, "It's a miracle."

"Indeed it was, Missis McCracken," Asa replied. "Indeed it was. But, it ain't over yet. General Urrea is still in south Texas, and there's others up north. The Comancheros are still raiding and looting the settlements, and the Comanches think Texas is up for grabs. They're starting their own war. There's plenty of work to be done before the Republic is safe for folks to live in again."

Asa provided Boots and Molly with fresh horses and saddles, and though the afternoon had grown late, Boots knew that it was only twenty five miles further to Liberty. Instructing his men to wait for him in Lynchburg, he left with Molly for Tuck's Landing.

As the sun flirted with the horizon, Molly noticed many more live oaks twisting into the sky along the road. Some of their massive limbs reached outwards until they rested on the ground where clusters of prickly pear sprang up to greet them. Rivers of bluebonnet and scarlet paintbrush flooded the countryside. She breathed in the fragrance of spring and sighed, saying, "This certainly is beautiful."

"The whole country is beautiful," Boots added. "I grew up here. It's my favorite part of Texas. Even General Houston loves it here. He built a plantation here."

At their side, wisps of cloud gathered on the horizon becoming orange, then red and then deep violet. Surging up ahead of a southwesterly breeze the clouds broadened into masses as the sun dipped from view. From below the horizon the sun cast its crimson fire, rippling along the bottom edges of violet folds, which spread over the sky above them.

"This takes my breath away," Molly exclaimed, as she gazed into the sky.

"Sometimes I can't sleep after watching it," Boots replied. "And sometimes it makes me sleep like a baby."

"I used to watch the sunset at home, back when Emmet and Innis would be out planting in the spring. Sometimes their shadows would stretch all the way across the field, going up and down over the furrows. It was beautiful."

"Did you always watch the sunset alone?"

"Not always. Emily watched with me sometimes."

"What about your husband? Didn't he ever watch the sunset with you?"

"He mostly loved the farm. Well, he didn't like to farm exactly … I don't know what he liked."

"I understand."

Molly could smell water, and knew they were approaching the Trinidad River. When they reached the high banks, they paused to look down into a swath of twinkling moonlight in the water below.

"Beautiful, isn't it?" Boots asked.

Down a steep trail she could see a long raft-like ferryboat tied to a dock. Riding down the grade, they boarded the ferryboat, and an operator towed them across. "Thanks Manuel," Boots said as he disembarked. Then up the east bank of the Trinidad he led them, and turned south onto a lane, which led through a stand of overhanging live oak along the high bank.

"Hold up there!" a man yelled at them. Onto the path the man stepped, leveling what looked like a large bore escopeta at them.

Molly pulled back her reins, and her horse nickered. Darkness hid the man's face, but his silhouette was massive.

"Evening, Klaus," Boots greeted the massive man. "You can put that shotgun down. It's me. Boots Williams."

Molly wiped perspiration from her brow and let loose of her breath, asking, "Why didn't you tell me that you knew who he was?"

"I wasn't expecting Aunt Ruthie to post a night watch. It's a good idea though, with the war and all. This is Klaus Folkvar, Aunt Ruthie's ferryboat operator. He runs it during the day, and Manuel takes it in the evening."

Klaus doffed his hat, bobbed his shadowy head and hung his weapon over his forearm.

"He's worked for Aunt Ruthie since he was a young man. About six years, isn't it, Klaus?"

"Six years," Klaus answered.

Boots dismounted and said, "This is Molly McCracken."

Bobbing his head yet, Klaus greeted her saying, "Pleased to me … meet y'all."

Boots led them up the lane and across a mowed lawn overhung with pecan trees. From there Klaus took their horses to a corral next to a barn where Molly could hear the whinny of other horses. Ahead stood a white-washed, two story house with rows of unlighted, double-hung glass windows. Up a wide set of steps, Boots led her across a broad and deep front porch to a bench-like swing that hung from the ceiling and offered her a seat.

"Why don't you wait here while I talk to Aunt Ruthie," he suggested. "She doesn't know we're coming and it's late. I don't want to frighten her. Don't want to get myself shot either."

Taking a seat, she glanced around the porch as Boots tapped on the door. Then he let himself in saying, "Sorry to bother you this late." Molly could hear him from the porch asking, "Can I talk to you?"

"Bootsie? Is that you I hear out there? Bootsie?" Molly guessed that the reply had come from his Aunt Ruthie, and inside she could hear thumping on the floor as if someone had commenced dancing.

Light spilled through the window onto the porch floor when someone lit a candle inside. She could see lace curtains hanging over the front window. Beyond the window she could see a stairway, next to it Boots sat with Aunt Ruthie on a serpentine-back sofa, and in the far corner she noticed a Boston rocker with curved arms. Next to the rocker she could see a small round table, and upon it stood a thick candle in a heavy candleholder. A rippling flame atop the candle gave its flickering light to the living room and gave off a thin ribbon of smoke, which streamed up to a sooty spot on the plaster ceiling. By the size of the spot, the table had apparently held a candle there for a considerable amount time. As Boots and Aunt Ruthie talked they faced each other, hand in hand.

Boots and Aunt Ruthie talked and laughed for a long while. Molly couldn't hear what they were saying, but watched when they stood, and watched as they walked together to the front door. Boots pulled a peg-lamp from a socket at the foot of the stairway and lit it. Aunt Ruthie emerged first from the doorway onto the porch, and then Boots came out holding the flaming peg-lamp.

Aunt Ruthie was wrapped in a lavender twill housecoat. Molly admired the handy work, aware that her own floppy shirt and baggy trousers were an embarrassment after endless days spent in the wilderness. Raising her hand to her hair, she felt a mass of dirt and debris imbedded in her tendrils and she shuddered. She wanted to crawl under the porch and hide from shame for the way she must look.

Aunt Ruthie grasped her shoulders with both hands and said, "You look just fine, darlin'. So, you're the poor gal that lost her family. Oh my, do I feel bandages under your shirt here?" She squeezed up and down Molly's arms. "You poor thing." Around Molly she wrapped her arms, pulled her close and hugged her adding, "I'm sorry all them terrible things had to happen to you. We'll start asking folks about your husband right away. His name is Emmet? Is that right?"

"Yes, ma'am. Emmet McCracken"

"How long has it been?"

"Since he's been missing? About four weeks."

"Bootsie says the army doesn't have any record of him."

"That's right," Molly affirmed. "His name wasn't on their roster. Everyone thinks he's dead."

"Do you think he's dead, darlin'?"

"I don't know, probably."

"Of course, darlin'. We'll ask all the folks passing by anyway. Most folks passing through Texas have to cross here at the Landing. Sooner or later we'll talk to someone who knows about him. If he's looking for you, he might even show up here himself."

Molly couldn't resist Aunt Ruthie's affection, and returned her hug. She didn't know Aunt Ruthie, but already she'd given her hope of finding out what happened to Emmet and had also awakened in her a deep need, one that Emily used to fill. She needed someone who cared, needed someone she could reach out to, someone who understood what she had gone through. A tear slipped unexpectedly from her eye and tumbled down her cheek.

Aunt Ruthie took Molly's hands in hers and stepped back. Holding them up, she said, "Let me have a look at you, darlin'."

She was taller than Molly, rangy and long of arm and leg. Molly couldn't see Aunt Ruthie's face very well but could feel her empathy. Aunt Ruthie slipped her arm under Molly's arm and hooked it. Turning toward the front door she suggested, "Tell you what, darlin'. Let's you and me go on into the house. I've got a room upstairs you can use and it's got all the trimmings. I can tell you're tired."

Molly agreed and together they entered the house, followed by Boots. Behind him Klaus carried the sea-chest as Aunt Ruthie led the way upstairs. Walking the full length of the second floor hallway, Aunt Ruthie opened a door and entered a room. Boots followed, and with the peg-lamp lit a candle atop a mirrored vanity.

In the light Molly could see Aunt Ruthie's face, gaunt and angular with features that reminded her of Boots. She looked quite a bit older than Boots though, very old, probably in her mid-forties. Aunt Ruthie's hair was gray, sprinkled with white, and tied into a bun on top of her head. Pieces of hair had fallen astray and floated around her head when she walked, and jiggled when she talked.

"Well, what do you think?" Aunt Ruthie asked. The folds under her chin smiled as she smiled at Molly, and her eyes had squinted into happy arches.

"It's beautiful," Molly replied.

Curtains hung over a glass window. The walls were whitewashed plaster and the floors varnished plank. Molly had expected a structure of squared logs or adobe. She pushed on the bed, a large, rigid bed with a feather mattress, linens and a coverlet. All her life she'd only known creaky rope beds. She'd heard about feather mattresses, but only rich people could afford them.

Toward the vanity Aunt Ruthie nodded. "There's towels and a basin in those drawers there. On the other side, behind that cabinet door, there's a chamber set. In the morning you can put it out in the hall and one of my hands will empty it for you. Klaus will bring y'all a pitcher of water for tonight. Tomorrow we'll fix you up with a real bath. Would you like that, darlin'?"

Molly caught a glimpse of herself in the mirror, eyes wide, and her mouth agape. "I've never known such luxuries," she exclaimed.

"Well good, darlin'. Do y'all think you would like staying here then?" Her stray hairs gave emphasis to her inquiry.

Molly smiled at the stray hairs floating around her head, and replied, "I'd love to stay here, Aunt … Aunt …"

"Ruthie! You can call me that. Go on ahead, darlin'."

"Much obliged, Aunt Ruthie."

Klaus sat the sea-chest on the floor at the end of the bed, and whenever his eyes met Molly's eyes, his head commenced to bobbing. A mat of strawberry-blonde hair covered his thick forearms, and from under his collar sprang up tufts of hair. His beard bushed out curly and hid his mouth. The breadth of his face made him look like a huge bulge of hair with cherry cheeks and narrow eyes wearing a hat, a hat which Molly thought appeared too small for his head. She couldn't help smiling at him, and the curve of his eyes suggested that he was smiling at her.

"Pretty nice room, isn't it?" Boots asked.

"Yes. I never expected anything like this … It's very nice. You and Aunt Ruthie are being very kind to me. But, the thing is, I don't have any money. I can't pay for this." She looked from Aunt Ruthie to Boots and then to Klaus, whose head was yet bobbing.

Around her shoulders Aunt Ruthie reached an arm and gave Molly another hug. "Now, now, let's not fret over that, darlin'. First, let's get you well, get some clean clothes on you, and put some meat back on them bones of yours. You ain't hardly got nothing on your bones."

"I've been sick."

"So I've been told. Well, you just relax, and don't worry about money, okay?"

"Okay."

"I'll help you with your bandages when you're ready. I have a night-shirt you can wear and a dress for tomorrow. We'll have time to get better acquainted when you feel up to it. Goodness sakes, you got enough to fret about, darlin', so don't fret about money."

Turning to the doorway, Aunt Ruthie swished her hands at Boots and Klaus. "You boys go on downstairs. There's some leftover biscuits and gravy in the kitchen, if it ain't been filched by the hands yet. Put some on a plate and bring it up for her, too, would y'all please, Klaus?"

Aunt Ruthie followed Boots and Klaus into the hall and closed the door.

The next morning began with a tap on the door. Molly's eyes refused to open, but a persistent tap forced them open. "Yes?" she answered.

The door muffled Boots's voice, "I'd like to see you before I go."

"I have to get dressed." Out from under her coverlet she hurried. The sun was full up and shining through her window. She'd slept longer than she intended.

"I'll wait downstairs," he said.

"I'll only be a moment." She could hear his steps fade down the hall-way. Slipping on the dress Aunt Ruthie had left on the vanity, she noticed it was a little tight in the bodice and it hung below her ankles. Aunt Ruthie might let her hem it up. Her shoes lay in the corner, cracked, rotten, and separated from their soles. Glancing from them to the vanity, she decided to give her hair a quick brushing and go downstairs barefoot. When she stepped into the hallway she could smell fresh baked bread.

Down the stairs and across the living room, she entered the kitchen. In back she could see a sunroom full of windows overlooking the Trinidad River. Boots sat with Aunt Ruthie at a long table, and they were drinking coffee. Like two peas in a pod, one was coarse and young, the other was old and fair, but to Molly they cast matching smiles.

"Coffee's on the stove," Aunt Ruthie informed her. "And, there's bread on the counter. Help yourself."

Molly filled a cup, sliced off a thick piece of bread, slathered it with butter from a wooden dish and took a bite. As she enjoyed the fresh bread, she looked around the kitchen and considered Aunt Ruthie fortunate to have a stove to cook on. She didn't have to crane pots in and out of a chimney. At the end of the counter Molly noticed a pitcher-pump and basin and smiled at such a modern convenience. She'd never seen such a thing inside a house. Aunt Ruthie could pump water in her kitchen and didn't have to carry it from outside.

"I can see that this place has been good for you already," Boots said from the sunroom. His stubble was gone, and his hair was combed and parted.

Aunt Ruthie added, "That yellow dress is pretty on you. It don't look that good on me anymore, not since my hair went gray." Glancing down at Molly's feet she asked, "Y'all need shoes too, don't you?"

"My shoes fell apart," Molly explained.

"I've got extra shoes," Aunt Ruthie informed her. "We'll fix y'all up with something."

Pulling out one of a dozen chairs surrounding a long, polished oak table, Molly seated herself. Glancing out the windows, she could see across a covered back porch to the ferryboat below, with a wagon, horses, and passengers aboard. Klaus was pulling them across as Molly remarked, "The view from here is spectacular."

"Klaus can pull folks across in about ten minutes. The other hands take twenty minutes or more," Aunt Ruthie explained.

Boots added, "Because he's gargantuan."

"How many others do you have working here?" Molly asked.

"Justin and Manuel," Aunt Ruthie replied. "They live in the bunk-house out by the barn. There's more work here than Klaus can keep up with and they're both good hands."

"I wasn't expecting anything like this." Molly turned her eyes from the window to Boots and then to Aunt Ruthie. "I haven't seen glass windows since I was in New Orleans. And look at this door." Standing, she swept her hand over the door leading out onto the back porch. "I've seen panel doors like this in New Orleans, but only in mansions, when me and my sister were working as seamstresses. This is a mansion, isn't it?"

Boots sipped his coffee and then set his cup on the table as he explained, "This house was part of a plantation before Uncle Foster got himself killed. He cleared the fields and built this place. After he was gone, Aunt Ruthie sold off the fields and kept the house, and then bought the landing and ferryboat. She has a good head for business. It's worked out well for her."

Aunt Ruthie sipped her coffee and smiled.

"I love your bread, Aunt Ruthie," Molly complimented her.

"If you want more, just help yourself, darlin'. Make yourself at home. You belong here now."

Boots nodded. "Aunt Ruthie gets up early and makes bread fresh every morning. I think she uses the smell of it to get the men out of bed early and get them out of the house sooner."

"What men?" Molly asked.

"They're overnight boarders," Aunt Ruthie explained. "I rent rooms mostly to teamster drivers when they're passing through. Fits in good with my ferryboat business, don't you think? Most are on their way from New Orleans to the lower settlements and back. Right now freight hauling has all but stopped because of the war. Lately, I've been getting a lot of settlers passing through. They don't usually stay long and don't usually have no money. If they need to spend the night, I let them camp for free in the marshalling area up on top of the hill.

"Once in a while I get some government dignitaries, they seem to like it here, but I haven't had any lately. I got the only place in a hundred miles with a hot bath, a feather mattress, and a home cooked meal. The hotel in Harrisburg is nothing but a bunkhouse, men sleep on one side and women on the other. Ain't nothing but a blanket hung up betwixt them. Most folks don't like it there because the ruffians like to stay there." She turned to Boots and asked, "You ever stayed in that hotel in Harrisburg, Bootsie?"

"There's no hotel in Harrisburg anymore," he responded. "Santa Anna burned the whole settlement to the ground. There used to be a bunkhouse at the Ranger's station. I used to stay there when I was in Harrisburg, but it's gone, too." Standing, he stepped around the table and slipped his arm around Aunt Ruthie. As Aunt Ruthie stood, Molly noticed that she wore a plain, cotton shirt with the sleeves rolled up and buckskin trousers, not what Molly expected to see on a woman. The butt of a dueling pistol lay against her waist behind her belt.

Boots continued to explain, "I'll be heading out to Lynchburg this morning to join up with my men." On his head Boots placed his hat and said, "So, I'll be going now."

Molly followed them out to the corral. His horse was saddled and ready, but before he mounted up she grasped his arm and stopped him. "I'm sorry you didn't get to go with your men to San Jacinto, but I'm glad you brought me here, Mister Williams. Your Aunt Ruthie is wonderful and her home is beautiful. I don't deserve this."

"To tell you the truth," he confessed. "You couldn't have stopped me from bringing you here."

Aunt Ruthie gave Molly an odd smirk and then embraced him saying, "I'm going to miss you, Bootsie." Then she took Molly's hand, and said, "Come on back inside, darlin'. We got a lot of getting acquainted to do."

As Boots rode out, they went to the kitchen. Molly refilled their cups and took a seat across the table from Aunt Ruthie. "I don't know why, but I feel like I've known you for years," she began.

Aunt Ruthie pushed her chair back and sighed. "I'm sure glad you got away from them Comanchero's and from that cavalry Boots was telling me about. And, ain't that nephew of mine something, whisking you off, and bringing you here like this?"

Molly nodded. When Aunt Ruthie raised her cup, she noticed her forearms, strong for such a frail looking woman. Sinews and veins stood out on them. Her fingers had a certain grace to them though, long, but callused. This woman is no stranger to hard work, she thought, but neither was Molly. "What can I do to help around here?" she asked.

"You rest, darlin'. I've got plenty of help with chores. Klaus and the farm hands do the heavy work, running the ferryboat, and working the fields. I tend the cattle and do the cooking, housekeeping, and gardening." Aunt Ruthie took a deep breath and sighed. "It just ain't the same without Foster."

"Your husband?"

"Yes."

"What happened, Aunt Ruthie? What happened to Foster?"

UNCLE FOSTER

"FOSTER TUCK," AUNT Ruthie explained, "was a good man. They don't come no better than him. We got married and got us a little farm in Tennessee, but it was a farm plagued with boll weevils. We got it cheap, but them boll weevils sure got a lot more out of it than we did. He sold that place and got us nineteen hundred and twenty acres of prime river frontage right here on the Trinidad. Some land broker was representing an impresario down here named Vhelin, and the biggest thing was there weren't no boll weevils here. Foster only paid two hundred and twenty dollars for all of it, that is, long as he agreed to homestead it.

"My sister's husband, Avery, bought twelve hundred and eighty acres adjoining to us. He was Bootsie's pa. Bootsie was ten years old when we all came here and settled.

"Foster was a strappin' young buck back then and as handsome as they come. It's a shame what happened. We built cabins and put up a barn. Then we cleared as much land as we could that first year and put in a garden. Today, we're still using that old cabin. It's the one out by the barn. That's where the farmhands live. And we're still using that first old barn we built, too. The big one out back is the one we put up later. Everyone worked back then, even Bootsie and his little sister."

"I didn't know he has a little sister, Aunt Ruthie."

"He didn't tell you, darlin'? He didn't tell you what happened to his family?"

"No. All he told me is that you're his only kin."

"Well, it's a genuine tragedy what happened to Avery and my sister and my beautiful little niece. It still troubles me to this day."

"First tell me about Foster."

"Okay, darlin'. Well, that Bootsie was a hard worker. He was as big as his pa by the time he turned twelve. Takes after my side of the family, my sister's side, Elizabeth, that is. He reminds me of my pa when he was a strappin' buck. Bless his soul. Foster and Avery and Bootsie had about five-hundred acres put into cotton that second year and it was a barn buster.

"Avery used his share to buy the landing and ferryboat. That landing has always been here, far as I know. The folks that owned it fell ill and put it up for sale, so he bought it.

"My Foster had lumber shipped down, and he hired laborers to build this house. We finished it over the next two years and moved in.

"Avery was different though. He had his own way of looking at things, and he put everything he had into improving that landing. He built those docks, and put a new deck on the ferryboat.

"Things were going along just fine. We had over seven-hundred acres under the plow, and Foster wanted to get all the rest of the land put into cotton, too. Between him and Avery, that would have been three thousand acres of cotton, and it would have made us all rich."

"Sounds to me like you were already rich, Aunt Ruthie."

"Well, let me tell you about rich, darlin'. It ain't the land, or what we put into it, or what we take out from it that makes us rich, it's the folks that does the puttin' and the takin'. They're the ones that make us rich. I'd give everything I have right now to get my sister, and my Foster, and Avery back, and my precious little niece. One by one they got took away from me, and my heart is still aching for them. When I lost them, I lost everything. You may as well have cut my heart out. Y'all might look at me, and think I'm rich, but inside I'm a pauper, poor as dirt, except for Bootsie. If I didn't have him, I think I'd just shrivel up and pass away with all the rest of my kin."

"I lost everything too, but I have a niece, Aunt Ruthie. Just like you have Mister Boots."

"I know, darlin', I know. Bootsie told me everything."

"I don't know how to find her though. I know she's alive. I saw her. My heart aches every day for her, and it aches for the ones I lost, same as you. And, I'd give everything I have to get them back, but I don't have anything."

"You do, darlin'. You have more than you think. You just don't know it yet."

"What do you mean?"

"Bootsie sees it in you, and I see it in you, too, same as he does. When it's time for it to come out, we'll see if me and Bootsie are right."

"You never had any youngsters of your own, Aunt Ruthie?"

"I miscarried three times. That broke my heart, too."

"Me, too. I miscarried, too. Was Foster disappointed when it happened to you?"

"He was crushed. He wanted heirs in the worst way. He wanted them to carry on with what he started here."

"So, what happened to him?"

"Well, he wanted to put all that land under the plow. He bought more horses and more equipment for clearing, plowing and planting. Problem was there weren't enough hands to do everything he wanted to do. He decided that he had to buy slaves. He didn't want to, but all the other plantations had slaves, and they were expanding faster than him. Mexican law wouldn't allow slaves to be sold in Texas, so one winter him and Avery went off to New Orleans on a buying tour. Mexican law would let us bring slaves in, just didn't allow them to be sold here. Avery came back a couple weeks later, said he and Foster had been ambushed and robbed by John A. Murrell and his gang of freebooters, and that Foster had been killed."

"I've heard of him, Aunt Ruthie. When I lived in New Orleans, we heard about the things John Murrell did all the time. Folks had to travel together to protect each other."

"Avery said he'd killed one of them and thought he'd even wounded Murrell himself. Said he was surprised that he was just a mere youngster, perhaps in his early teens, but a blood-thirsty and ruthless murderer, nevertheless.

"Well, that seemed to take the gusto out of Avery. After that he let some of the fields go unattended. Without Foster we couldn't keep up with them anyway. We tried to keep Avery's spirits up, but he started slugging down a pint or two of squeezins every night, got real ornery too. I couldn't stand to be around him for very long, and I felt sorry for my dear sister, putting up with him when he was like that. He turned into a bona fide tyrant, getting mad, yelling, and bossing folks around all the time. No one could do anything right when he was around. We tried to do things right. We worked until our fingers bled, wanted to keep the farm going, but whenever Avery was around, it was like walking into a tree trunk with your eyes shut. We never knew what was coming next.

"Bootsie was turning thirteen back then and he wasn't going to take it anymore. He was going to stand up to Avery and let him have what for. He was over here raging to me about the goings on at his place and telling me what he was going to do. In his own way, I guess, he was confiding in me. I got him calmed down, talked him out of it, and talked some sense into him. It ain't easy talking sense into a thirteen-year-old, but I did it, and he settled down. We were always close after that, me and Bootsie. He wanted to stay over here in this house with me, because I was alone, said he needed to protect me. Elizabeth said it was okay, but I think she was afraid for Bootsie. Avery didn't care one way or the other. So, Bootsie started staying over here."

"He grew up in this house, Aunt Ruthie? You raised him?"

"I figured it would wear off after awhile and he'd go back home, but one night a band of Comanches paid a visit to Avery's cabin. Him and his family were still living in their first place, the one him and Foster had built out of logs they'd cut from their own land. I wanted them to move in here with me after my Foster was killed, but Avery was too proud. He said he'd build his own house and move into it. Well, them old logs of his had shrunk up and left spaces betwixt them. Avery said he liked it that way, because it let a breeze blow through the cabin at night when he was sleeping. Problem was it also let them Comanches have a peek inside. They drawed back their bows and let their arrows fly right betwixt them logs, let them fly right into Avery, Elizabeth, and my little niece while they were sleeping in their beds.

Avery tried to fight them off. We found him outside the next day, had nine arrows stuck in him. One of them stuck him in the neck. It looked like he bled out while he was fighting them. We found him in the dirt, but Elizabeth and my niece never got out of their beds. They just died right there.

"You should of seen Bootsie after that. It was a pitiful thing what that did to him. He figured he could have killed them Comanches himself and saved his family if he would've been there. Sometimes I think maybe he could have when I hear about the things he does now, but I'd never tell him that. He blames himself for what happened, thinks he killed them by not being there. It took him a long time to get past that, about three years.

"He was fifteen, didn't want to farm, didn't want anything to do with cotton. He blamed cotton-lust for killing his Uncle Foster and blamed himself for killing his own family. I sure felt sorry for the dear youngin', tried to get him to accept things the way they were and move on with his life. Finally, he decided he wanted to become a surveyor. He sold his pa's land and used the money to go off to the Davidson Academy in Nashville. I sold my land too, except for the house and a couple hundred acres. Bootsie sold me the landing and ferryboat."

"When did he get married, Aunt Ruthie?"

"What made you think he got married?"

"We were talking on the way here and he said that he had a home and a family once. He said everything was gone."

"I think he was talking about his ma and pa and his little sister. He's holding a lot of feelings deep inside about what happened. He might have let you get a glimpse of it, but usually he don't let folks see what's inside of him."

"Am I asking too many questions, Aunt Ruthie?"

"No, darlin'. Tell you what. Why don't we put some water on the stove for that bath I promised, and you can tell me about that family of yours." She opened a door leading from the kitchen to a small room with a bathing tub. On the other side of the bathing room she opened another door leading into a parlor. She'd converted the parlor to use as her bedroom.

The tapestries that covered the walls stunned Molly, so did the oval rug and the lace canopy over the bed. Beside the bed stood a chiffonier of high quality, imported no doubt. "This is beautiful," Molly said.

Aunt Ruthie stepped back into the bathing room and explained, "I let my guests use my tub here for a nickel. It's solid brass and has a drain going outside. Another nickel buys them supper. I eat after they're done eating. You can have supper with me, if you like. No charge for any of it. Want to look around outside?"

While water heated on the stove, Molly toured the outbuildings with Aunt Ruthie and the cabin where Klaus and the farmhands lived. From there they walked up the lane to the road and crossed into a rutted marshalling area where wagons lined up, and folks waited for the ferryboat. Alongside the road a bell hung from a post and crossbeam so that folks could call the ferryboat.

Pointing down to the river, Aunt Ruthie said, "Looks like Klaus is bringing folks across with a wagon right now. Looks like a freight hauler. First one I've seen in a couple days. Folks ring the bell when they want to get on the ferryboat, and Klaus has one on board to ring back at them, telling them to come on down and get aboard. We can't have folks going both ways up and down that hill at the same time … Would you like to ride the ferryboat?"

"Yes, I would, but not today."

"Sure, darlin'. Come on, let's get you back up to the house for that nice hot bath. I think the water should be ready by now."

After bathing and then laundering her floppy shirt and trousers, Molly hemmed the dress she was wearing, and helped Aunt Ruthie prepare supper. Retiring early, she listened from her bed as houseguests came in late. They clumped up the stairs, down the hallway to their rooms, and then went back downstairs again. Talking and laughing out on the front porch, she could hear them with Aunt Ruthie.

Molly put on her floppy shirt and trousers the next morning and helped Aunt Ruthie with morning chores. Every evening after that she changed into the yellow dress Aunt Ruthie had given her, brushed her hair into a fountain of auburn curls, and socialized on the front porch with Aunt

Ruthie and the houseguests. Standing to see who it was whenever a horse clopped up the lane, she waited for Boots to return. For three weeks she waited.

During a warm evening in May a Ranger crossed the yard. Molly noticed his red shirt and recognized Alsey Arnette. Behind him rode Captain Boots Williams. Both had turned up the front brims of their hats. She found the set of their hats odd and wanted to run to them.

Aunt Ruthie held her back. "You see the way Bootsie turned up his hat, darlin'? That means he's unhappy about something. We shouldn't be running over there to talk to them just yet. Let them come to us."

Riding past the house toward the barn, both men nodded straight faced to Molly and Aunt Ruthie without doffing their hats. Following them, in spite of Aunt Ruthie's warning, Molly went down the front steps and out to the barn, watching as they entered the corral, unsaddling and currycombing their horses.

Aunt Ruthie caught up with her, hooked her arm and pulled her away, suggesting, "Come on back to the porch and sit with me, darlin'. We'll know what's going on soon enough."

Waiting with the houseguests on the front porch, Molly determined before long that Boots and Alsey were not coming and wondered why they didn't want to talk to her and Aunt Ruthie. Then she heard hooves clopping up the lane toward the house.

From the shadows of the live oaks emerged cattle and horses in single file. Two Rangers drove them past the house. Right away she recognized Zachary Thaxton's bushy beard and noticed that the brim of his hat was also turned up. The other Ranger she didn't remember, one of the hard looking ones, and he'd turned up his brim. Another brought up the rear, driving a wagon loaded with household goods. She recognized her wagon and her goods, Emily's loom and spinning wheel, and her horses. She'd know the markings on her horses anywhere. The Rangers parked the wagon, put the horses in the corral, drove the cattle to pasture, and disappeared.

"I think they went to the bunkhouse with the farmhands," Aunt Ruthie reasoned. "They've got food back there. Just give them time to settle in. I can tell something ain't right. They'll come around when they're ready to talk."

The sun went down, twilight passed, and the Rangers never came to the front porch. Standing, Aunt Ruthie declared, "They're not talking tonight, darlin'. Let's give them until morning. I don't know what happened out there, but I can tell they're pretty upset."

Aunt Ruthie went to the parlor, and Molly went up to her room, put on her night shirt and crawled into bed. She tried, but could not imagine what had happened or why the Rangers wouldn't talk. How did they come by all of her and Emily's belongings? Moments of darkness became decades of worry as she tossed and turned.

Unable to sleep, she decided to write about this day in her diary and got out of bed. Writing always made her feel better when things weren't going well. Searching around for her candle and holder, she found it on the vanity, and remembered that she had no way to light it. Opening her door, she noticed that the peg-lamp in the hallway had been snuffed out, and everyone was in bed. Usually, she wrote in the afternoon when there was plenty of sunlight, and she always went to bed at sunset. She didn't need a candle, but kept one on the vanity anyway. The only place she would find a light this time of night was in the stove, down in the kitchen.

Draping the coverlet from her bed around her, she tiptoed out of her room into the hallway. Completely dark, she felt along the wall, and searched with her toes until finding the first step. Groaning painfully when she put her weight down on it, she didn't think the step had ever made such a noise during the day. Downstairs, the living room was dark and so was the kitchen, but the stove would still have life in it. She felt around for the kitchen doorway, and heard something splash in the bathing room.

Light streamed out from under the bathing room door, making the kitchen floor-planks look rougher than they really were. Her feet made long shadows all the way to the sunroom. It seemed to her awfully late for a guest to be bathing. Maybe it was Aunt Ruthie. She bumped into the stove and felt around for the firebox. It was warm yet. Lifting the latch with a poker, she opened it. A blue flame twirled up from the coals when she stirred them. As she reached in with her candle to catch a light, the bathing room door opened, and she jolted around.

"Who's out there?" Boots held up a peg-lamp, which illuminated the kitchen. "Pardon me," he said. "I didn't know it was you, Missis McCracken."

Oh, my, she thought, and lowered her eyes, embarrassed because he had seen her in a nightshirt. With one hand she drew the coverlet tightly together at her neck. "What are you doing up so late?" she asked him.

"I could ask you the same question," he replied. "It's a full house tonight. I had to wait until everyone went to bed before I could get a bath. I'll be sleeping out in the bunkhouse with the boys."

She explained, "I came down to find a light for my candle."

Crossing the kitchen, he lowered the peg lamp to her and said, "Here, light off this."

She watched as the flame climbed onto her candle and brightened the kitchen. She could smell the soap he'd bathed with, the fancy lavender scented soap from New Orleans that Aunt Ruthie kept in the bathing room. "Much obliged," she said.

"Having trouble sleeping?"

"Yes, but I'll manage." Lowering her eyes again, she had to admit that he was not entirely unpleasant to look at and couldn't understand why he made her feel so shy. Holding her candle up, she rose to her feet, and walked briskly to the kitchen doorway, all the while keeping her eyes fixed on the floor.

"You don't have to just walk off like that," he pleaded. "See, I … Wait! Can't you wait for a moment?"

Pausing at the kitchen doorway, she would not look at him, and spoke to the floor. "You didn't want to talk to me or Aunt Ruthie all evening. Why do you want to talk now?"

"It's not that."

Aunt Ruthie entered the kitchen wearing her housecoat. Glancing at Molly, then Boots, she asked, "Is everything all right out here?"

Boots replied, "Missis McCracken was trying to light her candle, and I came out of the bathing room and surprised her. Sorry, Missis McCracken."

"It's okay."

"So, why are you so glum, Bootsie?" Aunt Ruthie asked. "Y'all came here with a cloud hanging over you today."

"I wanted to wait until morning and see if the boys' spirits improved before I said anything, but I guess I can tell you now."

A FITTING MEMENTO

"THE REPUBLIC OF Texas furloughed the army without pay about a month ago," Boots explained. "They can't discharge them until they come up with the money to pay them, so they furloughed them instead."

"Does that mean you boys will be staying here at Tuck's Landing?" Aunt Ruthie asked. "There's nothing wrong with that. In fact, that's good because there's plenty of plowing and planting to keep y'all busy here for at least a month."

"No need to do that, Aunt Ruthie. I wanted to talk with General Houston myself, but he's off convalescing after he was wounded at San Jacinto. So I met with Colonel Karnes instead. I told him me and my boys don't feel right about leaving Texas undefended at a time like this. I told him we want to serve on a volunteer basis without pay because the Comanches are trying to claim land that the settlers own, and the Comancheros are turning outlaw against us.

"Karnes said he wanted to assign us to serve under him in the south-western territories, and he's paying each of us thirty dollars a month. It's a fraction of what they owe the army, but the Republic considers it necessary because there isn't anyone else out there to oppose the marauders. The only thing is we have to furnish our own horses, rifles, pistols and whatever else we might need while we're on campaign."

"Were you able to ask Colonel Karnes about my husband, Emmet?" Molly asked.

"I did. In fact, I've been asking everyone about him. So far, no one has any recollection of him."

"He must be dead," Molly sighed. "You said the army has been furloughed for a month. He would have been looking for me. It's two months since he left to join up with General Houston, and no one has seen or heard anything from him. I guess there's not much else for me to think."

Aunt Ruthie put her arm around Molly and said, "I know this is hard on you, darlin', and I feel bad for you. It's hard on me, too, but folks go missing all the time. He's not the only one who ain't coming home from the war. All we can do is accept it and move on."

"I know Aunt Ruthie." She leaned her head against Aunt Ruthie's shoulder. "Obliged." Shedding not a tear, she had sensed for some time that this was coming.

Glancing over at Boots, Aunt Ruthie asked, "You'll still be working for the Republic of Texas as a Ranger then?"

"There's twenty of us now. Colonel Karnes assigned others to our unit. The rest are on patrol south of San Antonio. We'll meet up with them after we deliver Molly's restitution."

"Restitution?" Molly asked.

"Yes, we caught the Comancheros that ambushed you and your brother-in-law. I knew it was them by the things they had with them. I recognized your belongings. Remember when I found them strewn all over the Gotier Trace down toward Matagorda?"

"Yes. That's when you brought my sea-chest to me."

"They must have gone back to fetch your belongings after they smuggled those supplies up to General Urrea. They were probably fixing to sell them or trade them."

"How did you find them?" Molly asked.

"First thing Colonel Karnes did, after he assigned us to serve under him, is send us to San Antonio to give the ashes of the Alamo defenders a proper burial. Santa Anna burned their bodies, you know. From there he sent us out on campaign to liberate Laredo from the remainder of Santa Anna's forces. They're trying to make a last stand there. We had a little skirmish with them, and I'm proud of the way my boys handled it, but we were outnumbered and finally we were forced to retreat.

"On our way back to San Antonio we checked on some of the ranchers along the way. One of them told us he'd seen a dozen Comancheros hiding out along the Medina River. They'd been conducting raids in the area. So, we went off after them and found their camp. The Comancheros weren't there when we got there. That's when I noticed your belongings, and I figured the wagon holding them was yours, too.

"Just before sundown we took up positions along the trail they were using. When they returned, we fired on them. They fired back on us, but we put two of them down right there in the river. The rest turned and ran for it. Asa McClellan was hit. So, he stayed behind while me and the other boys pursued them.

"When the Comancheros realized we were after them, they turned to fight. I pulled off a quick shot and took the closest one right out of his saddle. After that, they scattered off into the hills. So, we pursued them. A few got away. The rest we captured. We questioned them about the one called Buffalo Head, but no one would admit to his whereabouts, and none of them fit his description. We hung them all right there, and we left them hanging for the other Comancheros to see if they came back.

"We returned to their camp to collect your things, and found Asa McClellan had passed from his wound. So, we took him to San Antonio and buried him proper with the defenders of the Alamo. Then we returned the Rancher's cattle and horses that could be identified from their brands and anything else they could identify. After that, me and the boys brought your belongings to you along with the Comanchero's horses, cattle, their guns and all their gear. Consider it your restitution for what they did to you. If you sell everything, you can probably get five hundred dollars or more. That should pay your way to New Orleans, or anywhere else you want to go." His voice trailed off as he concluded, "It'll give you a start on a new life."

"I need a moment to take all this in," Molly said. To the sunroom window she went to consider everything he'd just told her. Beyond the window she could see someone sitting on the back porch in the dark and she recognized Zach. The glow of his cigar illuminated his face when he took a pull. Then the glow faded in the darkness and drifted down to his lap where he held his cigar between his fingers.

What she wanted wasn't money or a new life; the only thing she wanted was to save her niece. The terminus of her purpose was to rescue Amy, and she believed that was the reason her life had been spared. She needed the Rangers and understood that she didn't have a chance without them. But, there were so few of them to protect such a large area.

Fearing that they would never be available to help her, she considered her options. She could hire someone to help her. Maybe, she could hire furloughed soldiers who were waiting for the Republic to pay them. They would jump at the chance to earn a fee. She could organize a rescue party or offer a reward, or both, and Lynchburg was her best bet. There would be soldiers there. From Tuck's landing she would go to Lynchburg as soon as her restitution could be sold.

Noticing the unusual way that Boots was looking at her, she asked, "Is there something else you wanted to tell me?"

"You don't have to leave. You could stay here."

"I can't do that."

"I'd be afraid for you anywhere else."

Aunt Ruthie touched her arm, agreeing with Boots saying, "I'd like you to stay here, too, darlin'."

"Aunt Ruthie, I have to find my niece. She belongs with me. We're the only family we have for each other. It's like you and your nephew over there." Turning to Boots, she asked, "Will you help me find her, Mister Williams?"

"Missis McCracken." His hands, and the peg-lamp which he held, drooped to his sides. "I'm sorry. I really am. You know I can't do that right now. Were still fighting what's left of Santa Anna's forces, and the Comancheros that took sides with him, and the Comanches, who are claiming our land for themselves."

"But, you had time to bring this restitution to me. Can't you take time to rescue her? That wouldn't take long, would it?"

"Well, Missis McCracken, you told me your niece was carried off by the Kiowa. That means we'd have to go up across the Comanche Barrier to find her. We can't just ride into a place like that and expect to come back with our scalps still attached to our heads. The Comanches are at war with us and there's thousands of them up there. After we establish the peace, maybe, we can go up into Kiowa territory and try to find out where they took her."

"Obliged, Mister Williams." Toward the living room she turned, understanding now that she would have to rescue Amy herself. She couldn't count on Boots, the Rangers, or anyone else. She would have to find her own way. "Please excuse me," she said. "I'm not feeling well." Crossing the living room, she started up the stairs.

"Y'all need anything, darlin'?" Aunt Ruthie asked.

"I just need to rest, much obliged." In her room she sat before her candle and made her final diary entry for that day. It was up to her now. She would start in Lynchburg, pay any price, and do whatever was necessary to find Amy.

Updating her diary solidified her decision to go to Lynchburg, and she needed gear, good gear, like the Rangers had. Retiring late, she rose a few hours later and dug around in her sea-chest. Taking out her black dress, it seemed fitting to wear it. For the sake of the Rangers she would mourn for Asa McClellan by wearing her black dress.

The bread dough was ready for the oven before Aunt Ruthie came to the kitchen. She'd gladly given up her bread-baking chores when Molly offered to take them over. "Morning," she greeted Molly. "I see y'all are wearing your black dress today."

"I'm wearing it for Asa McClellan."

"I think the boys will appreciate that, darlin'. They seem real strange with grief over what happened." Grabbing a basket, Aunt Ruthie went out to the henhouse to collect eggs for breakfast.

Opening the sunroom door and windows, Molly let the heat from baking out of the kitchen. Then Aunt Ruthie returned from the henhouse, washed and cracked a dozen or so eggs into a skillet. The Rangers came in without speaking, and took places behind the chairs around the long table, standing respectfully.

Molly noticed that Zach had slicked his hair back, and while standing next to him and filling his coffee mug, she could smell on him the hair oil Aunt Ruthie kept in the bathing room. He'd trimmed his beard and pocketed his cigar. Politely, he held his hat in front of him and said, "Y'all done a right fine job with breakfast this morning, Missis McCracken, and y'all fixed yourself right pretty in that black dress."

"Obliged, Mister Thaxton. This is my mourning dress. I'm wearing it in honor of Mister McClellan. Why don't y'all have a seat?"

"Yes, ma'am, we will after a moment. First, I need to give y'all something." Lifting his hat, he revealed to her a bundle of leather about the size of a melon. Rolled tight and folded on the ends, it was lashed with leather laces. "This is yours, ma'am. It's the scalps from them Comancheros that ambushed you and killed your brother-in-law."

Plopping onto a chair, Molly fanned a flush of horror with her hand and replied, "That's disgusting Mister Thaxton. We are not savages like those men. I can't believe that you'd do such a thing as this."

To Molly Boots explained, "First, we turned them in to Colonel Karnes to prove we're doing our job. Then it was his idea to pass them on to you. He thought it would mean something to you and so did we. What them Comancheros did to you and your brother-in-law was wrong, and we made them pay."

Showing his uneasiness, Zach continued, "I know it ain't no fitting gift for a lady like you, Missis McCracken, but it proves them Comancheros didn't get away with it." To her he presented the bundle.

"Asa gave his life for those," Boots added.

Reluctantly, she took the bundle. Hard, almost black, the bundle was surprisingly light. Placing it on her lap, she folded her hands over it, and said, "I am truly sorry for your loss gentlemen, and I'm thankful for what you've done to bring me justice."

The Rangers took their seats, as Aunt Ruthie passed around a skillet piled with fried eggs, thick slices of bacon and then a platter of fresh bread. With long faces they ate their breakfast. When they were finished, Boots clanked his cup on the table and said, "Any time you boys are ready."

Rising up, they scooted their chairs under the table and left the sunroom. Boots stood last, and as he did he said to Molly, "It was thoughtful of you to wear your mourning dress for Asa today."

"I can see that he meant a lot to you," she replied. "I really am sorry, Mister Williams."

"I rode with Asa McClellan and Arlan Hodge when I first joined the service. You never got a chance to know Asa, but he always had a way of making us laugh when things weren't so funny. I'm going to miss him for that mostly. But, I have to tell you that this is the way he wanted to go. Him and I have talked about this before. We both felt the same. That probably sounds strange to you, doesn't it?"

"No. It's not strange. It's just sad." A wave of distress washed over Molly as it occurred to her that she would be crushed, if Boots had been killed instead of Asa. She was glad that he was alive. To her chest she clutched the leather bundle, searched his sad eyes, and felt compassion for the grief she found in them, adding, "I've come to understand how it has to be for the job you do and what it means to those who care about you. You were made this way for a reason, Mister Williams, and I wouldn't change you, even if I could."

Giving her a familiar half-smile, he asked, "You wouldn't change me?"

"We are all indebted to you, Mister Williams. Like you said, there isn't anyone else to oppose the marauders. We need you, all of you. I wouldn't change you for anything."

Out the backdoor he glanced. She could see that the Rangers had mounted up and were waiting for him atop their horses. They were listening to the conversation between her and Boots inside.

"I have to go," he said.

Grasping his arm, she pulled him down to her height so that those outside could not listen, and whispered in his ear. "I want to ask before you leave, what are you going to do with Asa's repeaters, and his horse, and his saddle?"

"What's that?" Boots hooked her arm and walked her past Aunt Ruthie, through the kitchen and into the living room. "Are you saying that you want his repeaters, his horse, and his saddle, Missis McCracken? Why would you want his belongings? We gave you all the Comanchero's horses and gear, and you still have the pistols I gave you, don't you?"

"Your old pistols are no match for his repeaters," she argued. "You know that and so do I."

"Molly, those repeaters give us an advantage. They're changing the way we fight our enemies, and there aren't enough of them to go around. We need them. I was planning to re-issue Asa's repeaters."

"What about Asa's horse?" she asked. "I need a horse that's better than any of those Comanchero's horses."

"Then you're not staying here?" he asked.

"I can't stay here."

"You're not thinking about going after your niece by yourself, are you?"

Aunt Ruthie stuck her head through the doorway from the kitchen and asked, "Darlin', can you come in here and help me for a minute?"

"I have to go." Boots turned, went through the kitchen, and past Aunt Ruthie to the back door.

Molly chased after him, believing that the repeaters would give her an advantage, too.

Catching Molly by her arm, Aunt Ruthie thoughtfully said, "I can see what you're trying to do, darlin', but you're going about it all wrong. You just stay right here and let me go out and talk to him, okay?"

"Okay, Aunt Ruthie."

Molly watched Aunt Ruthie as she dashed out and stopped Boots before he mounted his horse. The other Rangers dismounted and gathered around her. What a diplomat she was, Molly thought, as she watched from the sunroom. What was she saying that had so captivated the Rangers? They were nodding their heads, apparently agreeing with something she said. Zach pulled his hat off, and the others pulled theirs off. Then Boots stepped up on the back porch and said, "Can you come out here for a moment, Missis McCracken?"

Stepping out onto the back porch, she took a bundle from him, rolled up leather, tied with laces on the ends, and very heavy. Untying the laces, she unrolled two Paterson repeating pistols and gaped at them, saying, "These were Asa McClellan's, weren't they? I didn't think you would give them to me."

"Me and the boys want you to have them." Raising one of the unloaded repeaters, he examined the oiled frame, cylinder, and long barrel. The trigger emerged from the frame when he cocked it. Then releasing the trigger, he let the hammer down easy with his thumb and explained, "The boys figure this would be a fitting memento for everything those Comancheros put you through. We want them to become heirlooms for your family, and we'd like you to write in your diary about how you came by them, and about Asa, so folks will remember him."

Taking a repeater in each of her hands, she said, "It's an honor to have these, and it will be an honor for me to write about Asa, and what he did with them."

"Don't get any big ideas about these repeaters, Missis McCracken," Boots warned her. "Just because you get five shots each doesn't mean someone can't take you out with an old single-shooter. That's what killed Asa McClellan. He put a couple holes in one of them Comancheros. Then that Comanchero pulled his old single shooter and shot Asa straight on. Always use your head first. Then back it up with your pistols if you have to. Do you remember how to strip these down and load them?"

She shook her head.

"Would you like me to show you before I go?"

"What about the other Rangers?" She noticed that Aunt Ruthie was waving them off.

"I told them I'd catch up. Did you eat breakfast yet?"

Again she shook her head. He offered his arm and walked her inside to the long table where some of the house guests had gathered for breakfast. As he pushed her chair in for her, he elaborated, "Those repeaters are very dangerous when they're loaded. After you eat, I'll show you how to load them. Then I'd like to take you out back and give you some pointers on how to use them properly. Would you like to do that?"

"Yes, I'd like that very much."

"You've sure changed since I brought you here. You're a lot prettier, you're healthy looking and you're hair is pretty."

"Well, thank you, Mister Williams." She smiled, the first smile she could recall since he'd returned to Tuck's Landing.

When Molly had finished eating, Boots removed the barrel from one of her repeaters, pulled out the cylinder and loaded it from the ammo wallet he kept in his inside jacket pocket. Over the ends of the chambers he smeared lard when he was finished and explained, "This keeps the chambers from going off all at the same time. You'd be unhappy if that happened when you're shooting. Why don't you load the other one?"

She broke down the other repeater, loaded it and reassembled it, and smeared lard over the end of the cylinder the same way he had.

"You seem to have a knack for this," Boots observed.

"True enough," a houseguest commented, as he ate breakfast and watched them. "It's a shameful pity that a nice lady like her should need to know how to do a thing like that."

"Are you ready to take them out back and try them?" he asked.

She nodded.

Behind the barn, out of sight from the house, he cut a blaze in the side of a live oak and said, "Let's see if you can hit that."

Stepping back a pace, he stood behind her and reached around to place one of the repeaters in her hands. The weight strained her wrists and she asked, "Aren't we too close to that tree?"

"In most cases," Boots continued, "folks would use these up close, like we are to this tree. Go ahead and use both hands. You'll have more control that way, one hand around the grip and one underneath, like a cup and saucer. It'll be a long time before you can shoot one-handed. Don't squeeze the life out of it either. Just hold it firm, like you caught a dove. Hold it hard enough to control it, but not hard enough to hurt it. Now pull the hammer back with your thumb. That's it. Don't put your finger down until you're ready to shoot, okay?" Withdrawing his hands he said, "Go on ahead, squeeze it slow and gentle."

The repeater leapt in her hands and the report deafened her, as if someone had boxed her ears. The shot struck the bark left of the blaze, and at this point she wasn't sure if possessing Asa's repeaters was such a good idea after all.

"That's alright," he said. "You did just fine. Try it again. Squeeze it slower this time. That's it."

Her next shot struck the blaze.

"Keep going," he urged her.

She fired again, but the recoil numbed her wrist and made her forearm ache. She began trembling and her last shots missed the tree completely. With the other repeater she missed five times, and was glad when it was over. She turned to Boots, feeling quite displeased with her first shooting lesson.

“I have to leave now,” he informed her. “You’ll get better if you practice. Try to get out every day and practice. You’ll be surprised how fast you’ll improve.”

Grasping her by both of her shoulders, he beseeched her, “Please don’t run off into Kiowa territory by yourself. Will you stay here? Will you wait for me?”

She had to consider her response before answering.

TOWING-THE-LINE

BOOTS'S EYES HAD such intensity, his voice so soft and earnest. Molly didn't want to disappoint him, but didn't have a choice. "I have to find Amy," she replied.

"Okay," he agreed. "I will help you. So, here's what I can do, Molly. When I get back to San Antonio, I'll talk to Colonel Karnes about Amy. But, you need to understand that I am assigned to the southwest territories, and Amy is in the northwest. We don't know the country, and if he agrees to let us search for her we'll need a guide. I know an agent up in Nacogdoches, Colonel Martin Casey. He negotiates with tribes all over Texas. I'll send a letter up to him and see if he'll help us. That's the best way, Molly. He's an expert in affairs like this. Anything else right now would be suicide."

Interlacing her fingers, Molly lowered her forehead to her knuckles and almost cried. "That's all I ask, Boots. It's all I ever wanted. I just want you to try."

"I'll come back as soon as I can … So, will you agree to stay here for now? Will you be here when I come back?"

Molly replied. "I have a few things I need to do. Then we'll see, but for now, yes, I'll stay at Tuck's Landing."

Together they crossed from the barn to the yard where Aunt Ruthie waited for them. Boots mounted up, doffed his hat, and then nudged his horse down the lane.

Molly went to her room, changed into her floppy shirt and trousers, and helped with morning chores. In the afternoon she went out with Aunt Ruthie to examine her restitution. The Rangers had stacked everything in the barn. The farmhands, Justin and Manuel, helped her load her wagon, and into Liberty she took everything. The horses and cattle took the longest to sell, but within two weeks she'd sold everything, even Emily's loom and spinning wheel, and bankrolled eleven hundred and forty-three dollars, more money than she'd ever seen in her life.

At the mercantile in Liberty she purchased buckskin to make trousers, like Aunt Ruthie's. She also wanted a jacket, like the jacket Boots wore. Leather would protect her from thorns and briars. She picked out supple leather and purchased a quantity for jacket making. Wanting also a good pair of boots, she hired the local cobbler to fashion a pair after the Ranger's boots, with tops that would pull up over her calves to her knees for riding or chores and roll down when they were not needed. Inside the boots she had the cobbler add inner pockets in which she could hide weapons or money. She also had the cobbler make a pair of shoes that would lace ankle-high like her old shoes. Those became the first new shoes she had since she was married. When she took delivery of her boots and shoes, she also picked out a suitable hat, made of leather, flat on top, and broad around the brim to shade out the sun.

The teamsters were beginning to move freight across Tuck's Landing again, and once every month they brought a load of fresh goods to the mercantile in Liberty. When Aunt Ruthie saw the goods going in, she would hitch up a wagon and take Molly shopping. During such an excursion a fresh bolt of dark-green muslin caught Molly's eye. Purchasing five yards for a new dress, she also fancied a set of hand-painted porcelain stud buttons and bought them. New buttons were a luxury that she and Emily had never known. They always saved old buttons for new clothing, traded them with their neighbors, or made tatted buttons out of thread.

Returning from the mercantile, Aunt Ruthie drew her wagon near the marshalling area before turning up the lane toward the house. Molly glanced over at folks in line waiting for the ferryboat, and then she hollered, "Look! Over there, Aunt Ruthie! Pull in behind those folks over there! I know those folks. They're from Gonzales."

Alongside a familiar looking wagon, she recognized the fluffy white beard of the man driving and the lacy bonnet on the elderly woman next to him. "Is that you, Henry Hort and Missis Schauble? I'm so happy to see you folks again."

"Molly McCracken? Sakes alive," Henry exclaimed. "Hey, Annie, it's Molly McCracken. Last time we saw you was … Let's see."

"San Felipe," Molly reminded him.

"Yes, that's right. San Felipe. When we pulled out, you and your sister were waiting for your brother-in-law to bring your little niece, Amy, back from the Comancheros. How'd that turn out?"

"She's still missing, Henry, and Innis was killed."

"Dad blame it, I knew he should have stayed with us that night. I couldn't talk to him though. No one could talk to that man."

"That wasn't when he was killed, Henry. It was after that, down in Matagorda. We went down there looking for Amy."

"Oh, I see. And, she's still missing?"

"The Kiowa have her."

"Sorry to hear that, Molly, real sorry."

Missis Schaubel leaned forward to look at Molly and asked, "How's your sister, Emily?"

"She got the cholera and died at Missis Powell's Tavern."

"What a horrible thing," Missis Schauble's voice faltered and her eyes reddened. "We've seen so much cholera these past weeks. Youngins mostly and elderly folks like us. I don't know why we were spared from the rotting death, but here we are, on our way back to nothing."

"It won't be easy," Henry declared. "But, we'll rebuild that mercantile back in Gonzales. Me and Annie Schauble here have decided to throw in together and be partners in business."

Molly smiled at both of them, and said, "Then congratulations are in order. So, tell me where you went from San Felipe. Did you go to Louisiana?"

"We made it as far as the Sabine," Missis Schauble explained. "We talked about crossing over and going all the way to New Orleans, but the roads were real boggy. Sometimes the horses had trouble keeping their heads above the mud holes they was so bad. It wore us out. We were getting skinny and sickly, too, so we decided to make camp with other folks along the Sabine. We figured if Santa Anna pushed his way that far, we'd just hop across the river into the States.

"Folks had camps stretching twenty miles up and down that old Sabine, and it was the most pitiful sight you ever seen, Molly. They had next to nothing. Their shoes were rotting off their feet, and their clothes had turned to rags. They were tying their blankets up in the trees to make tents, and their youngins were running around and doing their business anywhere they felt like it. When they weren't coming down with the dysentery, or the whooping cough, they were getting the cholera, and that was the worst. Very few that got the cholera ever got better."

"Were y'all starving?" Molly asked.

"We had meat. The folks that were able formed up into hunting parties and brought back everything they could get that was walking around on four legs. They'd split everything up amongst us, and sometimes folks would give us a big old catfish. There weren't many days when we didn't have something simmering in the kettle.

"What bothered us most was the stench and filth we came to live with after awhile. You put that many folks together without no accommodations and living conditions go down pretty fast. I couldn't stand it. We didn't have nothing to make soap and keep ourselves clean, so I decided to start bo'ling everything. I bo'led our clothes, and I bo'led our blankets. I bo'led our supper, long as we had something to eat. We didn't have no coffee neither, so I even bo'led what greens I could find and made them into tea. That's what we drank every day. I kept that kettle on the fire day and night. We stayed as clean as I could keep us, not like the rest of them poor folks. We didn't leave no garbage lying around neither. We buried everything we couldn't use."

"Would y'all like to come on up to the house and spend the night?" Molly asked. "We'd have a chance to catch up. You're the only folks from Gonzales I've seen since I left."

Missis Schauble turned to Henry and he nodded. "All right then," Henry said, and turned his wagon around.

After supper they sat out on the front porch with Aunt Ruthie and the house guests and recalled better times. In the morning Henry drove their wagon aboard the ferryboat and Molly waved them off, watching until they disembarked on the other side.

After chores, she spent the next few afternoons sewing together a new dress and proudly wore it with her new shoes out on the front porch with Aunt Ruthie and the house guests.

The riding leathers took longer, especially the gloves. Stitching the tough leather was difficult and time consuming, breaking several stout needles, requiring double thread, and a great deal of patience. The results provided her with a good pair of gloves and a pair of durable trousers. She also had the cobbler make her a belt.

Cutting out her riding jacket, she fashioned it after the jackets the Rangers wore, with a collar that would turn up, and lapels that would overlap and tie down for cold weather. Just above the front hem of the jacket she attached pockets for spare cylinders, and over the pockets she attached tie-down flaps to shed rain and keep the cylinders dry. Inside the jacket she sewed in a pocket for an ammo wallet, and with scraps she made a wallet. When finished, she rubbed blood wood into the jacket, trousers, and boots to blacken them. If necessary, she wanted to blend into the shadows. To rainproof her outfit she rubbed in bear oil. Pulling the jacket on, she found it warm but comfortable, and decided to try it out while she practiced shooting.

On her way to the barn Aunt Ruthie stopped her and asked to join her. Admiring Molly's handiwork she said, "Y'all have done a lovely job with your new clothes, darlin'. That dress you've been wearing is as good as I ever seen, and that riding outfit you got on, my, my. I can throw a stitch or two, but not like that. I've seen riding outfits that don't look near as good as that one."

"Would you like me to make a riding outfit for you, Aunt Ruthie? I offered to pay you for my room and board, but you wouldn't take any money. It's the least I can do."

"You do plenty around here, darlin', with morning chores and all. But, I must admit. That is a fine looking riding outfit you're wearing. It's not like anything I've ever seen on womenfolk. I wouldn't turn one down, if y'all offered me one."

"Consider it done, Aunt Ruthie. I'll start cutting it out this evening."

Aunt Ruthie followed her behind the barn, and she carried with her a block of fire wood under her arm. Standing the block on the ground, she backed away from it, drew her dueling pistol and fired. The block flipped over, as a cloud of sulfurous smoke rolled across the field. "How's that for an old lady?" she asked Molly.

"I don't think you're old, Aunt Ruthie. I think you're awesome."

"Obliged, darlin'."

Setting up the block again, Molly pulled a repeater from behind her new belt. It wobbled in her hand. Upon the palm of one hand she rested it, like a cup and saucer as Boots had taught her, and she fired. The repeater recoiled upward and all but wrenched itself from her grip. It hadn't kicked like that before, not that she recalled. Again she fired, and the ball splattered into the dirt. The recoil sent a stab of pain deep into her wrists. Three more shots went into the dirt as the recoil inflamed her wrist. Lowering the empty repeater, she declared, "This thing is hurting my wrist, Aunt Ruthie. It's heavy as an anvil and it kicks like a mule. The more I shoot, the worse I get. I'll never be as good as you."

Aunt Ruthie chuckled. "You ain't strong enough for a horse-pistol like that. That's all. If you want to shoot like me, you'll have to strengthen up your wrists, and you need more strength in your forearms too. That ain't natural for womenfolk." To Molly she presented her forearms, palms up. Making a fist, she flexed the muscles in her forearms. Opening her hands and turning them over, she displayed the veins and muscled tendons standing out on the backs of her wrists and hands. "These ain't pretty hands, darlin', but they can shoot a man if they have to."

"Your hands can do that, Aunt Ruthie? You don't need a pistol?"

Aunt Ruthie threw her head back and laughed. "My gracious, I think I found a smart aleck in you. I like that."

"I work hard around here, Aunt Ruthie. I think my wrists are already strong enough from the work I do."

"Well, you've haven't been out on the ferryboat with Klaus yet. You've seen how hard he works, and you've seen the strength that six years of towing the line has given him."

"You want me to tow the ferryboat? That's man's work. I can't do that. Look at Klaus. He's built for that kind of work. I'm not built like that. I could never tow folks across the Trinidad like he does."

"Maybe not like he does. And maybe you can't tow them all the way across, darlin', but you can tow them as far as you can, and the next day you can tow them a little farther. If you want strength enough to handle them repeaters, you'll do what you have to do. If not, well darlin', that's okay too. I like you fine, just the way you are."

The next afternoon, when morning chores were done, Molly changed into her new riding outfit and went out on the ferryboat with Klaus. She noted that the ferryboat was fitted with a plank deck of oak and side rails, and it was about a third the length of the sternwheelers she had seen in New Orleans. Fore and aft gates were latched while away from the docks. Klaus opened one or the other, allowing passengers to embark and disembark when the boat was secure.

Above the docks on opposite sides of the Trinidad stood oaken beam structures, which held large wooden pulleys bigger than wagon wheels. Around the pulleys a hemp rope fed out to the ferryboat. The rope was thick enough to secure a ship, and from the bottoms of the pulleys it attached fore and aft to the ferryboat. From the tops of the pulleys it spanned the river, and threaded through a smaller set of pulleys on the ferryboat railings, allowing the rope to slide across a deck span of about twenty paces, where Klaus could pull or walk with it.

Molly gave the rope a try. Her hands were too small to close all the way around, but she was able to tow the ferryboat about a quarter-way across the Trinidad, before her muscles gave out. The teamster driver aboard was patient with her slow progress, but seemed to be taken up the whole time with gawking at her leather riding outfit. He offered to help, but Klaus stepped up and took over.

Another teamster boarded, and Molly tried again. Lame and tired, she towed the ferryboat ever so arduously. Her arms ached, and pain began to radiate into her shoulders and back. She stretched, shook out her arms, and turned the chore over to Klaus.

A family drove their wagon and a team of horses on board, and a young girl watched Molly as she sat beside her parents on the seat-board. Klaus closed the gate, and once again Molly attempted to tow the line as the ferryboat drifted away from the dock. Slowing with each tug, she then tried folding her arms over the rope for a better grip and walked with the rope rather than pulling it, but her legs soon gave out as well.

"Why y'all dressed like a backwoodsman?" the young girl on the seat-board asked.

Her mother agreed and said, "A woman ain't supposed to dress like a man. Showing yourself off like that makes men-folk think thoughts." To her husband she turned a narrow eye adding, "It ain't lady like."

The young girl's father stepped down from the wagon and complained, "I ain't got all day to get across this here river. Let me pull that rope for y'all."

Molly gave him a sideways glance and let loose of the rope. Opening her hands, she looked at the blisters that were forming on the pads of her fingers and palms. "You're right," she admitted. With the tow rope no longer in her hands, her wrists, shoulders and back began to throb.

Klaus stepped in front of him, and said, "Let mm … me do that."

The man looked at Klaus in an odd way, then he mocked him by asking, "You sure y'all know which way to pull on that there rope?"

Heartily, the man's youngsters laughed at Klaus.

Then Molly spoke up in his behalf saying, "Why don't y'all get back in your wagon and mind your own business."

"Until my rig rolls off the other side," the man insisted, "this here ferryboat is my business."

Klaus jerked the rope so hard that the man staggered backwards, fell to a sitting position on the deck planks, and went speechless. His youngsters and his wife held their peace as he jumped to his feet, and scrambled up onto his wagon.

Beneath his beard Klaus smiled. When he saw Molly watching him he bobbed his head, and continued bobbing it until the ferryboat bumped into the dock on the other side. He opened the gate, and the man cracked his whip, driving his family up the hill.

"You handled that very well," Molly commended Klaus.

"Sometimes the things a man duh … does says more than the th … things he says."

"That's very wise of you, Klaus. Anything else you might have said out there would have just made him get madder."

His cheeks brightened, and his head continued to bob.

Across the river the bell rang. On top of the hill Molly saw a teamster waving at them, and he seemed anxious to board. Changing direction, Klaus prepared to pull the ferryboat over to pick him up, but Molly went back to the house and stayed off the ferryboat until her muscles and blisters had time to heal.

When she returned, she wore her floppy work clothes, rolled her sleeves up, and put on the gloves she'd made for riding. Tying up her hair, she pulled her hat on over it, and looked very much like a ferryboat hand. The passengers paid little attention to her. A quarter-way across, her wrists and arms gave out again, but a month of towing the line gave her the strength she needed to tow the ferryboat about three-quarters of the way across. During the evenings, when she was off the ferryboat, she'd take her repeaters out behind the barn for shooting practice.

"Would y'all like me to go out shooting with you, darlin'?" Aunt Ruthie asked her on a hot evening in June.

"Of course," Molly replied, as she thumped down the front porch steps. Behind her belt she'd tucked her repeaters, and over them she'd pulled her floppy shirt to keep them hidden from the houseguests. Behind the barn she stood up blocks of firewood, backed away from them, and said, "You go first, Aunt Ruthie."

Drawing her pistol, Aunt Ruthie cocked and fired, knocking over a block with a single, fluid motion.

"How can you do that so easy?" Molly asked. "You're so fast I can't see what you're doing. Are you cocking it when you pull it out, or do you leave it cocked all the time?"

"Carry around a cocked pistol?" Aunt Ruthie laughed. "I ain't got no death wish. I have known a few stupid people who carried around a cocked pistol, but they ain't around no more. It's a bad way of dying, too, with your bowels all blown out from the front side. Takes days, maybe a week, before you die. Don't ever do that, darlin'. I only cock it after I pull it out and when I'm ready to shoot. I cock it and pull the trigger at the same time."

"It's like lightening, Aunt Ruthie. I still don't understand."

Laughing again, Aunt Ruthie added, "That's the whole idea, but it don't come natural. It takes time, and lots of practice. In time it will come to you, too. Try it darlin', and let me watch you so I can see what you're doing."

Squaring her shoulders, Molly also spread her feet and drew a repeater. As it came out, the hammer caught under her floppy shirt. Shaking it free, she raised it one-handed, like Aunt Ruthie had raised her pistol. It felt secure, stable, and not as heavy, but when she pulled the hammer back, her thumb slipped off. Reaching with her free hand, she pulled the hammer back with both thumbs and fired. With strength to control the recoil, she also brought the barrel back on target and fired again. Three more times she fired, and when the smoke cleared she lowered the repeater and asked, "How'd I do, Aunt Ruthie? I couldn't see where they went."

"If y'all keep shooting like that, the boys won't need to plow my field." She slapped the tops of her thighs and laughed, adding, "And you're shooting up the alfalfa, too. Don't worry about it though. The cattle won't mind a few holes in their alfalfa."

Stuffing the empty repeater behind her belt, Molly tried to laugh with Aunt Ruthie, but it didn't come easy. "I don't know what I'm doing wrong," she said. "You told me I needed more strength in my wrists, so I've been working with Klaus. I'm holding on to the repeater better when I shoot, but I still can't hit anything. There must be something wrong with these repeaters. They're not as good as Boots said they are."

"Okay! Okay." Aunt Ruthie gave Molly a reassuring pat on her shoulder. "Here's your problem. There ain't nothing wrong with them repeaters. I was watching you while you were shooting, and it looks like you're scared to death of them horse-pistols, and that's understandable. They're powerful and they make a lot of noise. You need to respect them for what they can do, but don't let yourself be afraid of them. You're familiar enough with them now. You know what they're going to do, but you're not trusting them yet. You have to trust them. You're closing your eyes every time they go off. You're blinking, darlin'. You can't see where the ball is going, because your eyes are shut when you pull the trigger."

"I'm not blinking. I'd know if I was blinking."

"Can you see the barrel rise up when it fires? It should look like an upside down hammer for an instant, like you're holding a hammer head in your hand and the handle is sticking up the wrong way. Do you see that?"

"No."

"Can you see the ball flying down range?"

"No."

"It's there, darlin'. It's flying ahead of the smoke, and you can see it for an instant, just before the barrel jumps up in the way. Try to watch for that next time. It's just a little streak, and it's fast, but your eye is faster. By the time that barrel jumps up, it's over, and the ball already landed out in the alfalfa somewhere. Try it again with that other repeater of yours."

Drawing her other repeater, it too caught on her shirt. Shaking it free, she held her eyes as wide open as she could, raised the repeater and fired, knocking over a block of firewood. "I did it," she squealed. The following shots missed, but she said, "I think I saw it once, Aunt Ruthie. That little streak you were talking about."

"Yes, that's it, darlin'. When you get so you can see the ball fly every time you shoot, you'll know where it's going before you pull the trigger. You won't even think about it. You'll just know."

"Is that what you're doing when you shoot, Aunt Ruthie?"

"Yes, darlin', and that's why I only need one shot. And, that's why I never miss."

"Aunt Ruthie, I've been wanting to ask you something."

"Go on ahead, darlin'."

"Have you heard anything from Boots. It's been over a month."

"I haven't, but I expect to see him any day. He's not usually away more than a month."

In her room Molly cleaned her repeaters and put them away for the night. After chores the next day, she went out again on the ferryboat. When another month of towing the line had passed, she began to feel the strength in her shoulders, arms, wrists, and hands. She could pull the ferryboat across the Trinidad more than once. Klaus became a close friend, a benefit she hadn't expected. More than a job, she realized the ferryboat had become his evocation. Like a proud father, he taught her everything he knew about handling it.

When the ferryboat touched the dock at Tuck's Landing, Molly unlatched the boarding gate and swung it open to disembark a freight hauler. Cracking his whip and yelling, he drove a team of eight horses and a substantial wagon load of crates up the hill. An old buckboard pulled out from the marshalling area and turned down the hill toward the dock. Descending on wobbly wheels, the rickety buckboard was drawn by a swayback mare. Molly's heart went out to the passengers as she noted their extreme poverty. Waving them aboard, she also waved down another team from the marshalling area. There was room on the ferryboat for both.

Wedged between an elderly man and a middle age woman was a teenage girl, late teens, perhaps eighteen or nineteen years of age. Two early teen boys dangled their feet from the back as they took in the excitement of the ferryboat. The buckboard clunked onto the ferryboat, and Molly approached to collect the toll. An elderly man held a dime out to her.

"Xavier?" she gasped. "And Maudie? Is that you?"

"Molly McCracken?" the woman on the other end of the seat-board asked. "I not think I will to see you again. This is nice surprise!"

"Maria?" Molly squealed and clapped together her hands. "Maria Benson, and these are your boys back here, aren't they? They've grown so much. Look at them. Where are your little boys? Are they sleeping in back somewhere, and your baby? Where is your baby girl?"

"She is not …" Maria could only shake her head.

"Oh, Maria, are they …?"

"Yes."

"I'm sorry, Maria." Behind the teamster she closed the gate, latched it, and collected his toll. Turning to Klaus, she asked, "Can you take this one for me please?"

He bobbed his head and took hold of the tow line.

Turning again to Maria, she asked, "What happened?"

Maria was unable to speak, stricken with grief, and red in the eyes. To Xavier, who held yet a dime out to Molly, she turned and nodded, saying, "Please, please." Pushing his hand back to him, she clarified, "You keep this. You are my good friends. There's no charge."

"Gracias," he said and slipped the dime back into his coin pouch.

"What happened to the youngsters?" she asked Xavier.

He began to elaborate, saying, "We go to river called Sabine, and there we make our home with many others who run away from Santa Anna."

"Yes, yes," Molly said. "I've talked with Missis Schauble and Henry Hort about the refugee camp on the Sabine. Were you with them?"

"Sí, we go with them to river called Sabine. We make our camp close to them, and with each other we help to get food and water, and wood for our fires. Señora Schauble she uses very much wood. We bring much wood for her, and she cook much food for us, and she give us tea she make from greens. Together we drink lots of tea, but little ones, they do not like tea. They do not drink it."

"What happened to Maria's youngsters?"

"The baby she not go to Sabine with us. She has cough that whistles, and youngest boy he has cough, too, when we get to Sabine. He is very sick. We have to bury him with others who get whistling cough. So, we make place beside road to bury so many others. I call it Valley of Sorrows that place because everyone is very sad. It is not good place, Señora McCracken. I do not want to go back there."

"And what about the other boys," Molly asked.

"The other boys, they get the rice water, very sick. Señora Schauble, she gives laudanum but is very little, not enough. The youngest boys they cannot eat. They cannot stand up, and they get very small. They waste away, so the next one he die, and then the next. The two who are the oldest, very slowly they get okay. Then they are better but they are very thin and very weak. It is sad time for us, very sad. I cry sometimes too much. And, now we are going home."

Dropping down on one knee, Molly slipped her hand inside one of her boots. "Just a moment," she said. From the pocket inside she withdrew five gold coins and handed them to Xavier. "Take this," she said. "It's enough to buy a new wagon, a good horse, and the supplies you will need to put up a cabin before winter when you get to Gonzales."

"I can't take this, señora. I did nothing to earn this. It would not be right for me to take this."

Closing her hand over the coins, she smiled at Xavier. "These boys look strong enough to build a cabin for you. All you have to do is to show them what to do. They are your family now, Xavier, these boys, their mother, Maria, and your daughter-in-law, Maudie. You have lost so much in the war, but now you have been placed together. I don't want you to suffer anymore, so take this money and use it to take care of your new family." She reached over to his pouch and stuffed the coins inside.

"Gracias," he said, as the creases around his eyes filled with dampness.

"Thank You," Maudie whispered. "Y'all don't know how much this means to us."

Maria smiled and reached out to Molly, grasping her hand in both of hers. "I have not expected such good things like this. Bless you," she sobbed.

Over her shoulder, Molly noticed that they were nearing the other dock. When the ferryboat bumped, she opened the gate for her friends.

"Will you come back to Gonzales?" Xavier asked, as he drove the buckboard onto the dock.

"I don't think so," Molly replied.

He made the sign of the cross, and said, "Bendito sea Dios."

"Obliged," Molly replied. "Bless you, too."

He turned his attention to the road and cracked his reins. The others turned around and waved their goodbyes until they were out of sight, and Molly went back to the tow rope until evening.

After supper she went out for more shooting practice, and Aunt Ruthie went with her. Behind the barn she pulled her repeater, shook it loose from her shirt, and knocked down five out of five blocks.

Aunt Ruthie squealed with delight. "That's it! That's it!" Clapping her hands, she continued, "I think you're catching on. There's one last thing I need to tell you about though. It's the most important thing."

"What's that, Aunt Ruthie?"

"You're getting strong, sure enough, but that ain't all you need. Womenfolk will lose every time when it comes to strength, no matter how strong you are. The only thing that gives you an edge is your speed. The things you're doing so far, you're doing good, but now you have to do it faster than anyone else. Once you work that into your style, no one will be able to stop you."

When Molly was finished with practice she returned to her room. Before turning in for the night, she faced herself in the mirror. Faster than everyone else, she thought. Humph! Pulling an unloaded repeater and cocking it, she watched in the mirror as the hammer caught on her shirt tail. She could tuck her floppy shirt into her trousers, but she liked her shirttail out, it kept attention away from the rest of her, and it kept her repeaters hidden. Men-folk didn't gawk, and womenfolk didn't criticize. She wanted to keep it that way.

Sticking her thumb out as she pulled her repeater, she learned to lift her shirt tail and keep it from snagging, first with one hand and then the other. She practiced pulling both of them at the same time, cocking them together and watching in the mirror for ways to conserve motion and improve her speed. If her repeaters got tangled in her shirt when she really needed them, she knew it could cost her life. Every night from then on she practiced in front of the mirror before going to bed.

A third month on the ferryboat gave Molly a remarkable hardness she'd never known. Her wrists and arms grew strong. Her back and shoulders felt like they were knitted together with strands of steel. Veins and muscles stood out on her wrists and the backs of her hands. Pulling her gloves off, while Klaus took a tow, she stepped away from the tow rope, opened and closed her hands, and turned them over to admire the progress she was making with them. Noticing that her gloves had worn through the finger pads, she resolved to make a new pair the first chance she had, and while pulling them back on she heard someone yelling from the dock across the river.

With his face shaded by his hat and his hands cupped around his mouth, he shouted, "I should've known Aunt Ruthie would put you to work on the ferryboat the first chance she got."

"It's Boots," Molly yelled to Klaus. "Help me pull us in faster." As the ferryboat drew close to the dock, she climbed the gate and leapt the gap over the water to the dock where Boots was waiting.

Watching her as she landed on the dock, he said, "Aunt Ruthie used to get mad at me for doing that. She said it was too dangerous. Said I'd fall in the river and get crushed between the dock and the ferryboat." Stepping back, he examined her up and down, adding, "Look at you in those old work clothes and that big hat. You look like a farmhand. Has Aunt Ruthie got you out pitching hay, too?"

Molly couldn't help smiling at him, and replied, "In the mornings I help Aunt Ruthie with house chores, after that I've been working on the ferryboat with Klaus."

"Did Aunt Ruthie really want you to work with Klaus?"

"It was her idea. It's strengthening my grip."

"Your grip? Why do you need to strengthen your grip?"

"For shooting."

"I see. Has Aunt Ruthie been teaching you to shoot, too?"

"Yes, and I'm doing pretty good. You should go out back with me after supper and I'll show you."

"If Aunt Ruthie is teaching you, you probably are good. She's one of the best I know."

"Where've you been, anyway? It's been over three months."

"I know it's been awhile, and I feel bad because it took so long for me to get back here. I've got good news though." He offered the crook of his elbow and said, "Come on up to the house with me and I'll tell you."

THE FESTIVAL

AUNT RUTHIE TROTTED past her houseguests and down the front steps to meet Molly and Boots as they crossed the yard. "Bootsie," she yelled. "When did y'all get here? I thought I heard your voice. Manuel said he saw you in the corral, but when I went out there you were gone."

Wrapping his arms around her, Boots lifted her and twirled her around, and then set her down. Aunt Ruthie slipped her hand into his and pulled. "Come on in the house and let me fix you something to eat. You look starved half to death." With her free hand she poked at his sides saying, "I ain't never seen you so skinny."

Wincing, he laughed at her, and said, "I've got something for Molly first."

"Now, hold on there. I'm not done looking at you. Don't they ever feed you when you're out Rangerin'? You're getting too skinny. You're taking after your ma's side, tall and skinny, just like her. Will you be staying long? I hope you can stay awhile."

"About a week. I'm here to set up a festival in Liberty and recruit for the Service. Colonel Karnes has been authorized to add two hundred Rangers to his regiment."

"Two hundred?" Molly asked.

"Me and the boys have been out on campaign for the best part of three months straight without leave. Folks have been making their way back to their homesteads in Victoria, Goliad and Refugio, Gonzales and San Antonio. They've been plowing their fields and rebuilding their houses.

Most of them hardly have anything to defend themselves with. The marauders are taking advantage of them, while the Comanches are trying to take over their land. So, me and my boys are out there under-manned and stretched thin. Colonel Karnes says he wants to build up the Service, crush the marauders, and drive out the Comanches. That's why I'm here recruiting."

Aunt Ruthie tugged on his arm. "Before you go running off to set up your festival, why don't y'all come in and eat? I've got a big batch of beef and biscuits on the stove." Up the front steps she practically dragged him.

Glancing over his shoulder at Molly, Boots shrugged, and said, "I guess we can eat first. Then I have something to show you."

The bell rang down at the marshalling area. Someone was calling the ferryboat. Molly was glad to be away from the responsibility for the rest of the evening, and followed them into the kitchen. In the sunroom the houseguests had already taken seats around the long table. After helping Aunt Ruthie serve them, Molly took a seat, served herself supper, and inquired of Boots, "Tell me about this recruiting festival you want to set up."

"The last few weeks I've been working my way through the settlements, setting up these recruiting festivals. Folks have been cooperative, they fix vittles and donate livestock, we usually roast a hog or two. Then I run the horse races and shooting contests and give out prizes to the winners. The town folks get pretty excited over it, and when it's over, sometimes they dance all night."

"Sounds like fun," Molly commented. "Most folks haven't done anything like that since the war."

Boots nodded, "It gives them a chance to celebrate our independence from Mexico and gives me a chance to see who has the best horses and the most talent. The ones that seem right for the Service, I offer them an assignment and head them off to San Antonio."

"I'd like to help you with the festival," Molly offered.

"And I'd like to have you help," Boots accepted and pushed his empty plate back. "I have something to show you, if you're ready. Are you interested?"

"Yes."

Out to the corral he walked her, ushering her in with a broad sweep of his hand saying, "Her name is Angel. I told Asa's family about you and they agreed to sell her."

Astonished, Molly gaped at the pale-gray Arabian. Angel had a broad chest, large nostrils and wide-spaced eyes, eyes which were lower on her head than the horse that Boots rode. Angel's small muzzle fit in Molly's cupped hand, and while stroking Angel's neck she marveled at the horse's pretty eyes and long lashes. The name tarried on her tongue. "Angel," she said. "That's a pretty name, and you're such a pretty girl."

Angel bobbed her head as if she understood what Molly had said.

"And smart too," Molly added. To Boots she said, "This is a very nice surprise. I never expected anything like this."

"Want to take her out for a ride?" he asked.

Nodding, Molly said, "Wait here. I want to change out of my work clothes first." Up to her room she dashed, put on her riding leathers, and returned to the corral.

Boots already had both horses saddled. Looking up and down at Molly, he smiled and said, "Look at you now. That's the fanciest riding outfit I ever saw. You made that, didn't you? Nice job. I'm also noticing how much better you're looking, too." Glancing down at her feet he added, "And, look at those boots."

Reaching down, she rolled them up to her knees, shiny and black. "You like them?" she asked. "They're just like yours, but they're made for me."

"I'd say it looks like you're fitting right in here at Tuck's Landing."

"I love it here." Stepping into her stirrup, she swung her leg over the saddle and took up Angel's reins. "How much do I owe you for Angel?"

"Nothing. She's a gift."

"This is an expensive horse, Boots. I can tell she has breeding just by looking at her. She must be worth six months wages or more. I insist that you let me pay for her."

"I insist that she's a gift," he countered. Closing the corral and mounting up, he twisted around in his saddle to look at Molly.

She wondered about the dreamy look in his eyes and asked, "What is it? Why are you looking at me like that?"

"Just thinking about Tuck's Landing, thinking about how you've become part of things around here, and thinking about how much Aunt Ruthie likes you and thinking …" He stopped midsentence, turned his eyes toward the lane and nudged his horse forward, adding, "Just thinking is all."

The thud of Angel's hooves echoed back from the house as they crossed the yard, and when they were on the road they faced into the wind. Together they trotted the short two mile distance into Liberty, a small town with a single street, lined with log buildings, some plank, and some stone. Many buildings had glass windows, and others had only shutters. The bank was made of limestone, and the law offices gave the town a feeling of prominence. Town folks were in the street. Boots knew most of them, quite a few Molly also knew. The mercantile was open and busy.

Past Liberty, Molly glanced down at Angel's flowing mane and back at the sway of her long tail. Her shoulders bulged with unfurled energy, flexing in stride. Molly could feel her strength pulsing beneath her.

When they'd passed a line of freight-haulers, Boots kicked his horse into a gallop, leaving behind puffs of dust.

Angel followed effortlessly.

Boots turned his head and yelled above the wind, "This is as fast as most horses can go! Why don't you see what she can really do? See what Angel's bred for!"

Molly kicked her heels and hollered, "Git!"

Angel stretched out into a blistering, heart pounding race. Molly rose up on her haunches and flexed her knees with each powerful stride. The wind began to sting her face, and she squinted as she blew past Boots. The brush along the road began to blur and the release of energy made her want to scream. Long and hard she screamed, and Angel seemed to like it, leaping into greater speed. Molly screamed until her lungs hurt and leaned over her pommel, screaming and imagining that she was airborne. She wanted to soar up into the clouds with Angel.

The horse's breath began to labor. Molly slowed her to a canter, and then to a trot. The horse shook its head and blew a snorting breath that told Molly she liked to run. Twisting around, Molly watched Boots galloping up behind her, about ten lengths back. Reaching down, she patted Angel's neck, stroking her and saying, "Good run, girl. Good run."

Cantering up beside her, Boots commented, "I think the two of you were meant for each other. That was something to see."

Molly patted Angel's neck again saying, "I guess I need to get out more often. I haven't been out for a ride in weeks."

"What was all that screaming?" he asked. "You sounded like a Comanche. All you'd have to do is wag your tongue a little to make it into a war cry."

"I don't know." Again she gazed up into the sky, imagining that Angel could fly. "It just came out of me," she explained.

"I could hear anger," he observed. "I suspect it's your niece, isn't it?"

"I suppose it is," she admitted. "You haven't said anything about her."

"Remember I said I had good news?"

"Yes. I remember. You said that down at the docks when you arrived. I wanted to ask you about it. Then I thought Angel was the good news."

"This seems like a good time to tell you, now that we're alone. A couple weeks ago I met up with an Orcoquisac brave in Lynchburg. He works for the Service now. Said he did some trading with the Kiowa. Then he came over to our side and joined the Service as a scout. He spent quite some time with the tribes during the war, and he said he remembers seeing a little blonde haired girl with the Kiowa, and that they had taken quite some liking to her, because of the color of her hair."

Molly pulled back on her reins and stopped in the middle of the road. "Ugh!" she groaned, and lowered her head. Pausing for several moments to collect her thoughts, she said, "I have to go," and to the side of Angel's neck she pulled the reins to turn her horse around.

Sensing Molly's anxiety, Angel turned and reared up, whinnying on her haunches.

"Hold on." Boots grabbed Angel's bridle and eased her down to the road. "Where are you going?" he asked.

"You don't understand. If I know she's alive and know where she is, I have to go to her. I can't stay here."

"If you go up there, they will kill you, or worse. You <u>have</u> to stay here for now. The time isn't right."

Molly covered her face with her hands and wept. "There has to be a way," she sobbed. "There has to be. What about this Colonel Casey fellow you told me about?"

Releasing Angel's bridle, he reached over to Molly's shoulder and explained, "I haven't heard back from him yet. I told you about the Kiowa because I thought you'd take comfort in it. I thought it would ease your mind, if you knew she was all right. I didn't want to get you all fired up to go after her. Just give it some time, Molly. It sounds to me like she's being cared for just fine. She's safe. You don't need to worry about her."

Pushing tears from her cheeks, Molly admitted, "I can't help but worry about her."

"Well, worrying won't bring her back. We know she's cared for, and that's what's important. The time will come, I promise you, when we can go up there and get her." He turned his horse toward Liberty asking, "Are you okay with that?"

Molly's heart sank, but she nodded her agreement, and she nudged Angel toward town.

"What say we stop and talk to some of the town folks about putting on that festival?" he suggested. "You still interested in helping me with that?"

"Yes," she said. "But, I've been thinking about something else you said. I want to ask you something."

"Okay."

"I'd like to try out for the Ranger Service."

He almost smiled. Then he lowered his chin and pursed his lips asking, "You're serious, aren't you?"

"Yes. You saw me ride. I've got a good horse now, thanks to you, and I'm a good shot. I think if I enter those contests you're holding at your recruiting festival, I can win."

Pausing for several moments, his eyes softened and became almost sympathetic. "We'll see. When it comes time, I'll talk to the competitors. If they agree to let you enter in the contests, then I'll let you compete. But, I can't offer you an assignment in the Service."

"What if I win?" she argued. "If I can beat those other competitors in every contest, doesn't it prove that I'm the best? Why wouldn't you offer me an assignment?"

"Colonel Karnes would never allow it, to begin with. And, it would disrupt the boys if I did. He knows that. I don't want the boys thinking about anything else when we're on campaign. Your presence would divide their attention. I have to keep them together, keep them single-minded. I can't lead them if they're divided. Does that make sense?"

"Yes, it does," she sighed.

"Besides," he added. "When we go out on campaign, we go for weeks at a time. We eat together, sleep together, and do everything together, and the boys can get pretty rough at times. You wouldn't like living with them, Molly. I would be afraid for you and not just because of our enemies."

"But, I ..."

"You have to trust me on this, Molly. The Ranger Service is no place for a woman."

Entering Liberty, they talked with some of the town folks at the mercantile and after making preliminary arrangements, Boots and Molly returned to Tuck's Landing.

The next afternoon they went again to town and finalized their plans. That evening, after supper with Aunt Ruthie, Boots invited Molly out for shooting practice. Behind the barn they stood up several blocks of firewood. Then she stepped back and pulled one of her repeaters, knocking down five blocks with five successive shots, and then breaking down her repeater to exchange the spent cylinder for a loaded one.

The bell rang from the marshalling area; someone was calling the ferryboat and she informed Boots, "Manuel has the ferryboat this evening."

Boots beamed with approval. "If I hadn't seen you shoot with my own eyes, I wouldn't believe it," he said. "I think you might be faster than me." Standing the blocks up again and adding a few more, he squared off next to her. "On three, show me again what you can do with that repeater ... One ... Two ... Three."

At the same instant, their repeaters exploded into action. Molly's fifth shot knocked down her fifth block, as Boots's fourth shot knocked down his fourth block and then his fifth.

He exchanged cylinders, smiled, and acquiesced, saying, "You are faster. I think you'll be tough competition for them boys at the festival. You should be proud of what you've done so far."

"I never thought of it as something to be proud of. It's just something I have to do."

"It's important that you know there's more to it than just shooting straight," he explained. "There's things you haven't learned yet. You might have to use your repeaters someday, and if you do, your target won't be a block of wood, and it won't be standing still. Most likely, you won't be standing still either. You might be running for your life or riding Angel. Have you ever tried shooting at a moving target from the back of a galloping horse?"

"No, I haven't."

"Well, if I can get you in the games Sunday, we'll see how you do. Then you'll know what you have to work on."

"Fair enough," she replied.

By Sunday, Molly and the town folks had the festival ready. They'd blocked off Market Street on both ends and gathered together to share what they had, setting up planks to use as tables and roasting two hogs in a pit overnight. Riding Angel to town, Molly wore her riding leathers; she wanted to enter Angel in the horse races.

Boots drove a wagon for Aunt Ruthie, along with a load of houseguests who didn't want to miss the excitement. When he discovered that Molly wanted to race Angel, he advised her against it saying, "It wouldn't be fair to the others. Folks around here can't afford a breed like her. There'll be five heats and you'll win every time. The others will get discouraged and drop out before it's over. You'd probably be the only one left running. So, let's just keep her a secret for now. What do you think?"

Molly agreed to keep Angel out of the races. When she looked around, she noticed that almost everyone in the little settlement had come out for the festival. Even General Houston had come to town, though he had been home on his plantation recovering from his wound at San Jacinto. He arrived in a carriage, and an entourage of family and military aids assisted him, providing him with a chair. Young and old, rich and poor joined together as one, with General Houston looking on. They ate and laughed, and commenced to dance whenever the fiddler struck up a tune.

Molly volunteered on the service line and dished up vittles equally to everyone. Travelers and teamsters from both directions stopped in for mesquite barbeque pork and fixings. Travelers passing through, some of the poorest folks she'd ever seen, rode in bare-back, wearing broad sombreros. They tied their horses on the outskirts and joined the festivities, putting down vittles as if they hadn't eaten in days and slipping leftovers into their satchels. Molly didn't mind though and was pleased with the openness and generosity of the town folks. Some of the poor folks left when they were finished eating, and some of them stayed to watch the horse races.

General Houston didn't eat much, didn't look like he felt well either, and he seemed weary from the endless line of town folks who wanted to talk with him about the war. Finally, he motioned his aids over. They helped him up and whisked him away.

When the food was gone and the dancing died down, the races began. Molly cheered as twenty seven horses and riders galloped away with the starting gunshot out of Liberty. Observers cheered them along to the marshalling area at Tuck's Landing, where Klaus officiated the turn. The race finished at the festival, and the slowest riders were culled down to the last race. The town folks were crazy with excitement, yelling and applauding when the grand champion won the last heat.

With pomp and ceremony, Boots awarded the winner a silver belt buckle. Provided by the Ranger Service, it was a forged circle holding a five pointed star. The young man who won seemed to be proud to have it, holding it high and turning so that everyone could see.

Standing at the back of the crowd were two of the poor folk travelers Molly had noticed earlier. To her they seemed unusually intrigued by the valuable silver buckle. Perhaps they were interested in entering the contests and do their best to win one of the buckles.

Boots was ready to begin the shooting contests. Gathering the contestants together, thirty four of them in all, he asked if they were willing to allow a woman to join the competition.

One of them withdrew immediately saying, "If y'all are turning this into a picnic for girls, then why don't y'all just have us run a one-legged sack race with the youngins while we reload? But, y'all will have to do it without me." Brushing racing dust from his clothing, he stomped away.

Another commented, "Me and these boys over here don't much like the idea, Captain Williams." Indicating the others with him, "but we'll let her compete. Who is it, anyways? We don't want a bunch of little girls running around here shooting guns."

"It's Molly McCracken," Boots informed him.

"Missis McCracken over there?" He pointed at Molly. "She's okay. Why didn't y'all say so in the first place? Bring her on over and let's get this going."

Molly tugged on Aunt Ruthie's sleeve and asked, "Why don't y'all shoot with me?"

Aunt Ruthie replied, "I ain't trying out for the Rangerin' Service, darlin'. You go on ahead. Just go and have some fun."

The competition began with rifles. Molly didn't have a rifle, so Boots loaned his rifle to her, warning her that it would kick hard. For targets, the town folks had sawed off slices from an oak log and set them up at ten paces, one target for each competitor. After each round of shooting, they would move the targets back to twenty, thirty, forty, and then fifty paces. The best five shot target would win.

The first shot rocked Molly backwards. She wasn't used to shooting a rifle and missed. The second shot numbed her shoulder and it also missed. She dropped out after that. When five rounds of rifle competition were completed, Boots determined the winner and awarded him a buckle.

The town folks applauded with the same fervor as they had for the horse races, and the poor folk travelers were also applauding. They were looking up at that silver belt buckle, and while the town folks were whistling and yelling, one of them turned his gaze toward Molly. When the brim of his sombrero turned high enough for her to see his face, her heart skipped a beat. His face was scarred from his forehead through his nose, and highlighted with tattoos. She recognized the disfigured Comanchero who had ambushed her on Gotier Trace.

THE TWENTY-NINTH ASSIGNMENT

THE TOWN FOLKS fastened crosscut slices up on fence rails that they had erected for the pistol competition. The smallest group of five shots would win.

Anxious and fearful, Molly ran to Boots to tell him she'd just seen a Comanchero at the festival.

Giving her a quick smile, he returned his attention to the competition.

Tugging frantically on his sleeve, she insisted, "I just saw one of the Comancheros who ambushed me and my brother-in-law."

Again he gave her his attention and asked, "I thought you wanted to shoot in the pistol competition?"

"One of the Comancheros who killed Innis is here at the festival. I just saw him."

Opening his eyes wide, Boots glanced around and asked, "Comanchero? Where?"

"Over there," she said, gesturing toward the rear of the crowd. "In the back, over there."

"I don't see him."

Over the crowd Molly could not see. Jumping up, and then jumping again, she looked for the disfigured Comanchero, adding, "I can't see him anymore. He's wearing a sombrero. There's two of them. The other one might be Buffalo Head."

"Buffalo Head?" Boots rocked up on his toes and glanced again over the crowd. "There's lots of folks out there wearing sombreros," he said, and he shook his head. "Wait! I see them running between them buildings over there."

Molly tightened her hat and clenched her jaw. "They killed my brother-in-law in cold blood, Mister Williams. I'm going after them."

Extending his arm to block her way, he warned her, "They'll kill you in cold blood, too."

"Then I'll follow them. I'll find out where they're going."

"Just wait here …" He turned to the crowd and shouted at them, "Listen up, folks!"

Excited about the pistol competition, the clamorous crowd did not notice his plea, some applauding yet the winner of the rifle competition. With a commanding voice, Boots yelled at them again, "I said listen up!"

Falling silent, the crowd turned to him. The winner of the rifle competition lowered his prize buckle as Boots pointed across the street and elaborated, "Two Comancheros just ran between them buildings. They're murderers."

The shooting contestants sprang into action and Boots directed them saying, "Anyone who's willing, why don't y'all split up and see if you can seal off the town before they get away."

While his back was turned, Molly slipped away. Running across the street, she dashed between the buildings the Comancheros had run between. In back she found an alley, desolate and quiet, imposing a sense of grave danger upon her. Before stepping into the alley, she decided she should wait for Boots and looked back for him. She could see contestants running down Market Street. Boots was not with them.

Drawing one of her repeaters, she stepped out, pausing to scan the deserted alley. The rear entrances of businesses lined her side of the alley. Lining the other side of the alley, she noted a row of cabins and a few larger homes. Doors and windows stood open everywhere to relieve the heat of summer, she guessed. Folks didn't worry much in Liberty about thievery. They didn't own many things worth worrying about, and they always kept an eye on each other, except today. Everyone was at the festival today.

The alley reminded her of a long corridor lined with shadowy rooms. Taking a step, she glanced inside an open window, and thought she could see shadows, ominous figures, and armed oppressors. Blinking and looking again, they were only shadows. Next, she looked in an open doorway and saw more dark shadows. Only two doors remained before she reached the rear of the mercantile. Taking a few more steps, she checked inside all open windows and doors. Then someone stepped out from between the buildings.

Recognizing Manuel, Aunt Ruthie's farmhand, she lowered her repeater and breathed a sigh of relief. Against his lips he held an extended finger, shushing her. Turning, he pointed to an open door at the back of the mercantile. Passing him, she carefully proceeded to the mercantile doorway and saw only a sliver of what was inside. In that sliver she recognized the disfigured Comanchero, and he was filling his satchel. Buffalo Head would probably be with him, and he terrified her.

Again she glanced down the alley for Boots, and wondered what else she should do. Now that she'd found the Comancheros, she couldn't leave without confronting them. The more she thought about it, the more her stomach roiled. Tremors sank into her hands, and down to her knees. Her legs felt like jelly, and she could feel the color drain from her cheeks, as she realized that she would be killed if she went in there. He would want to kill her, as much as she wanted to … kill him? She hadn't thought about it that way before and couldn't say that killing him was what she really wanted. She wanted justice, yes, but by killing him? She was not certain. Now that she had the opportunity, it didn't seem right, as if a small voice was telling her it wasn't right.

Staggered in the breach of confrontation, she faced a moment that she had not expected, and away from the door she quietly backed up, bumping into Manuel and jolting around. Shaking his head and tugging at the fringe of her jacket, Manuel pulled her around the corner, drawing her into the space between the mercantile and the next building. He whispered to her ever so softly, "You not go in there, señora. Is very dangerous."

Inside she heard footsteps, running footsteps, and a man leapt from the doorway. The disfigured Comanchero ran across the alley and away from her, the one she'd seen inside the mercantile. Into the alley she stepped and raised her shaky repeater, adding her free hand, saucer-like to steady it, she cocked it. Having the opportunity to pull the trigger, she couldn't do that to another human being. Who was she to pass judgment on him? What gave her the right to take his life?

Between two cabins across the alley he scampered without looking back. His satchel bulged full with goods, too full to tie the flap down. Behind him the flap fluttered as he ran away. She lowered the hammer, and lowered her repeater to her side. Again Manuel pulled the fringe of her jacket, pulling her back into the space between the buildings. Then she heard more footsteps coming from inside, tapping rapidly across the plank floor.

Into the alley leapt Boots, stopping and looking around.

"Boots?" she whispered.

Spinning toward her, she heard his repeater click. Gasping, she fell backwards into Manuel, and both of them landed in the dirt.

"What are you doing back here?" he groused. "Are you trying to get yourself killed?"

"I'm … I'm …" she stammered.

"Did you see them?"

Across the alley she pointed, and said, "That way."

Peering between the cabins, he sidestepped for a better view. In the meadow she heard hoof beats fading, but couldn't see anyone. The disfigured Comanchero had gotten away. Buffalo Head had probably taken their horses back there and met him, and he probably got away too.

Town folks galloped up the alley on horseback, pulling up where Boots, Molly, and Manuel stood. "Want us to go after them?" one asked.

"Go on out that way." Boots pointed between the cabins. "I'll get my horse and catch up."

Out to Market Street he dashed, and Molly ran behind him. "My horse is back at Tuck's Landing," he reminded her. "Can I take Angel?"

Molly stopped halfway across the street, and he stopped to look back at her inquisitively. She wanted to go with him, wanted to see Buffalo Head and the disfigured Comanchero brought to justice. Angel could outrun the other horses, but she agreed that allowing Boots to take her horse was the only sensible decision. After all, he was a Ranger and she was not. "Go on ahead," she said. "Take her."

Mounting Angel, Boots galloped up Market Street with his knees perched high and his feet in stirrups adjusted to the length of Molly's legs, not his. At the sight of him she would have smiled had her experience in the alley not been so unsettling.

At the festival, the womenfolk had broken into small groups and vigorously discussed the state of the Republic and the problems they were facing. Molly stepped in alongside Aunt Ruthie and touched her arm asking, "Can I talk to you?"

"Of course, darling'. My word, looks like you're upset about something. Y'all didn't try to go after them Comancheros, did you?"

"Not here, Aunt Ruthie, over there. Let's talk over there." To the pistol shooting range, which the contestants had vacated, she took Aunt Ruthie and asked, "Did you ever have to shoot anyone?"

"That's quite some question you're asking. You went after them, didn't you? What happened? I didn't hear any shooting."

"I had him right in front of me, but I couldn't do it, Aunt Ruthie. I just couldn't do it." Molly hung her head.

"Of course you couldn't, darlin'. That's nothing to fret about. What was he doing, running away from you?"

"How did you know that?"

"Just putting things together is all. There was a time when I would have let him go, too, just like you did. But, I'm different now. There's no doubt in my mind, if I had the chance I would have put him down. I've been through times when folks were struggling a lot more than they are now, even with the war and all. There was a time when folks couldn't sleep at night least they keep one eye open. Those were hard times, darlin'. Times like that change folks. Not like it is now."

"Did you ever shoot anyone?"

Aunt Ruthie gave her an unusually long, sober gaze and admitted, "Men have fallen in front of me."

"You didn't have thoughts about doing it?"

"When a man's swinging a tomahawk at your head you don't have time for thinking thoughts."

"Was that the only time, Aunt Ruthie?"

"Well, darlin'. There's been trouble at the landing a few times and one other time up at the house. It's nothing to be proud of though. I'm not given to talking much about it."

"I'm just trying to understand what made you do it."

"Necessity, darlin', pure and simple. When y'all come to the place where you know you're going to die or else, you have to make a choice. Either you're going to give in and die, or you're going to do something about it."

"And, you don't have any regrets."

"Oh no, don't never think there won't be no regrets. If you survive, and in situations like that chances are you might not survive anyway, but if you do, you'll regret it the rest of your life. You'll just learn to live with it, like I do. There's faces in my head I can't never get out. They're like ghosts that never leave me be, but I'm still here in spite of them, and I'm still alive."

"It seems like it's given you a certain hardness, Aunt Ruthie."

"Hardness, darlin'?" She chuckled. "What you see that looks like hardness is fifteen years of heartache and regret. That's what makes folks like me look hard. It's heartache and regret."

"Then why do you stay here?"

"I love this land, and I love Bootsie." She offered Molly the crook of her elbow adding, "Getting kind of fond of you too, darlin'. Just so y'all know, having the nerve to shoot someone ain't worth the worry. If it happens, it'll be over before you can think about it. The thinking part starts afterwards and then you won't be able to make it stop. It just eats at you for the rest of your life. All you can do is try to be prepared for it, before it happens."

"I already have things that eat at me, Aunt Ruthie, like what happened to my sister and my brother-in-law, and my niece, and my …"

Aunt Ruthie put her arm around Molly and said, "I know. I know. Unfortunately, it's just the way of Texas, darlin'. Like you said yourself, why do y'all stay here?"

Molly thought for a minute. "What's keeping me here right now is my niece, Amy. After that, I don't know."

"Can you see yourself anyplace else?"

"No. I guess I can't."

"It's gotten into your blood then, just like me. It's Texas. I think you'll see it in time." Aunt Ruthie pulled her toward the festival. "Let's go on back with the other womenfolk before we start getting all teary eyed." They joined a circle and listened in on their conversation.

"It's always been like this!" a woman raged. "If it ain't Santa Anna butchering our men-folk and burning us out, it's Comancheros raiding our farms and our businesses, or it's Comanches trying to run us off our land. It's got to stop. We have to put a stop to these goings on."

"That's what this festival is all about," Molly interjected. "Didn't anyone tell you?"

Taken back by Molly's comment, the woman replied, "I was told it's some sort of celebration the Rangers are putting on for winning the war."

"It is that too," Molly continued. "But, mostly it's for recruiting men-folk into the Ranger Service."

"Oh, I see."

"Do you have anyone competing today?"

"Yes, my husband and my oldest."

"Captain Williams will probably be talking to them later about the Service."

Molly moved to another group and explained Boots's intentions to them also. While she was speaking, a cluster of hoof beats drew everyone's attention to the end of Market Street. Boots led the men-folk into town, dismounted and tied Angel. Gathering together, he and the men-folk rejoined the festival.

"You haven't been gone very long," Molly observed.

"They're clever." Boots lifted his hat and raked his hair with his fingers. "When I rode into that meadow everyone was milling around out there. The Comancheros had split up. The town folks wanted to split up, too, and go after them. We followed one set of tracks, but they rode where the cattle run back in the pasture, and they got their tracks all mixed together. We couldn't follow them, so we went out the other way, and found the same thing. By now those Comancheros are probably joined up again somewhere, and they're sitting out there eating our food and laughing at us."

"We need more Rangers out there," one of the men declared.

Waddling out into the street, the mercantile proprietor carried a keg and announced, "I guess this here was too heavy for them to steal." Upon blocks of wood he set up the keg and tapped it adding, "Maybe, this will lift your spirits some."

The men-folk rounded up mugs and filled them, as the womenfolk grumbled about the men-folk drinking. Before long the men-folk were talking and laughing again. "Let's get that pistol competition going," one of them hollered.

The competitors squared off in front of their respective oak targets and between shots they reloaded their dueling pistols. Molly used a repeater to quickly put five shots into her target. When all the shooters had finished, their targets were compared, and Molly's five shot group was the smallest. She was delighted with her belt buckle when Boots awarded it to her, and she held it up for the town folks to applaud.

The next event was a moving target. A grain sack was filled with saw dust, and the town folks pulled it back and forth between two trees with rope and pulleys. A slice of oak was attached to the sack, and the best five out of five shots would win. Molly missed five times.

The final round was riding and shooting. Contestants had to shoot a block of firewood off the top of a fencepost with their pistols as they galloped past on horseback. The best five shots would win. Each contestant was assigned their own block of wood. Molly missed five times, dismounted, and threw her hat on the ground. She jabbed her repeater behind her belt and huffed at her untouched block of wood atop that fencepost.

Boots watched her, and she could tell he had restrained his laughter. "Don't even say it," she warned him.

He shook his head and pushed his palms out toward her. "I'm not saying nothing."

The party went full tilt after that. The town folks danced until the keg went dry, and well past midnight they split up and went home.

The next afternoon Boots paid visits to several of the men-folk who had competed and offered them assignments in the Ranger Service. Twenty-eight of them accepted, and of those, nineteen had served at San Jacinto. Pleased with the fruits of the festival, Boots prepared the following day to leave Tuck's Landing.

In the morning Molly put on her new green dress and covered it with a cotton apron while doing her baking chores. Boots came in early. After breakfast he turned to Aunt Ruthie and put his arms around her.

"When will I see you again, Bootsie?"

"Nacogdoches is my last recruiting festival," he explained. "Probably a week, then I'll be heading back to San Antonio. I'll stop in after that for a day or two."

He kissed Aunt Ruthie goodbye, and Molly couldn't take her eyes off them. Releasing Aunt Ruthie, he turned to Molly and said, "I want you to have something before I go." Opening a flap on one side of his saddlebags, he rummaged around inside. Pulling out a pair of neatly folded sheets of paper, he handed them to her.

"What's this?" she asked.

"You are my twenty-ninth assignment from Liberty."

Opening the papers, she found duplicate certificates, professionally printed with her name written in and signed by General Houston, Colonel Karnes, and Captain Williams. "I don't believe this," she said. "What does this mean? You're accepting me in the Ranger Service?"

"If you look again, you'll see that I've amended it to read, 'An Honorary Assignment.' You won't be paid, and you are not to be sent out on campaign. I am taking full responsibility for you. I don't see how Colonel Karnes can object to that, but you need to know that he can deny or revoke your assignment at any time and for any reason. Other than that, you are a fully sanctioned, honorary Ranger of the Republic of Texas. That buckle you won last Sunday proves you deserve it. You should wear it proudly."

"Oh, I will! Definitely, I will!"

"I have to swear you in now."

She repeated a pledge, signed both copies of the document and gave one back to Boots. Into his saddlebag he stuffed the document and then slung the saddlebags over his shoulder. "I need to be going," he said, and toward the sunroom door he turned.

Aunt Ruthie tended breakfast for the houseguests while Molly walked him to the corral. Behind his saddle he tied his bedroll and saddlebags. Then he turned and put his arms around her.

Gasping and surprised, she pushed him away asking, "What are you doing?"

Dropping his arms to his sides, he answered her with a question, "You don't want a hug and kiss goodbye?"

"I'm not Aunt Ruthie."

"But, you're like family."

"I'm a married woman."

"Are you sure?"

"No, I'm not sure."

"I'm not trying to court you, Molly. I care about you, and I care about your niece, Amy."

Sliding her arms around him, she accepted his affection, and turned her cheek against his shoulder. Until she released him, he embraced her.

At arm's length he held her, saying, "I won't try to kiss you, okay?"

At that moment it would have been all right if he had, but she wouldn't tell him that. She stood there watching him, as again his arms fell to his sides. "I'll miss you," she said.

He mounted up and opening the corral gate, she let him out. Turing he lifted his hat high above his head. She waved him on, and he nudged his horse across the yard and down the lane.

Unsure what to think about him, she also wasn't sure what to think about herself, hugging an unmarried man that way. She wished she knew what had happened to Emmet, and wondered about him, too, as she had been wondering every day for the past five months. But, she had to admit, she had been thinking about Boots every day, as well.

Changing into her floppy work clothes, she prepared to do morning chores and stuffed her repeaters behind her belt. Her experience in the alley taught her that she should be prepared for trouble at all times.

After chores, she began to realize that the novelty of spending her afternoons with Klaus on the ferryboat was wearing off. She loved Klaus, but towing the line became just another chore to her. She enjoyed the strength it gave her, but she was glad when the afternoons were over.

During the evenings she would put on her riding leathers and prepare for a rough practice out behind the barn. She taught herself to shoot right-handed, left-handed and with both repeaters blazing at the same time. She practiced shooting while crouching, lying down and running.

The bell rang for the ferryboat and the sound made her glad to be off for the evening.

She knew that when she aimed at a moving target, she missed every time. The target moved before her pistol ball got there. To improve her skill she hung a block of firewood on a length of rope from the limb of a live oak behind the barn and set it to swinging. Leading her target, she aimed ahead and shot at a point the block would swing into. Within a week she could hit the block consistently. Then she practiced until she could shoot a block of firewood off a fence post every time she galloped past while riding Angel.

Living up to her appointment as a Texas Ranger, she determined that she would train herself to do everything they could do. Her repeaters gave her the first real power she'd ever known. Their force became her force, emanating from her hands and fingers, and piercing her targets at the same instant she thought of pulling them out, as if an invisible force guided them.

She had the cobbler in Liberty attach her prize buckle to her belt. When she brought it home for the first time, she pulled it around her waist and smiled at her reflection in her vanity mirror. Tying up her hair, she set her hat over it and her heart sank as she realized that she would never look like a Texas Ranger, buckle or not. Her riding leathers revealed too much of her. She would have to cut out a new jacket, one that was fuller in the sides and longer. It would have to cover her hips.

At the mercantile a few days later she purchased leather for a new jacket and her eye caught on a small caliber rifle.

"A squirrel rifle," the proprietor called it.

"Will it kill a man?" she asked.

"What the devil?" he replied. "Kill a man? Why, it's a squirrel rifle. Like I said, it's for killing squirrels."

"I have tried the larger calibers," Molly explained. "But they are too much for me to handle."

"That's understandable," he replied. "They're rather hard for me to handle, too, and I'm nearly twice your size."

"A smaller caliber is less powerful. Isn't that correct, sir?"

"Yes, ma'am. It takes less powder, so it is less powerful."

"And, what caliber is that rifle, sir?"

"Thirty-six, ma'am."

"Thirty-six, you say? That's the same caliber as my repeaters." Slapping the butts of the repeaters under her shirt, and behind her belt she added, "These have been known to kill a man. If you put the same ball in a rifle, I should think it would do as well."

"I suppose it would," he said.

"I can use the same mold to make ball for the rifle and my repeaters. I'll take it."

With her new rifle she began practicing long range shooting at fifty paces, then one hundred paces and eventually two hundred paces. Using leftover leather from her new jacket, she stitched together a scabbard with a tie-down end flap for her rifle and attached it to her saddle.

More than two weeks had passed since Boots left for Nacogdoches. Though Molly had used the time to advance her shooting skills and improve her equipment, she was becoming concerned about Boots's absence. After supper she took Aunt Ruthie aside and asked, "Do you think I should ride up there and look for him?"

"Up to Nacogdoches?" Aunt Ruthie asked. "I don't think he'd want you to do that, darlin'."

"I could ride along with the freight haulers. They won't let anything happen to me."

Aunt Ruthie folded her arms and asked, "What if he ain't there? Then what will y'all do? Nacogdoches is a dangerous place, darlin'. Freebooters and land pirates are known to be hiding out there. They commit their crimes in the States and then skip across the Sabine into Texas, where the law can't follow them. Folks also tell me it's dangerous for womenfolk up there because the men-folk outnumber them ten to one. I've been told the men-folk steal womenfolk up there."

Searching for an answer, Molly was unable to think of one and said, "I don't know." Heading to the sunroom door, she added, "I'm going out to practice."

"We'll talk some more when you come back in," Aunt Ruthie called after her.

When she reached the barn, Molly heard the bell ring for a tow and didn't give it another thought. Preparing Angel for practice, she tried for the first time to shoot her rifle from horseback and discovered the impossibility of holding a rifle steady enough for an accurate shot while mounted. She practiced with her repeaters while mounted instead. Finished with riding practice, she put Angel back in her stall, hung her saddle over the rail next to the stall, and headed out to try a few freestanding shots with her rifle. Then she heard a popping sound on the river.

Realizing that what she had heard was the pop of a pistol, she became concerned and ran out for a closer listen. Rifles crackled, six or seven of them. Dashing toward the house, she met Aunt Ruthie.

Bounding down the front porch steps, Aunt Ruthie said, "Sounds like someone's getting impatient. Guess I better go down there and see what's going on."

"I'll go, too," Molly offered.

Across the yard Molly dashed with Aunt Ruthie, until Manuel emerged from the lane and met them. He gasped, "Men ring bell to cross river. I am towing ferryboat to get them, and I see man. I know this man. He is man in alley behind mercantile. With him there are many more men. So, I think it is not good for me to take ferryboat to get him and bring more men over here. I take ferryboat back to Klaus. Then one of the men, he climbs on rope and crosses river to take ferryboat away from us, so Klaus he shot him."

Rifles crackled from the river again as Justin ran in from the fields, skidding to a stop and raising a cloud of dust. Down the lane Aunt Ruthie dashed toward the road and extended her arm so that Justin, Manuel and Molly would not run ahead of her.

Down the riverbank at the dock Molly could see Klaus hunched behind a piling, and in each of his hands he wielded a dueling pistol. Across the river the Comanchero's rifles crackled. Their rifle balls splashed into the water next to him, and one splintered the piling he hunched behind. Aunt Ruthie whistled to get his attention and when he turned, she motioned him away from the dock.

When the shooting stopped, he stepped away from the piling, glanced up at Aunt Ruthie and then turned to watch the Comancheros reload their rifles. Aunt Ruthie whistled again, bared her teeth at him and motioned forcefully for him to get away from the dock. Up the hill he bounded, surprisingly agile for such a large man. Molly noticed that another Comanchero had climbed out on the rope, and he was pulling himself, hand over hand, toward Tuck's Landing.

Aunt Ruthie yanked Klaus out of the road when he reached her. Motioning everyone together she said, "I'm going to stay right here and keep an eye on them. Looks like they're fixing to commandeer my ferryboat. We have plenty of time before that man gets across the river and takes the ferryboat back to get the rest of them. So, I want y'all to go up to the house and get all the rifles you can find. Bring them here. Hurry, but don't let them see you. I don't want them to get any ideas about what we're up to, okay?"

Searching frantically in every closet and corner when they reached the house, Molly and the others also went out to the barn and gathered up all the rifles they could find. Some of the houseguests loaned their rifles, and two of them wanted to join the fight. One was a chunky man with chubby cheeks and a trim, black beard, who Molly had seen before. Wielding her new rifle, she returned with the others to Aunt Ruthie.

The ferryboat was now across the river at the opposite dock, and it was a considerable distance from where Molly stood at the top of the hill. She guessed four or five hundred paces, too far to shoot a rifle, but the distance didn't prevent her from recognizing the first Comanchero on board. A bead of perspiration trickled down her cheek as she watched him. That face, she thought, she would never forget that face.

EYES WHICH CANNOT SEE

KLAUS, JUSTIN, MANUEL and two houseguests took cover in the live oaks overlooking the Trinidad River. Molly watched across the river as six more Comancheros rode their horses onto the ferryboat with the disfigured Comanchero. One of them began to tow the ferryboat to Tuck's Landing. Filled with trepidation, Molly's heart began to pound all the way up to her temples. Her rifle felt slippery, so she rubbed her palms dry on her jacket and then placed them again on her rifle.

Calling Klaus, Justin and Manuel out from the cover of the live oaks, Aunt Ruthie motioned everyone together, including the two houseguests. "They're about as stupid as I figured," she observed. "They're all bunched together out in the open on that ferryboat. I want you boys to go with me down by the dock. We can sneak down through the trees, and when we get there, we'll stay out of sight and wait for them. Justin, you reload for Klaus. Manuel, you reload for me. We'll wait until they're almost all the way in. Then we'll cut them down. After that, we'll pull the ferryboat in the rest of the way."

"Why don't y'all just sit on top of the hill yonder?" the chunky man with chubby cheeks and a trim, black beard suggested. "We can pick them off with our rifles."

Aunt Ruthie turned to him, and Molly could see that she was not pleased. "I'm obliged for your willingness to help us, sir, but it's too far for your rifle, and I'm not going to have you popping off at them before they're close enough. So, with all due respect, sir, y'all best take yourselves and your rifles back up to the house, and defend the folks up there if they need it."

Showing offense, the houseguests returned up the lane to the house.

"Where do you want me?" Molly asked.

"I want you to stay here, darlin'. You'll be out of range."

"I'm going with you, Aunt Ruthie."

"I figured you'd say that."

"You can't stop me," she insisted.

"Figured you'd say that too, darlin'. Come on down with me then, but keep yourself under the dock and behind them pilings. Help Manuel reload and pass rifles up to me."

"I'm a good shot, Aunt Ruthie!"

"I know you are. So am I, and so is Klaus, but you ain't never shot at men who are trying to kill you. Neither has Justin or Manuel. You just watch, learn, and reload, alright?"

"I've faced these men before, Aunt Ruthie, and all I had was a pitchfork to fight them with. Now I have my rifle and my repeaters."

"By the time that ferryboat's in range of them repeaters, all those men will be dead."

"All right, Aunt Ruthie."

They spread out, Klaus and Justin went left of the road, Aunt Ruthie, Manuel and Molly went right. They descended through the thicket with an armload of rifles each. The ferryboat was about half-way across when they reached the dock, and the Comancheros seemed to have spotted them, for they had dismounted and hunkered down behind their horses. Klaus took a position behind the giant rope pulley and the framework that held it. Across the dock from him, Aunt Ruthie crouched behind a piling and aimed her rifle. Below the dock, in a space about four-feet high, Molly and Manuel crouched at the edge of the water with spare rifles, powder and ball, and from their position they could see the Comancheros.

The ferryboat stopped moving, and the Comancheros were shading their eyes with their hands and examining the dock. The creaky rope pulley slowed and then stopped. Very slowly, it started up again, but the rope had changed direction. The ferryboat was moving away from Tuck's Landing, and at that moment Molly thought that it might be better if the Comancheros would just tow themselves back and then ride away.

Aunt Ruthie mumbled, "We ain't going to let them get away with that! … Klaus!" she yelled. "Can y'all pull them in?"

He bobbed his head and stood his rifle against a piling. Grabbing the rope, he stopped it from paying out from the bottom of the pulley. His shoulders and thighs bulged as he leaned back, pulling the thick rope.

Scrambling around on the ferryboat, the Comancheros acted as if they were alarmed by the resumption of their direction toward Tuck's Landing. They rushed to the gate facing the landing, knelt behind it, and laid their rifles over the rail, preparing to shoot.

Aunt Ruthie's rifle make a sharp cracking sound when she fired, echoing back from across the river, but her rifle ball fell short, splashing in front of the ferryboat. The Comanchero's rifles crackled in response, splashing next to Klaus and landing in the deck planks in front of him. He turned his shoulder against the splinters and then yanked on the rope. The Comancheros, who were hastily reloading, toppled over as the ferryboat lurched, and their horses reared up behind them, nickering.

Molly exchanged rifles with Aunt Ruthie, handing her a loaded one, and asking, "Where's Justin? Why isn't he shooting?"

Aunt Ruthie shouldered the rifle. "He don't know what to do. He's just a boy."

"I'm going over there. Manuel can reload for you."

Aunt Ruthie's rifle cracked again, splitting the gate rail as her shoulder rocked back. "All right, darlin', but be careful. Don't expose yourself to their rifles."

With her new rifle cradled in her arms, Molly crawled under the dock to where Justin crouched with three spare rifles and two dueling pistols. The Comancheros rifles crackled again, and she could hear their rifle balls thudding into the dock and the pilings. "I'm going up there," she informed Justin. "Keep me loaded."

He nodded.

Once she was up on the dock, she knelt behind a piling next to Klaus. The Comancheros were reloading again, and Aunt Ruthie's rifle cracked from the other side. One of the Comancheros rolled backwards, having been hit while ramming a ball into his barrel. The others knelt with their rifles, but Molly had already raised her rifle against the side of the piling and had taken aim. She squeezed the trigger and watched her ball streak over the river to its mark, sprawling a Comanchero backwards. His rifle teetered from the gate rail, and tumbled into the river.

The Comanchero's rifles crackled again, whacking into Molly's piling and the pulley framework around Klaus. He was pulling them in, but he was also pulling them dangerously close to Aunt Ruthie and her.

Klaus strained against the rope, as Justin exchanged rifles with Molly. The rope was slowing down again, stopping. Aunt Ruthie's rifle cracked as Molly watched the Comancheros, all of them, set their rifles aside and grab the rope. They were pulling against Klaus. "Help him, Justin," Molly shouted.

Justin scrambled out from under the dock and latched onto the rope with Klaus. A muscular farm boy, he added his strength to the rope, but it did not move. Molly aimed the rifle, which Justin had given her, heavier than her rifle, and fired. It rocked her shoulder back, throwing her off balance, almost down on the dock. Then Aunt Ruthie's rifle cracked, and one of the Comancheros let loose of the rope, clenching his hip, and toppling over onto his side.

The horses reared up, and the Comancheros grabbed their bridles to steady them. When they released the rope, Klaus and Justin pulled hard, and the ferryboat lurched again toward Tuck's Landing.

Molly jumped down from the dock, collected her own rifle, and rammed a charge into it. Watching as the Comancheros took cover behind their horses and reloaded, she shouted, "Klaus, Justin! Get down! They're too close!"

Both of them jumped behind pilings as the Comanchero's rifles crackled. Aunt Ruthie fired back, and one of their horses fell. Molly fired, and another horse bolted, breaking through the side rail and plunging into the river. Klaus reached for the rope and pulled as the Comancheros again reloaded; he yanked the rope hard with Justin's help.

The ferryboat bumped into the dock. Justin dove behind a piling, and Klaus threw himself on the planks. A Comanchero ran to the gate and kicked it open as Aunt Ruthie fired. He doubled over, collapsing face down. Horses spewed forth from the ferryboat galloping up the dock without riders, five of them. As they separated, Molly saw the disfigured Comanchero hanging on the side of his horse, crouched in a stirrup and holding himself with one hand on the pommel. In his free hand he wielded a dueling pistol, leveling it at her as he bobbed and weaved. Her repeaters exploded together at him, her pistol balls streaking into him. From his hand his pistol fell, tumbling across the dock, and he seemed to dangle from his horse as it galloped past her.

Aunt Ruthie fired, but Molly couldn't see what was happening on the other side of the horses. Another man hung from the side of a horse at the rear. His hair was bushy and his beard pointed. His eyes were black as coal and evil. When his eyes met hers, they chilled her to her soul.

It was Buffalo Head.

He seemed to recognize her and raised his pistol against her. She thought she heard herself scream, and his horse looked like it had stopped in midair as her repeaters blazed at him. Long flames and billows of smoke pushed her pistol balls into him, ripping through his body. His eyes took on a look of disbelief. Losing his grip on his pommel, he fell to the dock, rolling several times with his pistol clamped tightly in his hand. Propping himself on his elbow, he raised his pistol at her. Molly fired both repeaters, tearing the pistol from his hand. Again he reached for it, and her next volley stopped him for good.

Swinging her repeaters around, she had one shot left in each, but the Comancheros were all dead. Buffalo Head lay before her, gazing into the sky with eyes which could no longer see. Blood oozed into a pool beneath his lifeless body, and dripped between the planks into the water below.

Another Comanchero lay next to Aunt Ruthie's piling. She stepped out and looked down at him, holding a rifle across her hips. Manuel climbed up behind her. Molly turned and saw halfway up the hill where the disfigured Comanchero lay. Beside him his horse nuzzled his body.

Klaus picked himself up from the dock and brushed off his clothes. Next to him Justin jumped up. Examining the end of the dock, Molly saw the Comanchero Aunt Ruthie had shot at the gate, and on the ferryboat she counted three bodies and a horse carcass.

Looking around, Aunt Ruthie shook her head saying, "Them Comancheros shouldn't have come to Tuck's Landing and commandeered my ferryboat. They just shouldn't have done that." Over at Klaus and Justin she looked and added, "Y'all did a brave thing, pulling them in under fire like that. And you, darlin'," she looked straight at Molly. "I saw what you did with those repeaters. I ain't never seen nothing like that before. I never expected to see you do nothing like that."

Molly tried to respond, but couldn't speak. Her repeaters were frozen in her hands in front of her, and they were beginning to tremble. Inside, she felt satisfaction, but on her face she felt tears, streaming tears, and they were dripping relentlessly onto the lapels of her jacket.

Klaus stepped up to her and eased her repeaters down to her sides, saying, "It's over. Let me ta … take y'all home now. Me and the boys will take care of everything else here." He turned her toward the hill, slid his arm around her waist, and walked her up past the disfigured Comanchero.

The houseguests had gathered together in the yard and watched as Klaus walked Molly to the front porch. One of them, the chunky man with chubby cheeks and a trim, black beard asked, "Is she all right?"

"She's fine," Klaus answered, as he helped her up the front steps.

"Things sounded pretty bad out there, is anyone hurt?"

"None of us is hur … hurt. It went pretty well."

"You're telling me no one's hurt after all that shooting?"

"I'm going back down there to bur … bury a few bad ones, but everyone else if fine." He took Molly inside to the stairway, and she walked herself up to her room.

On her vanity she laid her repeaters and next to them she laid her hat. Then untying and shaking out her auburn curls, she glanced at herself in the mirror. Tears streamed down her cheeks, and around her lips. She didn't recognize her lips. They'd become a thin, straight line under her nose. Pushing her tears away, she couldn't turn them off; then she noticed her eyes. Never had she seen such intensity in them, and it frightened her. Her own reflection frightened her.

Hanging her jacket over the mirror, she didn't want to see herself, didn't want to think about the way she looked. She didn't want to think about anything right now and seated herself on the edge of her bed. Her heart and her mind were racing, and her stomach had drawn up into knots. Wanting to lie back, she couldn't, and sat on the edge of her bed, staring at her jacket over the mirror. She knew what was behind the jacket, for she had seen herself in the mirror. She had seen a murderer, a cold-blooded murderer!

The houseguests came in when Aunt Ruthie came in. Molly could hear them in the kitchen below. Utensils clanked and chairs shuffled against the floor. Voices were muffled, but she could hear them clear enough to understand what they were saying. Aunt Ruthie explained to them every detail of the battle. The houseguests were questioning her as Aunt Ruthie prepared their supper. Prepared their supper? Molly wondered how she could prepare supper after going through something like that.

When the talking stopped and the clanking subsided, Molly noticed that her tears had also stopped. From her water pitcher she filled her basin and washed her face, and listened as footsteps came up the hallway, followed by a tap on her door.

"I've got supper for you, darlin', but y'all have to open the door for me. My hands are full."

Molly let Aunt Ruthie in.

Holding a kettle with one hand, she had table ware in the other, and explained, "We've got bo'led beef and vegetables today. I figured y'all wanted to be alone, so I brought it up. Can you take this darlin'? It's getting heavy."

"Obliged, Aunt Ruthie, but I'm not hungry."

"Well then, why don't y'all just take it before I drop the darn thing, and help me put the rest down so we can talk?"

"I'd rather not talk right now."

"I know you wouldn't, darlin'. Just take this," she said.

Taking the kettle from her, Molly set it on the vanity, and Aunt Ruthie left the table ware next to it. She continued, "This ain't a good time to be alone. Things will just eat away at you all night. You won't get any sleep, and they'll keep eating at you until you're all ate up. Then you won't be no good to yourself, or nobody else."

"How do you stay so calm?" Molly asked.

"It's my job, darlin'. What we did out there today is my job. Same as staying calm is my job. Folks around here are looking to me for that, and I give it to them."

"Staying calm?"

"Yes, darlin'. No matter what. It keeps my boys level headed."

Aunt Ruthie closed the door and put her arms around Molly. She didn't say anything, just hugged her. Molly stiffened at first, hadn't expected that from Aunt Ruthie. She was expecting a lecture, a well intentioned, but lengthy and unnecessary lecture. When she thought Aunt Ruthie would release her, she did not, and she continued to embrace her tightly. Molly returned her embrace. In Aunt Ruthie's arms she felt sympathy and understanding, which was communicated without words. Finally, she held Molly at arm's length and smiled at her. Her eyes were damp, and Molly knuckled tears from her own eyes, as Aunt Ruthie said, "I'm glad you're here darlin', and it made me proud that you stood with me today. That's what being friends is all about. I'm sure you'll see that when things settle down." Then Aunt Ruthie opened the door and said, "Don't worry about chores. I'll have someone else do them. Take all the time you need. I'll be here when y'all are ready." She left Molly by herself in her room.

After an hour or so, she was hungry enough to eat, but not very much. Throughout the night, images of the battle haunted her. She tried to sleep, tossing to and fro, pistol balls kept exploding from her repeaters, and Buffalo Head gazed up at her over and over from that grotesque pool of blood. The horse nuzzling the disfigured Comanchero troubled her most of all. Would a good horse stand by a bad person? Shouldn't his horse know the kind of person he was? Whatever the horse liked about him, she realized that she had taken it away. More than once she dozed off and saw her own reflection in that vanity mirror, and it jolted her awake.

Morning came, and sunlight streamed through her window, telling her that it was time to start breakfast chores. She couldn't do it, couldn't face herself, much less the houseguests. The morning she spent in her room. Aunt Ruthie brought breakfast up, saying, "Morning," as she exchanged dishes and left.

The afternoon Molly spent with her diary, and that seemed to help. Writing always had a settling effect. Aunt Ruthie was right, she conceded. Only a true friend would stand up with another true friend in a fight.

Though her limbs were heavy with fatigue the next morning, she put on her green dress. As she pulled a brush through her hair, she noticed in the mirror that her lips didn't look as taught. Her eyes had lost the intensity she'd seen in them two days before, and they looked more like the hazel eyes she knew. Though the reflection of a murderer had left the mirror, she still felt like one. Taking a closer look, she noticed something else, something which wasn't there before, a scowl line. Rubbing her finger across her brow, she stretched her skin until the scowl line disappeared. Then taking her finger away, it reappeared. It hadn't been there before. She was sure of it.

When she reached the kitchen, she stoked the stove and started the bread dough, and about then Aunt Ruthie came out from the parlor, saying, "I didn't expect to see y'all this morning. Are you okay?"

"Okay," Molly replied. Devoid her usual joy, she filled the coffee pots adding, "I think I'm okay."

"Are you getting any sleep, darlin'?"

"A little."

"Good. I was afraid you wouldn't get any sleep at all."

"How about you, Aunt Ruthie? Have you been sleeping?"

"I don't sleep much like I used to, so I don't let nothing rob me of what little I get." Taking her egg basket down from the shelf, Aunt Ruthie turned to the sunroom. On her way to the sunroom door, Boots came in.

Aunt Ruthie set her egg basket aside, laid her hands against Boots's chest and laughed. "I'm so happy y'all are finally here, Bootsie." Studying his face, she added, "I can tell you're upset about something."

"Yes, I'm upset."

"Okay," Aunt Ruthie said to Boots. "Tell me why y'all are so upset. Did something happen up in Nacogdoches?"

"Nothing happened in Nacogdoches. When I rode in this morning, I saw seven fresh graves beside the road. I was afraid something happened to you and Molly. At least I can see now that y'all are okay. What happened anyway?"

Aunt Ruthie explained the altercation on the ferryboat and added, "Y'all should have seen Molly. She was something with those repeaters. I ain't never seen nothing like it before."

"I knew she was fast," Boots agreed, "but you never know what a recruit is capable of until they face their enemies." He smiled at Molly and said, "I'm proud of you."

Molly searched, but could not find a smile to give back to him, not yet. "Obliged," she said, and turned her attention again to the stove.

Aunt Ruthie asked, "So, y'all are done with your recruiting festivals? Can you stay awhile, or will you be going back to San Antonio?"

"Truth is I might be staying here for quite some time."

Laughing gleefully, Aunt Ruthie gave him a pat, saying, "I don't believe it. I don't believe I'm finally hearing this. I have to tell you, Bootsie, I've been waiting a long time for y'all to say you're coming home to stay. You can have a good life here. Everything will be yours when I'm gone, you know, and I'm getting too old to keep up with this place like I used to. I need you here."

"I can't say exactly when I'll be staying, Aunt Ruthie."

"Then something else is troubling you," she observed. "You always come here troubled, and leave here all at ease. That should tell you something about what being here does for you. So, what is it that's troubling you this time?" she asked.

"I need to talk to Molly first."

THE BAD THINGS THAT BAD PEOPLE DO

"SURE THING," AUNT Ruthie assured Boots. "I was just on my way out to collect eggs for breakfast. I'll go on out and do my chores. Y'all can stay here and talk. When I come back, y'all can tell me all about it." Grabbing her egg basket, she went out the backdoor toward the henhouse.

Molly could feel him looking at her, and shifted to him a side glance asking, "What'd you want to talk about?"

Hesitating for a long moment, he replied, "I can see that what happened on the ferryboat is hard on you."

"In a manner of speaking," she agreed.

"I understand. I'd rather wait and talk when you feel up to it."

"That's very thoughtful of you, Mister Williams."

"I'll hang out with Aunt Ruthie awhile."

"She will enjoy that. She loves you, you know."

"Yes, I know, obliged."

A few houseguests had trickled down from their rooms, and had taken seats around the long table when Aunt Ruthie returned. While frying eggs, she rehashed the ferryboat incident with them. As the houseguests ate their breakfast, Molly cleaned up the kitchen and became weary of listening to the same old story retold so many times.

Boots listened with growing interest and tarried long after the houseguests had left the table. When the sunroom had cleared out, he refilled his coffee mug. Molly sensed that he was waiting for her to say something, but was politely holding his peace. Clearing the table, she cleaned and stacked the dishes and then pulled off her apron.

"Where y'all going?" Aunt Ruthie asked.

"I'm going to change my clothes and do morning chores like always."

"Y'all don't have to do that today. You've done enough, darlin'. I'll do the rest."

"Obliged, Aunt Ruthie, but I need to stay busy. It keeps my mind off things."

Aunt Ruthie nodded. "That's all right, darlin'. You go on ahead and do what you need to do."

To Boots, Molly said, "I have to give it some time. It's not that I don't want to talk with you."

"Take all the time necessary," he replied. "I'll be right here hanging out with my favorite aunt."

After changing into her floppy work clothes, dumping the chamber pots, cleaning up after the houseguests and readying the rooms for the coming night, Molly went out to spend the afternoon on the ferryboat. Klaus would understand what was going on inside of her, and he wouldn't make her talk about it either. He never talked, and towing the line might make her troublesome thoughts go away.

As she turned from the lane onto the road, she noticed that folks and teamsters had lined up in the marshalling area, and they were holding their hats against a gust of wind blowing up from the river. Placing her hand on her own hat, Molly recalled how the ferryboat incident began on the very spot where she was now standing. Pausing, she examined seven fresh man-size mounds along the side of the road, and understood how they would become a warning to anyone passing by. Each grave was marked with a cross made from tree branches and tied together with the Comanchero's belts and clothing. Upon the crosses were hung their hats, and their boots.

Glancing back at the marshalling area, she looked for anyone she might recognize from Gonzales, as she always did. Noticing a woman, who sat in a wagon next to a man, she could also see between them a young boy, and a strawberry mole under the woman's left eye. "Elli-Lou?" she mumbled. Over to the wagon she dashed, yelling, "Elli-Lou?"

The woman, the man, and the young boy turned to her with startled looks on their faces. "Yes, I'm Elli-Lou," the woman confessed.

Molly cupped her hands to her chest, saying, "It's me, Molly McCracken. Remember me from Gonzales?"

"Is that you, Molly," she gasped, and covered her mouth. "You scared us. You look like a Comanchero. We were afraid you were going to rob us. What's happened to you? I didn't recognize you."

"These are my work clothes," Molly replied, as she held out the sides of her floppy shirt, and smiled at her old friend.

"Now, I recognize that smile," Elli-Lou declared. "But, you've changed so much. You don't look like the Molly McCracken I remember. What happened to you?" Opening her eyes wide, she glanced up and down at Molly, and said, "You're carrying pistols! Are you a Comanchero? Why are you wearing men's clothes?"

"Elli-Lou!" Molly exclaimed, and she felt her whole body sag with disappointment. Over her repeaters she pulled her shirt to hide them. "I work here," she explained. "Is that Franklin up there with you? I'm so glad he found you! Thank goodness he's alive and came back from the war to find you."

The man tipped his hat, and said, "Good to see y'all again, Molly. How's my old friend Emmet?"

"He's been missing since the Alamo."

"Sorry to hear that. I always liked Emmet. He's a good man, and a hard worker, never afraid to pitch in and lend a hand when I was falling behind. And I spent quite a few times throwing in with him, too."

"You say you're working here?" Elli-Lou asked.

"It's a long story." Molly shrugged. "Would you like to spend some time catching up? You're the only close friends I have left, and I could really use a close friend today. Are you and Franklin in a hurry?"

"We're making our way back to Gonzales, but we expect our farm was burned out. There won't be nothing waiting for us, but a lot of work when we get there. So, I guess there's no hurry. What are you thinking?"

"Aunt Ruthie has a boarding house over there." She pointed to the lane, overhung with live oak. "Do you think you could spend the night, so we can visit awhile?"

"You never told me y'all had kin in these parts, Molly."

"She's not kin. She just likes me to call her Aunt Ruthie."

"We don't have money to spare for a boarding house, Molly. We are preparing for a hard winter."

"Don't worry about anything. You'll be my guests tonight, meals included, and a hot bath if you want. Just stay and enjoy yourselves."

"What do you think?" Elli-Lou asked Franklin.

He nodded.

"I think that would be fine, obliged."

Molly climbed up and took a seat next to Elli-Lou. "Go ahead and take your wagon on up to the house," she suggested.

Franklin drove the wagon out of line and turned his horses toward the lane. Sitting next to Elli-Lou, Molly noticed that her skin was yet supple, unlike the other womenfolk she knew. Her nose was small and precise, and her dark hair was tucked inside a lavender bonnet. Most folks would think the strawberry mole under her left eye was a beauty mark. "Where's Uncle Elmer?" Molly asked her.

"He's not with us any longer," Elli-Lou informed her. "He's been suffering considerable these past few months at Cousin Ike's farm in Louisiana. It was a blessing when he finally passed."

"How sad. Are you still grieving for him?"

"He's the last kin of my ma, bless her soul, but I'm relieved that he's no longer suffering."

"How about you, Franklin? How did y'all fare in the war?"

His gaunt face, aquiline nose, and pouting lower lip gave him the appearance of a scavenging bird, but a lovable one. Molly had fond memories of him and Elli-Lou.

As the wagon approached the house he explained. "I fought with General Houston at Beason's. That's where I got hit with a ball from a Brown Bess. Then the doctor had to take my right leg off from my knee down. Never thought a Brown Bess could do that. I never thought them Mexican cavalry could hit the side of a barn with one of those blunder-Besses, but they got me all right. Took about three months before I was well enough to hitch a ride with a freight hauler up to Cousin Ike's in Louisiana."

"That's terrible," Molly said sympathetically and shook her head.

"I get around okay with my crutches," he added, glancing over his shoulder. "Got them back here in the wagon somewhere. I can still ride a horse, and I suppose I can still plow a field. I just have to make one leg do the work of two from now on."

Leaning forward to look across Elli-Lou at him Molly said, "I'm glad you found Elli-Lou again. I know she was fretting over you the last time I talked to her. There's been so much separation and heartache because of the war, it's all I hear about nowadays. I don't think anyone really knows how much devastation the war has caused folks. It's good to hear a happy ending like yours now and then." Looking down at the leg of his trousers tied in a knot below his knee Molly said, "I'll take your wagon over by the barn, and I'll put your horses in the corral for you."

Inside the house, she took them to the kitchen, heavy yet with the smell of fresh bread, bacon and eggs. Introducing her old friends to Boots and Aunt Ruthie, she offered them seats at the long table. Franklin stood his crutches in the nearest corner, and then hopped to a chair.

On the edge of the chair next to him sat his toddler. The little boy howled, "I'm hungry."

"Did y'all have breakfast?" Aunt Ruthie asked.

Elli-Lou and Franklin shook their heads.

"There's plenty over there by the stove. Why don't y'all help yourselves? I hate throwing good food to the hogs."

Molly loaded plates for them. As she set one in front of the young boy she asked Franklin, "Did you ever forgive me for that blackberry pie back in Gonzales?"

"Pie?" he asked, and then his eyes crinkled at the corners. "Oh, yes. I remember that pie, and yes I forgave you."

"What pie?" Aunt Ruthie asked.

The young boy had emptied half his plate before Molly set down plates for Elli-Lou and Franklin. She went on to explain, "Elli-Lou had taken ill in the spring when I was baking blackberry pies. So, after I put one of them pies into the Dutch oven, I started fixing an extra big supper. I took a kettle over to their farm, and the supper turned out real good. Elli-Lou stayed in bed, and I took a plate in to her. Then I cut a slice of that warm, blackberry pie for Franklin, and put it on his plate. I noticed that he got real quiet while he was eating it. He kept eating slower and slower. So, I asked him what was wrong. He said he thought he might be coming down with what Elli-Lou had. Then he left half that piece of pie on his plate, excused himself and went out to the barn."

Franklin looked up at Molly and chuckled. "I tried to eat it, Molly. I really tried."

"What was wrong with the pie?" Aunt Ruthie asked.

Elli-Lou set her fork down, laughed and said, "When I took the kettle and that pie pan back over to her, I told Molly how much Franklin loved that blackberry pie."

Molly continued, "So, I asked her how she liked it. Delicious, she says. I didn't tell her I made two of them, and when I tasted mine it was bitter. That's when I realized I forgot to add sugar to the filling. The sugar was still sitting there on the table in a bowl."

When their laughter quieted, Elli-Lou asked, "So, how did y'all end up working here, Molly?"

Molly explained everything that happened to Emily, Innis, and Amy. Elli-Lou's laughter turned into sorrow. She could not hold back her tears. Molly handed her a towel from the kitchen, since she didn't have a hanky.

Franklin dragged his sleeve over his eyes and said, "There weren't no better folks in all creation than Innis and Emily. I loved them like they was my own brother and sister." Hanging his head, he squeezed tears from his eyes with his finger and thumb. "All them good times we had together. All them good times. Who would ever figure it would turn out like this?"

"Why are you sad?" his toddler asked. He studied his parent's faces with big eyes as he cleaned his plate again.

Patting him on his little shoulder Franklin said, "It's all right, son."

As she watched them, Molly's eyes also welled up, and she apologized saying, "I'm sorry I had to tell you like this." She went on to describe her escape from the Comancheros, how Boots had brought her to Tuck's Landing, and the incident on the ferryboat.

"I had no idea," Elli-Lou shook her head. "No idea."

"Would you like some more breakfast?" Molly asked.

"Obliged, Molly, but I can't eat," she sobbed and blotted her tears. "I don't think I can stop crying. Emily was a dear, sweet friend, and I miss her so much." She covered her face with the towel and sobbed again, as Franklin reached over and laid his hand on her shoulder.

"Would you like me to put some water on for a bath?" Molly asked. "You'll feel better if you get a nice, hot bath."

Muffled by the towel, Elli-Lou replied. "Yes. Yes, that might be best. I would like that very much, Molly, obliged."

Most of the afternoon Molly spent running bath water for the family. In between baths, she laundered their clothing for them, and hung it out to dry in the hot sun.

Toward evening Elli-Lou offered to help Aunt Ruthie prepare supper. Franklin insisted on helping the farmhands with chores even though Aunt Ruthie urged him to stay inside. His son tagged along as he clunked out to the barn on his crutches.

Elli-Lou's spirits lifted after supper. She and Franklin seemed to enjoy chatting with Molly, Aunt Ruthie, Boots and the houseguests out on the front porch. "What will you do from here?" she asked Molly.

"We have some knowledge of where Amy is," Molly explained. "I'm hoping we can rescue her."

"Will you come back to Gonzales? Will you bring her home with you?" She looked at Franklin and smiled. "You can start over. We'll help you. If you like, y'all can live with us."

She glanced over at Franklin again and he nodded.

"I haven't thought that far ahead," Molly confessed. "I've been taken up with my present troubles."

Aunt Ruthie agreed. "More than your fair share of present troubles, darlin'."

"It's remarkable how you've come through all this," Elli-Lou concurred. "Most of us don't have to endure the kind of testing you've endured."

"Testing?" Molly asked. "Do you mean testing by the Almighty?"

"Yes."

"Why would he test me, Elli-Lou? I've always been faithful."

"But, look at what your troubles have done for you, Molly. Look at how strong they've made you."

"I was strong before any of this happened."

"Yes, you were." Elli-Lou lowered her chin, and looked away, adding, "I always admired your strength."

"Then he has no reason to test me, does he?"

Looking back at Molly she argued, "He always tests the ones he loves."

"Love? You call it love? What kind of love burns us out of our homes? What kind of love takes Franklin's leg from him, and devastates the good folks of Texas? What kind of love lets my sister die, and lets Innis get murdered, and takes Amy away?"

"Now it sounds like you're making him into something he isn't," Elli-Lou scolded her. "That's a dangerous thing to do, Molly. You're making him sound evil. You'll get his wrath instead of his blessing if y'all do that. You have to take what he gives you. You have to be humble with it, and try and find out what he wants you to learn from all the trouble he gives you."

"If he gives trouble to the ones he loves, Elli-Lou, then he doesn't really love any of us. You don't give your loved ones trouble, sickness, and death. You wouldn't give such a thing to your own youngsters, would you? No, I'm not against him. I'm against the trouble that befalls us. I just don't understand why he lets us suffer. He doesn't listen. If he did, I'd prove that I'm innocent, and I don't deserve any of this."

"It's because he wants folks to make amends," Franklin interjected. "I've seen it with my own eyes."

"You're saying he afflicts folks with trouble and lets them suffer so they'll make amends? I made amends before I was afflicted with suffering, and what about Maudie's little boy? He suffered with whooping cough until he died in Maudie's arms. How was he supposed to make amends? He didn't even know what amends are, much less make them. That doesn't make any sense, Franklin."

Franklin explained, "He don't judge folks while they're living, he gives all of us until we reach the end of our days. Folks, good and bad alike, get the same chance to make amends right up until the end. Now, if y'all let bad folks run around their whole lives doing bad things until they reach the end of their days, then they can do a lot of bad things to a lot of innocent folks, can't they? I've seen this with my own eyes."

"Maybe that's true," Molly disputed, "but what about the affliction that took Maudie's little youngster? That wasn't caused by the bad things that bad folks do."

"Yes it was. That's the way it's been since the beginning. Ever since bad folks started doing bad things, sorrow upon sorrow has heaped upon them. The ground they walk on has been cursed with thorns and thistles. Sickness and death turns them into dust. Their curse falls on all of us, Molly, and in the end it turns us all into dust. After that he judges us, and that's the thing to be afraid of, not the trouble what befalls us while we're living. Maudie's youngin' wasn't given as many days as the rest of us, but he went the same way all us folks go. The only difference is that he's not held accountable, because he's a youngin'. He just went straight on into the other side. I've seen this with my own eyes."

A teamster sprang up from his chair, clumped across the porch, and down the steps.

"Everything all right?" Aunt Ruthie asked.

"All right, ma'am," he replied. "I'm going out back to check on my horses."

"You just came from there."

"I think, maybe, there's some fresh manure that needs pitching out of the corral."

"It's dark," Aunt Ruthie protested, "and the boys will take care of that in the morning."

"It don't matter if it's dark, ma'am. I know manure when I smell manure, so I'll be pitching it out." Clumping down the steps he went to the corral.

"Was he offended by something I said?" Franklin asked.

Boots got up and crossed the porch also, saying, "I'll go out and have a talk with him."

Elli-Lou gave Molly a look of mortification, and Molly felt sorry for her. Giving her hand a pat she said, "It's all right."

Elli-Lou explained, "Ever since the war Franklin always gets riled up about religion." She hung her head.

"Don't feel bad," Molly assured her. "He said some interesting things. If folks don't agree with him, that's their problem, not yours. He sees things different than we do."

"The war can change the way you see a lot things," Franklin added.

"Franklin?" Molly asked. "You said you saw this with your own eyes. How did you see all these things?"

"Y'all see lots of things when men are dying all around you. Sometimes y'all see things when you're dying yourself."

"Is that what happened to you."

"I lost a lot of blood, Molly." Franklin dragged his sleeve across his eyes, and his hand was shaking. "That's when I started seeing things."

"Did y'all see a woman? Was she a woman in white?" Molly asked.

"I don't like to talk about that," he replied.

Molly felt her eyes widen and her mouth drop open. His reply made her recall her apparition at the Brazos. What she'd seen might not have been her imagination after all. About the same time the woman in white had appeared to her, she had also appeared to Franklin. "I've … I've seen her, too," she confessed.

"Did she say anything to you?" Franklin asked.

"She said the hand of the Almighty was …" Her eyes smarted when she said it. "… upon me." At that same moment she understood who had rescued her from drowning under the logjam that day, and she confessed, "I felt his hand lifting me out of the Brazos River when I was drowning."

"Is that so?" Franklin smiled at her, not an accusing smile, but and understanding one. "Didn't y'all just say he was causing all your trouble, burning you out, letting your sister die, getting Innis murdered, and taking Amy away? And, didn't I hear y'all just say he didn't love you?"

Molly shifted her gaze away from his, covered her eyes with the back of her forearm and whispered, "Yes … Yes, I said those things."

"Then why would he pull you out of the Brazos? Why didn't he just let y'all drown right then?"

"I don't know."

"I know why, Molly. It's the same reason why I'm sitting here right now telling y'all about it. It's because he loves you."

"But all those terrible things that happened," she sobbed.

"They are terrible," Franklin agreed, "and it makes y'all wonder why it's happening, don't it? There ain't nothing wrong with wondering, Molly, but when you start blaming him for all the bad things that happen to you, y'all make him into something he ain't, and you start believing things that ain't true."

"But I'm innocent," she added.

"We can't stop bad folks from doing bad things, Molly. Folks like to think the innocent will always prosper and bad folks will always be punished, but it don't work that way until the end of days. Folks don't like to think that innocent folks can suffer sometimes."

"Oh, my!" she gasped, and covered her mouth with her fingers. Suddenly, she understood. Indeed, he had been doing something about the bad things happening to good folks. He had chosen her. He wanted to do something about it through her and through other folks he'd chosen, like Franklin. "I've made a terrible, terrible mistake," she said. "I've been saying things I didn't understand. Now, I see that this is part of a plan. He knew what was going to happen to me before it happened, before I ever left Gonzales. He sent the woman in white to help me."

"He knew you would blame him."

"Yes, he knew, and he helped me anyway." Pulling a hanky from her pocket, she dabbed her eyes and said, "I'm sorry, Franklin. I was wrong. All those things I've been saying were wrong. I shouldn't be asking the Almighty to explain himself. He isn't obligated to explain his ways to anyone. I just have to trust him. That's what he expects from me. What I don't deserve isn't the bad things that happened to me, it's the help he's been giving me. That's what I don't deserve."

"Nothing can stop him, Molly."

"I see that now," she admitted. "I didn't understand, but now I do. I know what he wants from me." Turning to Elli-Lou she pleaded, "Forgive me. I didn't know what I was saying."

"I didn't know what I was saying either," Elli-Lou admitted. "He wasn't testing you. He was rescuing you. I'm sorry I said that."

"Yes, he was rescuing me," Molly declared, "and I've been ungrateful. I pray that he'll forgive me for that, and I pray he'll forgive all the others who accused me of wickedness. They didn't understand either."

"What do y'all think he wants from you?" Franklin asked.

Interlacing her fingers, she pressed them against her lips. Looking to Franklin, then Elli-Lou, Aunt Ruthie, and the others, she replied, "I think he wants me to help folks who are suffering like me."

The conversation transitioned to family, to farm, and then to politics before Boots and the teamster returned from the corral. Pausing as he crossed the porch, the teamster said to Franklin, "My apologies, sir, if I appeared rude before."

"Pay it no mind." Franklin replied.

"All you boys what fought Santa Anna done a good thing."

"Obliged, sir," Franklin replied again.

The teamster went in and retired for the night. One by one the houseguests went in as well.

In the morning the house seemed unusually quiet to Molly when she came down to start the bread. Aunt Ruthie went out to the henhouse, and Boots came in early from the bunkhouse, carrying a bundle of leather tied on the ends. He left it in the corner of the sunroom and went into the kitchen where Molly informed him that the coffee was ready.

"Would you like some?" she asked.

"Morning," he said. "Yes, I would." Taking a mug down from the cupboard, he filled it.

"You've been wanting to talk about something?" Molly asked.

"You feel up to it?"

"Yes, much as I can be." From the oven she withdrew a platter with two loaves of freshly baked bread.

Against the kitchen counter he leaned, sipped coffee, and began to explain, "The recruiting festival up in Nacogdoches went real well. I had a bigger turnout than Liberty. Afterwards, I sent thirty-seven recruits off to San Antonio. Some of them had just come down fresh from the States to help us fight Santa Anna. They didn't know the war was over. I explained that we're still fighting the Comancheros and the Comanches. All them boys I recruited seemed like good men."

"How come you're not going to San Antonio with them?" Molly asked. "Wasn't that your last festival?"

He took a long sip of coffee, hesitated, and then said, "I'm leaving the Ranger Service, Missis McCracken."

Stunned by Boots revelation that he planned to leave the Ranger Service, Molly set a pan of bread dough on the counter instead of in the oven. Turning to him, she asked, "Something happened in Nacogdoches, didn't it? You've been gone for over three weeks. I knew something happened."

"Nothing happened … Well, I guess something happened, but not what you're thinking," he replied and sipped his coffee again.

He seemed nervous, and it made her heart race. Fearing for Amy she asked, "Are you hiding something about Amy? Is it bad news? If it is, just tell me so I can deal with it."

"It's news, but not so bad." He set his mug on the counter. "Didn't think I'd ever hear something like that come out of you."

"I'm not the same person I was when I came here."

"No, you're not, Missis McCracken. You've got mettle. And, that's what I …" He stopped midsentence and looked down at his mug and then sipped nervously from it without taking his eyes from her.

"You must have slept on your tongue last night," she mused. "You don't seem to be able to say anything this morning." Into the oven she slipped the next batch of bread and closed the door. Cutting into a steamy, hot loaf, she asked, "Would you like a slice while it's hot?"

"Yes, ma'am, I would."

As he munched she inquired, "Does your tongue feel better now?"

"Mm … Yes!" he said, between ruminations.

"Then tell me why you're leaving the Ranger Service."

"I met with Colonel Martin Casey after the recruiting festival in Nacogdoches. He built a fort about twenty miles west of town, calls it Fort Casey. I spent a few days there before I came back here." Next to his coffee mug he laid the slice of bread he had been munching on. His eyes lost their luster, and his mouth went straight as he said, "He knows what happened to Amy."

KITCHEN ENCOUNTER

MOLLY DROPPED HER breadknife, thumping and clattering on the oak counter. "Happened?" she gasped. "Something happened to Amy?" Gripping the edge of the counter she asked, "What does that mean, Mister Williams?"

"I'm sorry, Missis McCracken. I don't know a better way to tell you, but there's more. You don't need to be upset. Just hear me out, okay?"

"Okay," she agreed.

"Marty knows folks who trade with the tribes, and he knows tribes who trade with tribes, also. He thinks the Kiowa traded Amy, and he thinks the traders know where she is. She might even be with tribes that he's had negotiations with. He thinks he can get her back in trade."

"Will you take me up there? I have to go up there."

"That's what I've been thinking about, Missis McCracken. You need to be there if he finds her."

"Is that why you're leaving the Service?"

"I can't help you rescue Amy and serve the Rangers, too. I had to make a choice, and I decided I want to help you."

"You can go back to the Service after we find her, can't you?"

"I don't have the heart for it anymore, Missis McCracken."

"I don't believe you, Mister Williams. You thrive on the life. I know you. You live for the danger. It quickens you, remember? And now I've had it happen to me, too, just like you said. I was quickened in that fight the other day. Things that only took a couple seconds seemed like they took hours. I could see my pistol balls flying, and I thought they were taking forever. No matter what those Comancheros did, I could do it faster. I liked it, Boots. I don't know what that means, and I don't know what it makes me, but I liked it. You can't tell me you don't have the heart for the Ranger Service, because I know what's in your heart. You showed it to me. The Service is in your heart, in your blood, and in your soul, the same as it's in me."

"You don't understand, Missis McCracken. There's something else that's gotten into me, and it's turning everything upside down. It's got me thinking about things I've never thought about before."

"What kind of things?" she asked.

"I've been thinking about living instead of dying. I've been thinking about building a life instead of fighting against it. And I've been thinking about raising a family."

"Listen to you," she said. "That doesn't sound like the Captain Boots Williams I know. What caused this big change all of a sudden? What in heaven's name has gotten into you?"

Grabbing her shoulders, he looked into her eyes and said, "You did, Molly. You've gotten into me. You've gotten into my heart, my blood, and my soul, and it's turning everything I thought I loved upside down."

"What's going on in here?" Aunt Ruthie walked in and set a basket of eggs on the counter. "Are you two arguing again? I can hear you all the way out to the barn." Into a basin she pumped water and began washing the eggs before cracking them into a skillet.

Boots's hands fell to his sides. Molly was stunned and speechless. Her feet were millstones, and her arms were made of lead. As if Boots had clamped her in a vise, she couldn't turn her head and couldn't unlock her eyes from his.

"Is something wrong, darlin'," Aunt Ruthie asked. Looking first at Molly, and then at Boots, and drawing a quick, deep breath she said, "Oh, my! Yes, I see! I think I'll just go back out to the henhouse and see if I missed anything." Out the sunroom door she scurried, taking with her a half full basket of eggs and leaving the other half in the washbasin.

Shock drained slowly out of Molly's arms and legs. Her eyes fell from his, and she turned to the washbasin. One at a time she began to clean the eggs and crack them into a skillet as she explained, "You already know I'm obligated to someone else, Mister Williams."

"I thought that was settled. I didn't know you still felt that way. How long has it been now?"

"Six months, one week, and two days."

"Since he left to sign up with Houston?"

"Yes."

"But he hasn't been looking for you. If he was either him or someone who knows him would have passed through here by now."

"I don't know that for sure." She stopped washing eggs and set the skillet off the stove. Grabbing the edge of the counter again she asked, "So, what's your point? Am I supposed to turn my back on him because I don't know where he is? I'm not that kind of person, Mister Williams. I can't do that."

"He's dead, Molly … Missis McCracken. Everyone can see it. Something happened to him after your brother-in-law went back to the farm to get you and your sister. Something happened that no one knows about. No one has seen or heard from him for over six months, and the army has no record of him. He's gone, Missis McCracken. You just haven't accepted it yet."

Tightening her grip on the counter, she looked down at the washbasin of eggs and said, "I need to find Amy."

"Would things be different if we had Amy?"

"We?" she asked him in return. "What do you mean, if we had Amy?"

"I'm being foolish," he admitted.

Turning, she reached out to his arm and said, "Mister Williams, you are the finest, most handsome gentleman that I've ever had the pleasure of knowing. I owe you everything, even my life. But, please forgive me. I'll never break my vows to Emmet until I know what happened to him."

"Would it make a difference if you knew he was dead?"

Her answer came slowly, but it came. "Yes," she admitted.

"Then you do have feelings for me?"

She dropped her gaze, shook her head, and turned back to the counter and the skillet.

"If you don't feel the same as I do," he persisted, "just say it. I need to hear you say it."

"I can't say that," she whispered.

"Why?"

"If I say it ..." She hesitated. "If I say it, I'd be ..." Her words would not come. As much as she wanted them to, she couldn't get them out. Her words boiled inside her, giving her great distress and turmoil and making her angry. He was making her angry.

"What?" he asked emphatically. "You'd be what?"

Picking up the bread knife, she thrust it into a loaf of bread, cutting slice after slice, and repeatedly thumping the blade against the counter. "Unfaithful!" she screamed. "Okay! I'd be unfaithful if I said that! And I can't do it! I won't do it!"

Grasping her hand, he gently removed the knife, laid it on the counter and said, "Having feelings doesn't make you unfaithful, Molly, and neither does admitting you have them. You're the most faithful person I know, and I admire that in you. I'm sorry I made you say it. Sorry I upset you, but I had to know how you feel. Maybe you didn't say the words I hoped for, but you did say what I wanted to hear. You said it without saying it, and now I know."

Lifting her knuckles to her lips, she bolted for the living room. Boots caught her at the kitchen doorway and held her, adding, "As long as there's any doubt about your husband, I won't speak about this again, okay? I give you my word. I have the greatest respect for you Molly, and if we can find Emmet, I'll go my own separate way. It's the right thing to do. Can you agree with that?"

She relaxed, but would not turn while he held her in his arms. "You have to let me go," she said.

He released her. She didn't bolt away, but turned then to face him. "You'd do that?" she asked. "You'd really do that?"

"I want you, Molly, but I want you like you are. I don't want anything to change you. I don't want to make you do something that would destroy the thing I admire in you."

"You're very kind."

"I know how you feel about me and that's enough for now."

"When can we leave?" Molly asked.

"I'm riding down to San Antonio first. I owe that much to Colonel Karnes. He's been good to me. After that, we can ride up to Nacogdoches."

"When will you leave for San Antonio?"

"I've been expected there for over a week now. I should leave this morning. I'll be there tomorrow. Then I'll probably be back the day after that. Can you be ready by then?"

"Yes. I'll get my gear together. I need a few things from the mercantile, and I want to get saddlebags like yours."

Reaching down he took her hand in his, but she pulled it away. Smiling, he said, "The way things are going is good. We'll see where it takes us from here."

"We'll see," she admitted.

After breakfast Molly watched him pick up the leather bundle he'd left in the sunroom. "That's not more scalps is it?" she asked.

Swinging it discretely behind his back, he said, "Well, yes it is. It's the scalps from those Comancheros you and Aunt Ruthie killed. Klaus took them before the farmhands buried them. I'm taking them to Colonel Karnes. He doesn't know about your honorary assignment yet. When I show him the paperwork, I want to show him what you did with it. There's a lot less chance that he'll revoke your assignment if I do that."

The next morning, Molly boarded the ferryboat with Boots, Franklin and Elli-Lou, and waved them off on the Atascosito Road toward Gonzales and San Antonio.

"You probably won't come back to Gonzales, will you?" Elli-Lou asked as Klaus closed the gate.

"Probably not to stay, but I'll come to visit after I've settled a few things," Molly replied. Watching until they crested the hill, she rode the ferryboat back to Tuck's Landing.

That afternoon, Aunt Ruthie took the wagon and Molly to the mercantile where Molly purchased cooking and eating utensils for her trip, wool blankets for a bedroll, a used military tent, saddlebags, lead ingots, gunpowder, primers, and a couple tins of Vesuvians. Everything fit in the wagon on the way back to Tuck's Landing, but when she went out to the barn to load her gear on Angel, she had a problem. She couldn't find enough places to tie everything on.

In her room, she emptied her sea-chest, and brought it down. Klaus was waiting for her when she walked into the barn with it.

"Let mm … me help you with that." He reached to take the sea-chest from her hands.

"Obliged, Klaus, but I've got it." She set the sea-chest on the ground next to Angel's stall and noticed a rifle standing there. "What brings y'all out here this afternoon?" she asked.

"I he … hear you're leaving us."

"Yes. In two or three days, probably."

"It's going to be lone … lonesome out there on the ferryboat without y'all."

"I'll be lonesome for you too, Klaus."

He bobbed his head, but he wasn't smiling. "Will y'all come back and see us?"

"I'll be back with a feather in my hat and Amy's hand in mine. Would you like to see that?"

"Yes, ma'am, I woo … would." His eyes told her that beneath that bushy, strawberry beard he was now smiling as he continued, "I thought y'all would like to have this." From the waist of his trousers he pulled a knife, double-edged with an ivory handle, and he handed it to her, hilt first.

Molly recognized it immediately, "It's Buffalo Head's knife," she declared, and took it from him.

"I got this, too." Turning, he picked up the rifle, which was leaning against Angel's stall.

"That's my brother-in-law's rifle," she squealed, taking it in her hands, she held it out in front of her. "I'm so happy to have this. Obliged, Klaus."

"I figured it was the one you told us about. I found it tied to Buff … Buffalo Head's saddle. The rest of the gear me and the boys are splitting up, the guns, horses, and gear. We'll sell most of it."

"You deserve it and more," Molly said, smiling and admiring the rifle in her hands.

"Aunt Ruthie pay … paid us a bonus," he informed her.

"Oh yeah? How much?"

"Month's pay."

"You and your boys earned it, too. Good for you, Klaus."

"Guess I'll be seeing y'all then someday." Doffing his hat, he went out. Looking back at her he smiled and bobbed his head.

"See you when I come back, Klaus," she called after him.

Standing the rifle against the stall, she knelt and slipped the dagger into the pocket inside her boot, and found that the knife was small enough and flat enough to be comfortable there.

Behind her saddle she tied her sea-chest the way she'd seen Boots tie it when they left the cabin on Gotier Trace. Perching it over her bedroll, which was on top of her tent, she lashed it also to her saddlebags. Around and under Angel she bound everything together, and then filled the chest with utensils, clothing, gear, and food. She put her foot in the stirrup, and when she swung her leg over her saddle the chest dislodged, sliding with everything else tied to it, around Angel's mid section. Hanging upside down, the top dropped open, dumping the contents onto the ground along with her tent and bedroll. Standing back, Molly planted her hands on her hips and noticed that Angel didn't seem any happier about the situation than she was.

Behind her someone chuckled. Turning to see Aunt Ruthie, she asked, "Are you laughing at me?"

"Can't help it, darlin'. How'd you like to walk around with a big old trunk tied to your belly?"

"That's not funny."

Loosening the bindings, she let the chest drop to the ground. Angel bobbed her head and snorted her pleasure with the release of such a burden from her underside.

"I don't think the Rangers carry this much stuff," Molly concluded. "I need to get rid of a few things."

Aunt Ruthie nodded her agreement and chuckled again.

Gathering her items back into the sea-chest Molly said, "Guess I'll forget this sea-chest, my tent, and my pots and pans, and my table ware, and just take my bedroll and saddlebags … I don't know if I can live out of a saddlebag."

"Sure you can, darlin'. You're a Texas Ranger. You always travel light. Y'all can do it. Tell you what. We've got a couple days yet. Why don't we jerk some beef? Then we'll load you up before you go. You won't need to take things for cooking that way. I'll have Justin butcher one of the cattle. You and me can strip it out and hang it in the smokehouse. We're getting low on beef anyways."

"That's a good idea, Aunt Ruthie."

"We'll stuff one of your saddlebags full of jerked beef. It should last you and Boots for a week or so."

Justin was cleaning stalls when Aunt Ruthie sent him out to process a head of cattle. In a small plank and dirt floor slaughtering room at the far end of the barn, he chunked out fresh cuts and passed them to Molly and Aunt Ruthie's preparation table. There they sliced thin strips from the chunks and basted them with a paste made from molasses and salt. Filling wooden crates with the prepared meat, they then carried the crates to the smokehouse.

At the back corner of the pasture, a hundred or more paces beyond the barn, there stood a tiny log building built on a knee-wall of field stones and clay. Molly couldn't stand all the way up inside; neither could Aunt Ruthie. Both sides Molly could almost touch if she extended her arms in the windowless structure. She wouldn't want to do that though, for the walls were layered with a sticky residue of black soot and animal fat, and the racks blocked her reach anyway.

Against the walls, racks had been constructed from stripped saplings and had been tied together with leather bindings. These also were coated with black residue. Over the racks Molly and Aunt Ruthie stretched rows of basted beef strips and then stepped outside while Justin filled an earthen pit at the center of the floor with kindling and chopped mesquite and lit it up. As he did so, he also sampled some of the raw jerky.

"Don't eat that!" Aunt Ruthie chided him. "It'll give y'all the worms."

"Then maybe I'll just take some of them worms and go cat fishing," he rebutted.

"You'll be eating it by yourself."

"That's the whole idea, ma'am."

"You are a truly repulsive boy, Justin. Just get out here and shut that door before the whole place catches fire."

Justin closed the door, which was shorter than he was tall, tightly fitted, and he barred it from the outside to wedge it shut. The fire he had built reduced then to smoke from lack of air to keep it burning, and the smoke began to trickle out between the logs. It trickled out in spite of the clay, which plastered them together. A light breeze caught the smoke, spreading it over the pasture, and filling the air with the sweet aroma of mesquite, beef, and molasses.

Justin groaned. "This is what drives us all crazy down there. We can smell it from the other side of the river. Can you imagine being over yonder on the ferryboat, smelling this, and not being able to eat none of it?"

Aunt Ruthie glanced toward the river where he pointed, and while her head was turned he poked another piece of uncured jerky from his hand into his mouth.

By the next afternoon the beef was fully cured, packed into wooden crates, and stored in the pantry. Molly filled one of her saddlebags with it. Barely able to close the flap, she munched on a succulent strip, as she tied down the straps. Over the stove she then melted lead and molded an ample supply of ball for her rifle and repeaters, placing the ball in a leather pouch. That way she could leave the mold, ladle, and lead ingots behind. In the other side of her saddlebag she had just enough room for her powder horn, primer tin, Vesuvians, sharpening stone, hair brush, hand mirror, and a few other essentials like sewing supplies and scissors, which she rolled up in a strip of cloth left over from the green dress she'd made. On top she stuffed her freshly laundered work clothes and floppy shirt. She never knew when she might need a change of clothes, and they would help keep everything else in place while she was riding.

As she was rubbing bear oil into her saddlebags, Aunt Ruthie came into the sunroom. "Looks like your gear's about ready," she said. "Looks like you got everything real compact, too."

"I'm leaving almost everything behind," Molly explained.

Aunt Ruthie touched her arm and said, "I wanted to ask you about something before you leave, if y'all don't mind."

"Anything, Aunt Ruthie."

"Well, it's about your room. I can't see leaving it empty."

"My room?" Molly slipped her riding jacket off and began to apply a fresh treatment of blood wood and bear oil replying, "You should rent my room out, Aunt Ruthie. Go on ahead."

"You won't take offense to me renting it."

"No offense. I'm obliged for everything you've done to help me."

"We can put your things in my room," Aunt Ruthie offered.

"Let's do it now." Molly slipped her jacket on.

They had set down her sea-chest in the corner of the parlor when Boots rode in, galloping past the parlor window to the corral.

In the sunroom they met him. Hugging Aunt Ruthie, he lifted her up and set her back down. Then he looked over at Molly, and said, "I did it."

"What did you do, Bootsie?" Aunt Ruthie asked. "Molly says you're leaving the Ranger Service. Is that what you did? It's all right if you did."

"Now I've got the best of both worlds," he said, smiling broadly. "It's better than I ever expected."

"So, are y'all in the Service, or not?" Aunt Ruthie asked.

Boots explained, "Remember the first couple years when I worked as a surveyor out of San Antonio?"

"I remember," Aunt Ruthie replied.

"And remember when I decided to join the Ranger Service?"

"I remember that, too. You wanted to put a stop to the depredations them marauders were committing everywhere."

"That's right. Then Santa Anna decided to drive us out. Now, the Comanches think Texas is up for grabs."

"Didn't y'all say Colonel Karnes was recruiting Rangers to drive them out?"

"Yes, and he's conducting a campaign against the Comanches right now, but it doesn't involve me and my boys anymore. Colonel Karnes assigned us to a sector up north of San Antonio. Me, Zach, Alsey, and Noah Smith will be riding the hill country. It's a sector about forty miles north by fifty miles wide."

"So, you're still in the Service?" Aunt Ruthie asked.

"Does that mean you won't be taking me to search for Amy?" Molly asked with alarm.

Boots continued. "I went to Colonel Karnes and turned in a hundred and seventy six certificates of assignment for the Service. Then I told him I was resigning … By the way, Molly, I also turned in your honorary assignment with the other assignments. He got a good laugh at first when he read it. Then I showed him the scalps from those Comancheros, seven of them, right?"

"Yes, seven," she replied. "Aunt Ruthie shot four of them."

"It looked like more, because some were in pieces. Anyway, Colonel Karnes was surprised, almost shocked. 'A woman did that?' he asked."

"Aunt Ruthie shot four of them," Molly protested. "Didn't you tell him that she shot four of them?"

"Darlin'!" Aunt Ruthie tugged on her sleeve. "I told Bootsie I wanted you to get all the credit. You did just as much shooting as I did. Maybe more, and I don't think I could have done it without you."

"Obliged, Aunt Ruthie."

"Anyways," Boots added. "I brought this for you." From his inside pocket he withdrew a sealed envelope and handed it to her.

FORT TERAN

MOLLY EXAMINED BOTH sides of the envelope Boots had given her from his inside jacket pocket. Breaking the seal, which was a lone star made of sealing wax, the official seal of the Republic of Texas, she then slipped a neatly folded paper from the envelope, unfolded it, and gasped, saying, "This is a letter of commendation from Colonel Karnes." Reading further she said, "For outstanding service and courage shown in the subjugation of the nefarious outlaw known as Buffalo Head." She looked up from the letter at Boots and said, "I wasn't expecting anything like this."

"I know of only one other Ranger who's got a commendation from Colonel Karnes," Boots replied.

"Who's that?" she asked.

"Me! I got it for them Comancheros we chased down on the Medina River."

"You never told us," Aunt Ruthie observed.

"I don't care to draw attention to myself," he said apologetically, "but you on the other hand, Molly. You need that kind of attention. Folks aren't going to accept that you're a Texas Ranger. I want them to know how capable you are, and that your service has been acknowledged by your superiors. It truly was outstanding service, and courageous, and you should be proud of it."

Molly shook her head. "I don't think I could ever be proud of doing something like that, but I appreciate the commendation. Say, there's another sheet of paper here. It's a bank script for thirty dollars."

"He's paying you, Molly. He said he don't expect any of his recruits to provide their services for nothing. He was pretty happy that you got Buffalo Head. Happier than you know, so are a lot of other folks."

Folding up the commendation, she asked, "So, now I need to know something, Mister Williams. What are your plans from here? Are you going back to patrol the hill country, or are you taking me up to Nacogdoches?"

"Well, I told Colonel Karnes I was resigning. He wanted to know why, and I told him about you and Amy, and I explained what Colonel Martin Casey told me up in Nacogdoches. Colonel Karnes is a good family man. He has youngsters of his own, and he understands the situation. Said he wouldn't let me resign. Instead, he sent me to meet with Mister R. C. Timble. Said he'd been thinking about it for some time.

"Then Mister Timble appointed me Deputy Surveyor of the Bexar District and gave me a raise. Me and the boys are going to be surveyors from now on. We'll also be patrolling the hill country as Rangers, but we'll be serving as surveyors too. That's our new assignment. There's a lot of surveying that never got completed, and a lot of folks who are waiting to stake out their land, build homesteads, ranches, and farms. The Rangers are the only ones capable of making that possible."

"What about Amy?" Molly asked.

"Colonel Karnes and Mister Timble gave me thirty days to put my affairs in order, Molly. Then they want me to come back. You and me can leave for Nacogdoches in the morning."

That night Aunt Ruthie put up an extra large batch of biscuits for supper, stashing the leftovers in a grain sack for the trip to Nacogdoches. Molly and Boots spent the evening on the front porch with her and the house guests, discussing old times and saying their farewells. In the morning Molly did her breakfast chores, changed into her riding leathers and then bid her room and her green dress adieu. Heading to the parlor to put her remaining belongings in her sea-chest, she had a second thought and rolled her green dress with her bedroll, just in case she had need for a dress sometime.

Boots was waiting for her by the corral. He'd already saddled Angel. Molly tied on her saddlebags, bedroll, water gourd, and a sack of biscuits. Then into its scabbard she slipped her new rifle and mounted up. Aunt Ruthie waved them off, smiling as she always did, but Molly could see sadness in her eyes, and the sadness seemed to catch in her own throat, too. Waving back, she turned her attention to the Atascosito Road running east ahead of her.

The sun stood only a hand above the horizon and straight in their eyes when Boots turned off the Atascosito onto an overhung trail that forked off in a northerly direction.

"You're not taking Old Boggy?" she asked. "They say it's a good road this time of year?"

Boots agreed, "This time of year it's dry. That's true enough, but the Orcoquisac Trace is the safest way to get from Liberty to Nacogdoches. It's an old native trail."

"I've heard of it," Molly confessed. "I don't think the teamsters go this way."

"We're bypassing the teamsters on the Atascosito," Boots explained. "It's shorter, and we're also bypassing any Comancheros or freebooters that might be going that way."

Comancheros didn't frighten Molly, not any more. His remark challenged her, so she asked, "Do you think we should go that way? Maybe it would be good for folks and the teamsters using Old Boggy for us to be there."

"I appreciate what you're saying, Molly, and I recall a time when I used to think the same thing myself. But the truth is we don't want to invite trouble that we haven't been assigned to. There's Rangers already assigned to do that."

"I understand."

"The Orcoquisac Trace is rougher than Old Boggy, but it's safer. We'll be riding through places where a wagon would have trouble. Most likely we won't see anyone else until we get to Fort Teran."

When the sun was full up, it warmed Molly's leather jacket a little too much. Perspiration began to trickle under her shirt. Wiping her brow with her forearm she noted to Boots, "It's going to be hot today." Pulling off her jacket, she tied it by the sleeves around her waist.

Lifting his hat, Boots also wiped his brow, adding, "Back in Liberty we can catch a breeze off the coast. Problem is the breeze doesn't make it up into these parts."

The further they went, the more Molly noticed the flat rocks that appeared in the soil around them, and in the distance she could see the land thrusting upwards into a rugged, tree-covered barrier, which they would eventually have to breach. "Is that a mountain range up ahead?" she asked, noticing that Boots's hat had soaked through the band.

He replied, "They call it the Kisatchie Wold. It's not high enough to be a mountain, but sometimes it looks like a mountain. That's because everything around it is so low. It runs all the way to the Mississippi."

She also noticed that the trees around her were larger than she was used to, enormous, bigger than any she had seen at home or in Liberty, and with trunks wider than the expanse of her arms. The height of them was dizzying, and when she looked up into the tree tops she had to glance back down to keep her balance.

Beside a small creek, where there was water and grazing for their horses, they made camp that evening. Stifling, hot, and arduous, Molly was glad the day was over. After a supper of jerked beef and biscuits, she spread her bedroll, hung her green dress on a tree branch, and upon her blanket she sat.

"You brought a dress along?" Boots asked.

"I wasn't going to. Then I thought I might need a dress sometime, and I wouldn't have one. It doesn't take up much space in my bedroll."

"Well, suit yourself," he agreed. "So what do you think so far?"

"About what?"

"About traveling with me?"

"It's not so bad. I'm not bouncing around on a seat-board all day long. And, I don't have to haul out a kettle and cook for everybody, and I don't have to carry water either."

"Traveling light has its advantages, doesn't it? You seem to be taking to it quite well."

"I grew up riding horses. I've always liked to ride. My pa gave me a foal when I was little before he moved us to New Orleans. I was about ten, I think. I named him Daisy. When I was older, me and Emily would go exploring." Molly laughed. "It must've been a sight to see two little girls riding bareback on Daisy. Back then, we thought every little hill we climbed was a mountain."

Laughing, Boots said, "Only you would give a stallion a name like Daisy. Why'd you call him Daisy anyway?"

"He was kind of creamy-yellow with brown spots, and he reminded me of a daisy, so that's what I called him."

"Then he must have been Nez Perce?"

"What?"

"They're a Native tribe up in the Northwest Territories. They breed horses with spots like you said Daisy had. They're mountain horses. The Nez Perce breed good horses, too. How'd your pa get one like that way over in Louisiana?"

"Traded somebody for it I suppose. He was always trading something. Now that you mention it, Daisy didn't like the pasture much. He always liked to be out in the woods or running the hills. He never wanted to go back home when we took him out. Neither did me and Emily, but we always went back and so did he."

"Then you had some tomboy in you?"

"Riding horses doesn't make me a tomboy."

"Riding out in the wilderness and not wanting to go back home does." He smiled.

"I don't think so. I knew a tomboy once. There was one back in school. She'd make your ears burn with her swear words, and she could fight like one of the boys."

"Did you ever slug anybody?"

"Me?" Molly shook her head. "That's not important."

"It is if you're a tomboy."

Holding her doubled fist up to him she said, "Just how bad do you want to find out, Francis?"

"Where'd you hear that?"

"I have my sources."

"Did Aunt Ruthie tell you that?"

Mocking him, she shook her fist and said, "Ranger Francis Williams. Has a nice sound, doesn't it? Makes me want to put my green dress on you and see if y'all can ride sidesaddle."

"Hey!" He straightened his mouth. "It's Francis Jacob after my grandpa. Folks used to call me Jake when I was growing up."

Molly lay over on her side, pulled the corner of her blanket over her and said, "It's getting dark, Francis. Good night."

"Humph! You're pretty funny for a tomboy, aren't you?" he grunted and then added, "Good night." Rolling onto his side, he laid his head on his saddle.

Cool air began to settle over their camp, but sleeping on rocky ground was not something that Molly's body was easily accustomed to, and lent itself to frequent bouts of tossing and turning. And she discovered right away that Boots had taken up log sawing as a nighttime occupation. She didn't recall that he snored when he brought her from the cabin on Gotier Trace to Tuck's Landing.

The second day on the Orcoquisac Trace was worse than the first due to Molly's lack of sleep and the increasing daytime temperatures. Angel snorted frequently, and they stopped wherever they found water. Molly watched as Boots cupped water over his head with his hands, tossed his hair back and then covered his head with his hat. "You can stay cool a long time this way," he advised her.

Removing her hat, she too drank, soaked her head and then set her hat over it. "You're right," she agreed.

The trail took them over a low place on the Kisatchie Wold, which she had been observing since yesterday, and their ride downhill became easier, but hotter. What little breeze they'd enjoyed before they reached the ridge they'd left on the southern side of the Wold, and the northern declivity seemed to Molly like a descent into Aunt Ruthie's oven.

Before the sun rested on the horizon, they arrived at the rocky banks of the Neches River. To her right, through the trees, Molly could see a fortification wall of pointed vertical logs and a lane that led into it.

"Fort Teran," Boots announced, as he turned onto the lane and rode through the gate. A dozen or so chickens clucked and flapped away from him as he cantered in. To the right of the gate a healthy looking sow nursed a litter of shoats in a small pen.

Doors and window shutters were standing open among ten cabins that lined either side of the fort's interior. The center was a broad, earthen plaza with a flagless flagpole and a well lined with stones. Young girls were playing tag and twirling around the flagpole. A woman was lowering a rope and bucket over a low stone wall and into the well. Another woman, who was holding an infant, came to the doorway of one of the cabins to watch. Apparently, more than one family was living on the grounds. At the most prominent cabin in front, Boots and Molly dismounted where two men were unloading a wagon.

The men carried large sacks over their shoulders into the main cabin, one of them reemerging. A broad-shouldered man, he wore a linen shirt stained with perspiration and soil. Over his spreading midsection his suspenders were buttoned down to his trousers front and back. Pulling his hat off, he wiped his face with his hand, and shook it into the dirt. "Good afternoon folks," he said. Wiping his hand on his soiled trousers, he then offered it to Boots. "I remember you, Captain Williams. You stayed here just a couple weeks ago."

"That's right, Sam." Boots shook hands with him and then rubbed his hand on his own trousers.

"Y'all brought someone along with you this time, Captain Williams. Is there some special occasion?"

"No, sir, this is Ranger McCracken."

Molly nodded, "Evening, mister."

"You got a woman's voice," Sam exclaimed. "Ranger you say?" He smiled, and braced his hips with his hands, as he examined her silver-star belt buckle and the butts of her repeaters. "So, y'all couldn't recruit enough men-folk up in Nacogdoches? Now y'all are putting womenfolk in the Service? That ain't right, Captain Williams. Womenfolk ain't made for fighting. I know folks that would walk through her like she was a clump of weeds." He pawed at the air with his fingers and said, "What's she supposed to do? Scratch their eyes out?"

"Look here, Sam." Boots snapped at him. "She gunned down Buffalo Head and his whole gang, and Colonel Karnes gave her a commendation for it."

"I heard about that," he said. "It weren't too long ago neither. So, that was you, Ranger Mic ...?"

"McCracken," she said. "I didn't do it single-handed though, but I did shoot Buffalo Head and two others."

"Dad-blame-it!" Sam exclaimed and extended his hand to her. "I'm Sam Pallet, Ranger McCracken. Pleased to meet y'all. You're some kind of local hero from what I hear. Welcome to Fort Teran. This here fort is mine now that Santa Anna's been defeated."

Shaking his hand, she then rubbed her palm on her trousers and asked, "You say this fort used to belong to Santa Anna?"

"Before the war it did, yes ma'am," Sam explained. "About five years back a fellow named General Terán was sent up here by the Mexican government. He's the one what had this fort built. Had a crew of carpenters brought down from Nacogdoches to do it. You can see it in the quality of the buildings they put up. General Terán was trying to close off the Alabama Trace over yonder. It's an old native trail that freebooters were using to smuggle slaves into Texas illegally. At least, it was illegal back then. Ain't no more. There'll be lots of folks traveling through here now.

"I'm opening up a trading post in this first cabin here. I got shelves built, and I'm bringing in supplies. We already got a dozen or so folks farming along the Neches. Someday this will be a real town. I'll have a boarding house and tavern over there on the other side. Got plenty of cabins to work with. Me and my family live in that one, behind the trading post, and I got a couple tenant families living here, too, until they get their land cleared, and their own cabins built."

"Sam," Boots broke in, "We plan to spend the night. We'd like to use one of those cabins."

"If y'all got two bits, it's yours."

"You charged me a dime last time, Sam."

"There was just one of you last time. Now there's two of you, and y'all be wanting supper too, right?"

"That cabin you gave me last time has chiggers, Sam. Your beds don't have bedding on them, and they smell like something died in them."

"I told y'all I was making it into a boarding house. I just ain't got around to cleaning it out yet."

"I'm not paying two bits to stay in that cabin. Two bits is a lot of money, Sam. It's a dime each. Take it or leave it."

"Ma's got a pot of bear meat simmering in the chimney over yonder." He pointed to his own cabin, which had a flat-stone chimney on one end, with a trickle of smoke rising from it. "And, she's making cornbread," he added. "Your supper's included with that two bits, Captain Williams."

Boots stepped into his stirrup, swung his leg over his saddle and nudged his horse toward the gate. Molly mounted Angel and followed him thinking that they'd be sleeping on the ground again tonight.

"Now hold on a minute," Sam called after them. "Y'all don't have to just ride off like that. Can't we jaw-bone about this a little more? How about two dimes and two cents? Your supper is worth two cents, ain't it?"

"Two dimes," Boots yelled at the gate. "And that includes supper. Just like last time."

Riding alongside Boots Molly whispered, "I don't want to sleep in a cabin that's infested with chiggers." Looking back, she noticed that Sam's face had gone red.

Boots whispered back to her, "I just made that up."

"Dad-blame-it!" Sam yelled. "Two dimes then!"

Boots pulled back on his reins as Sam yelled, "Y'all got one jagged old hard streak in you, Captain Williams. So, make yourself at home, and I'll bring your supper when it's ready."

The cabin was standing open when Molly tied Angel to the hitching rail next to Boots's horse. Pulling down her saddle and gear, she took it all inside. Over one of the rope beds she opened her bedroll, folded her green dress, and left in on the table. "I don't smell anything in this bed," she noted.

Boots smiled and said, "Don't tell Sam that, okay?"

A table standing in the center of a plank floor held a pitcher of water and basin. Around the table stood sawed off pieces of logs rather than chairs. Sam brought in a pan of cornbread and a fair sized bowl of meat and then huffed away with the two dimes Boots paid him.

Molly pulled off a chunk of meat and tasted it; she found it to be kind of sweet, dense, and gamey, reminding her of a combination of venison and pork. She liked it, pulled off another piece and took a seat. "Are there a lot of bears in these parts?" she asked.

Chomping his own chunk of bear meat, Boots had taken a log-seat across from Molly. "Yes," he mumbled. "In fact, folks around here are known to train their curs just for hunting bear."

"Did you ever go bear hunting?"

"I did once. It wasn't around here though. It was before I went off to school. I was fifteen. Some friends invited me to go along with them on a hunting trip. We made camp deep in the woods, and from there the dogs did the rest. All we had to do was follow them. They sniffed out an old bear and ran him into the thicket, ran him into the deepest, darkest thicket that old bear could find, and the dogs ran right in after him. We could hear them yelping and hollering in there, and that old bear was growling back at them. From all the thrashing and crashing, I figured there was a fight going on between that old bear and them dogs, so my friends elected me to run the log."

"Run the log?" Molly asked. "A lot of men-folk have been killed doing that?"

"I was just a stupid kid then, so I run the log and I crawled in there among them yelping dogs and that scrappy old bear and shot him. Now that I think back on it, I only had one shot. I don't know what I would have done if I would have missed."

"I can't believe you did that."

"I did, and I got to keep his hide for doing it. I used that old hide as a blanket for a long time. Still got it back at Tuck's Landing, even though it's worn out."

Using her boot knife, Molly cut the cornbread into sections, lifted one out for Boots, and another for herself.

"Where'd you get that cute little pig sticker?" Boots asked. "I never saw anything that fancy in the mercantile back in Liberty."

"It was Buffalo Head's dagger," she explained as she slid it back into her boot. "And, it's not that little. Do we need to worry about bears when we're traveling around here?"

"Only if they see you first."

Molly swallowed hard on a bite of cornbread. "Really?" she gasped.

He laughed and coughed into his fist. And, as he did, she heard a cluster of footsteps running up from the Neches River into the fort.

"Ma! Pa!" a boy was yelling.

Molly went to the doorway and saw three young boys running up to Sam's cabin. Running ahead of the other two, the oldest reached the cabin first. Against their heads the other two held down their straw hats, running bare foot, shirtless and wearing only their trousers.

"Ma! Pa!" the oldest yelled again.

From the cabin a woman emerged.
"Ma, we seen a man's body down in Shawnee Crick."

SHAWNEE CREEK

BOOTS JOINED MOLLY at the cabin doorway and asked. "What's going on?"

"Those boys over there are telling their ma they found a man's body in a creek somewhere."

"Well," he said, setting his hat on his head and adjusting it. "Let's go see what this is all about."

"We was wading up the Shawnee Creek," the oldest boy told his mother. "We was up there spearing frogs and catching crawdads and such." He held up a sapling, which he'd splayed into sharpened tips on one end, and the younger boys also held up their spears as the oldest continued, "Then Joey saw him looking up from under the water. Scared the bats out of him, too."

Sam Pallet stepped out of his cabin, holding a bowl of meat in hand and a fork in the other. At his sides his suspenders dangled, and his belly sagged over his trousers. "A body?" he asked through a mouth full of food.

"Yeah, pa, we found him just laying there on the bottom of Shawnee Creek looking up at us."

"Suppose we better go down yonder then and see if it's someone we know. That's a fine looking spear y'all made, son." He handed his bowl and fork over to his wife, and pulled his suspenders up over his shoulders and observed, "We only got a couple hours of daylight." Toward the boys he walked, stopped, and then turned back. "Oh yeah," he added. "Better take a shovel." Around the side of the cabin he disappeared.

"How far is Shawnee Creek from here?" Boots asked the oldest boy.

"About a stone's throw, mister."

"Y'all can't throw a stone that far," the next boy argued. "It's two stones, maybe three."

"It don't matter," Boots said. "We'll go with you."

"All right, mister."

By then Sam had returned with a shovel and a rifle. "Can't be too careful," he said. "We get all kinds around here."

Down a stony trail to the river's edge the oldest boy led them. Mosquitoes swarmed over them. The river was low and flat rocks were exposed on the bottom.

Sam explained, "It's a solid crossing place when the water's up. That's why the trails cross here, because of this rock bottom. Going east is the Alabama Trace. The Coushatta Trace is going north and south from here, and the Orcoquisac Trace goes west, the way you folks came in. The river's usually a lot deeper than this. When the water's up where it's supposed to be, y'all can't see the bottom. It ain't rained here since last spring, so everything is low. We can walk right across. No swimming necessary." He waded out into the lazy current, ankle deep, then knee deep, and then ankle deep again. The others followed.

A cloud of mosquitoes surrounded each of their heads, as he turned right at the shoreline. Swatting and spitting the pesky insects, he twisted and wound along the edge, climbing over logs and boulders, and wading around brush piles. He led them to the mouth of a broad but shallow creek where he paused and said, "You boys go on up there. Show us where you found it. We'll be coming along right behind y'all."

The younger boys looked at each other and then at the older boy as if they were too frightened to proceed. "I ain't going back up there," the middle boy declared.

The youngest began to weep, and Molly put her arm around his shoulders. "It's all right," she said.

The oldest boy ridiculed the younger ones, saying, "Y'all are chicken." He stuck his thumbs under his arms, flapped his elbows, and clucked like a chicken.

"I ain't no chicken," the youngest cried out, digging tears from his eyes with his fists.

"Come on then," the oldest commanded them. "Let's get on up there." He waded up the middle of the creek, ankle deep, with the younger boys close behind. Rounding a bend, he waded waist deep into a hole and then up again. Sam went through the hole after him, then Boots, and then Molly.

At the next bend the oldest stopped with his back to them and held out his hands. "Right here," he said. "I can still see him. He's down there in the bottom of that hole by this here bend."

They surrounded the deep hole at the bend, and Molly could see that it was about three feet deep, with a man looking up at them. His eyes were open and clouded over, mouth agape. His arms drifted up at his sides, and his swollen fingers seemed to reach for the surface. Bare to the waist, his britches were tattered, and he wasn't wearing shoes.

"Let's get him on up out of there," Sam suggested.

Sam and the boys lifted his shoulders and arms. Boots and Molly took his legs. "He's a Negro man," Boots observed.

"He looks like a white man to me," the oldest boy remarked.

"The water does that to him," Boots added. They laid the man's body on the bank. Boots blew his breath and said, "Whew, he's been in there awhile. He's getting pretty ripe."

The two youngest boys turned, dropped to their knees and retched on the ground.

Molly let go of his leg. "Whew-wee!" she breathed and then lifted her arm to bury her nose and mouth in her shirt at the bend of her elbow.

"I don't have no slaves," Sam explained, "and I don't know anyone around here who does. I don't know where he comes from, or how he got here." He turned and began climbing up the rocky bank. "We'll have to drag him up here where there's enough soil to bury him. I'll start digging."

Speaking into her elbow Molly asked, "Do you think he's a runaway."

"He's not a runaway. Folks wouldn't do something like this to a runaway." Boots indicated the man's midsection. "Look here. He's been cut from stem to stern and sewn back together again. Not a very good job of it either." Reaching down he pushed the man's eyelids closed.

"Did he have surgery or something?" Sam asked from the top of the riverbank as his shovel shushed soil into a pile. "Maybe, an army surgeon did that," he suggested. "You think he fought in the war?"

Boots pushed against the stitches, which held the man's abdomen together, and said, "There's something inside him. He's all lumpy. I think he's full of rocks. Someone cut him open, filled him full of rocks, and sewed him back together again."

"Maybe, they forgot their shovel," Sam called down. "Maybe, they wanted him to stay in the bottom of that crick. If it weren't for the draught this summer, this crick would be full up, and you'd never find him."

"Did you notice this here?" Molly asked. "What are all those raised lines on his shoulder?"

Boots ran his thumb over the raised design on the man's shoulder and remarked, "I'd say it's some sort of decoration, wouldn't you? It looks like chords, but I think it's scar tissue. I think it was cut into him on purpose, but it wasn't done recently."

"He was a slave though, wasn't he?"

"Most likely," Boots said.

"He was young and strong," Molly observed. "That would make him worth a lot of money, wouldn't it? Why would anyone do this to someone worth a lot of money?"

"Well, Molly, a slave owner can't be held accountable for what he does with his slaves. They're his rightful property, to do with as he pleases."

Molly shook her head and mumbled, "That's not right."

"Let's get him up here." Sam tossed his shovel into the dirt pile. Molly could hear it land as Sam said, "Let's get him buried before I puke my supper like them youngins over yonder," Kicking his feet down the bank, he took hold of the man's head and lifted. "Are y'all going to help me? Hey, look here, the back of his head is gone."

Turning the man's head, Boots examined the back of it, and said, "He's been shot," and rolled the body over. Strings of raised scar tissue laced the dead man's back, and behind his head Molly could see an opening about the size of her fist.

Boots observed, "He's been whipped more than once," Pointing to a small puncture above his ear, he added, "He was shot right here. It came out the back of his head over there."

"Well," Sam added, "At least he didn't suffer, and he ain't from around here neither. That's the important thing."

"He's still a man." Molly insisted.

"So?" Sam turned his palms upward.

"So, he didn't deserve this. No one deserves this."

"So, who are you supposed to be? You're talking like one of them stinking abolitionists?" he squawked. "You sound just like them. If you're an abolitionist, there's a lot of folks who won't be too happy knowing we got an abolitionist in the Ranger Service. Y'all know what I think, Ranger McCracken? I'm thinking y'all don't belong here."

Boots reached over and touched her arm. "Leave it be, Molly. Our job is keeping the peace and making Texas safe for innocent folks."

"But Boots, how do you know this man wasn't innocent?"

"Let it go, Molly." He turned to Sam. "She's not an abolitionist, so put that thought out of your head. She doesn't need that kind of trouble. She just hasn't seen anything like this before, that's all."

"Well, y'all better get used to it then, Ranger McCracken, because you'll see it all over Texas. You'll find it everywhere you go."

Boots squeezed her arm. "We'll talk about this later."

"Y'all best take his advice, Ranger McCracken, because slave trading is big business around here, probably the biggest business in Texas. You start messing with that, and you can end up like this poor feller here. We get slave traders coming by here almost every week. They bring them in from Louisiana and sell them to folks who want them down here in Texas. Y'all can't run a plantation without slaves, you know. Mexico wouldn't let them in, so folks used to smuggle them. But, with Santa Anna gone, it's like opening the flood gates. We've even had the Mystic Clan come here."

"The Mystic Clan?" Boots asked. Suddenly intense, he narrowed his eyes. "The Mystic Clan has been here at Fort Teran?" he asked again.

"Yes, sir, Captain Williams, more than once. Those kind of folks know all the back ways into Texas."

"What's the Mystic Clan?" Molly asked.

Boots squeezed her arm again and shook his head. She understood that she might be asking too many questions, and he didn't want her to say anything more. From then on she determined that she would hold her peace and try to learn more about what had happened. And, for the first time since leaving Tuck's Landing, she began to feel uneasy.

"Let's get him up that hill," Sam insisted. "It's getting dark, and it'll be hard to see our way back."

They rolled the man onto his back as the younger boys wiped vomit from their mouths and rubbed their hands on their trousers. Then the boys helped Sam lift the man's body. Together everyone slipped and stumbled up the loose rocks until they reached the top of the creek bank, where Sam had dug a shallow grave. They laid the man in the ground, and Sam shoveled soil over him. "This ain't the first time this happened," he confessed. "I just wish they'd clean up their own messes when they come through here, instead of leaving them for me and the other folks that live around here."

"I'd like to have a look around before we leave," Boots announced. "But, it can wait until morning."

"If y'all want to see their camp, I'll show you where it is, back up the Alabama Trace a little ways."

"That sounds easy enough to find, Sam."

"When the traders got slaves with them, they camp in a clearing over there. When they come by without slaves, they stay at the fort in that cabin where y'all are staying tonight." Sam tossed in the last shovel of soil, and they all started down the bank into the darkness of Shawnee Creek.

"How much do you charge the traders when they stay at the fort?" Boots asked.

"Nickel each."

"Including supper?"

"Yes, sir, Captain Williams. There's usually a dozen or so of them. The boarding house business pays real good when that many are staying there."

"Then y'all owe me two nickels, Sam."

"What?" he yelled.

"You charged me a dime each."

"You're saying y'all can't let a man earn an honest living, Captain Williams?"

"Yes, sir, if it's an honest one. If you charge me the same as you charge everyone else, then it will be honest, won't it? So, pay up, Sam. You owe me two nickels."

"Dad-blame-it, Captain Williams!" Sam fished around in his pocket and pulled out a dime. "Here!" He handed it over.

As they waded down Shawnee Creek to the Neches, Molly began to have trouble in the dark with the slippery rocks along the creek bottom, stumbling over them and falling into the shallow water. She heard splashing more than once and knew that the others were stumbling as well, but couldn't see who it was. When they reached the Neches, the open space brightened enough with twilight to see where she was walking. She was relieved when they climbed the road to the lane, which took them back into Fort Teran.

The cabin was dark when she entered. Every muscle in her body ached from carrying the dead man's body up that creek bank, ached from riding all day and from tossing and turning on the rocky ground all last night. She wanted to light a candle, but Boots had already flopped onto his bed. She fumbled with her saddlebags, but couldn't find her Vesuvians in the dark, so she rolled onto her bed, and laid her repeaters at her sides. The ropes sagged almost to the floor, creaky and hammock like, but comfortable. A sawing noise had already begun to rise from Boots's side of the cabin.

"I don't think I'll be able to sleep tonight," she said.

"Huh? What?" Boots mumbled.

"I said, I can't sleep."

"Something wrong?"

"It's that man we found tonight. I can't stop thinking about him."

"He's just a man, Molly. It happens all the time."

"But, I feel bad for him, like we should be doing something about it."

"You can't do that, Molly. You can't let it bother you. It's just a job. Try to look at it that way. That's what you wanted when you asked for that Ranger assignment."

"I wasn't expecting anything this awful."

"We live in an awful world, Molly. Unfortunately, in our line of work you and me have to see things like that. Tonight you were getting down into the dirty part of the job, the part folks don't like to talk about."

"I don't know if I'm cut out for this."

"So, you're just now figuring that out?"

"It's giving me the shakes, and they won't quit."

"I can always take you home, you know. Do you want to go back to Tuck's Landing?"

"Tuck's Landing is a wonderful place, Boots, but I can't call it home. I don't have a home."

"You can always call it home, Molly. You're welcome there anytime. Aunt Ruthie loves you to pieces, and so do …"

"Don't say it, Boots. I'm not ready to deal with that just yet. I have enough to deal with right now."

"Do you want me to take you back? We can leave in the morning."

"No."

"You'll get past this, Molly. Just try to sleep on it. You'll feel different tomorrow."

"I haven't had any dealings with slaves before," she added. "No one back in Gonzales had slaves."

"No one in Gonzales could afford them," Boots added. "But, I need to tell you to be more careful about what you say to folks. They might take it the wrong way. Like Sam did tonight."

"Boots, what do you think about slavery?"

"It doesn't matter what I think."

"I need to know. I want to know where you stand on this. Do you think the man we found out there was innocent?"

"Probably, but no one knows for sure, and you'll never get folks to talk about it."

"You wouldn't help that man if he was still alive?"

"That's a hard question. Men have gotten themselves killed for helping slaves. It goes against what folks believe is right. Not just here in Texas, but all across the states."

"Well then, I think you should take me back to Tuck's Landing."

"I didn't say I believe it's right, Molly."

"Then, would you help him, or not?"

"It depends on what he did. If he's a runaway, I'd be obligated to return him to his owner, but catching runaways isn't my job. Other folks do that. If he was an outlaw, I'd treat him like any other outlaw."

"And, if he was an innocent man?" she asked. "Would you help him then?"

"Innocent or not, helping a slave can cost you your life."

"Would you do it, or not? Tell me the truth!"

"I'll tell you this. I know natives who are good men. Some of them I'd even call friends, and I'd help them if they needed help. And, I've seen Negro men and womenfolk living with natives. They're runaways. They run up into the native territories, and sometimes the natives will take them in and teach them their ways. All they want is to raise their families and be free. But, you're asking me if I would help them? I suppose I would if I wasn't a Ranger. You can't be a Texas Ranger and help slaves. Those two things just don't go together."

"Then I don't want to be a Texas Ranger anymore," she said.

"Maybe I don't either," he admitted and became silent for a long time.

He wasn't sleeping. Molly could tell by his breathing that he wasn't asleep, and he wasn't at ease either. He was just silent. "So," she asked, "what is the Mystic Clan?"

"The Mystic Clan is folks you don't want to know."

"Are they all kin or something? Is that why they call themselves a clan?"

"There's more than one family," Boots replied. "They call themselves a clan, but it's more like a secret brotherhood of freebooters. Some say there's thousands of them, and they're led by men of high standing, bad men, and government officials, who make up their Grand Council. Folks say they meet under a big old sycamore tree up in Arkansas along the Mississippi. They call it 'The Grand Council Tree,' and that's where they coordinate all their illegal activities across the states. They smuggled slaves into Texas for a long time. It's a sad and dangerous state of affairs, because they're well armed, well organized, and ruthless. You can't call them out.

They won't face you. And if you go after them, they'll lay in wait somewhere and ambush you when you're not expecting it, or they'll cut your throat while you're sleeping and laugh while you're bleeding out. All they want is to keep you out of their way."

"Oh, much obliged, Boots. I'm sure I'll get a good night's sleep after hearing that. Is that why you stopped me from talking to Sam?"

"Yes! We know Sam is doing business with them. He told us so out there tonight. We don't know if he's a clansman or not. He might be, and that's why you have to be careful what you say to him. You can't take a chance with a man like him. If there's other clansmen around here, and he says something to them, we could wind up dead, like Uncle Foster."

"Uncle Foster? You're talking about Aunt Ruthie's husband?"

"That's right, my Uncle Foster."

"Aunt Ruthie told me about him. She said he went to Louisiana with your pa to buy slaves, but he didn't come back. She said they were …" Molly stopped mid-sentence, as she put things together. "She said they were ambushed by a gang of freebooters! Are you saying it was the Mystic Clan?"

"My pa told me it was John A. Murrell himself who ambushed and robbed him and killed Uncle Foster."

"I remember Aunt Ruthie said that. I know about Murrell and his freebooters," Molly added. "We used to hear about him all the time when we lived in New Orleans. Folks were scared to death of him."

"That's why folks join the Clan, Molly. They're scared to death and figure it's safer to join them than to fight them."

"So, you're saying that John A. Murrell is a member of the Mystic Clan?"

"He isn't a member of the clan, Molly. He is the Mystic Clan."

"Oh, my! You're saying that he's the founder? And, you're saying he's the one who killed your Uncle Foster? That's why you were so intense out there tonight, isn't it? I understand now, and you think Murrell has been coming here to Fort Teran?"

"It's possible. I don't know for sure. This is the kind of place where he would go. He'd feel safe here. It's remote, and it doesn't get a lot of travelers. Tomorrow, we'll search that campsite Sam told us about. Maybe, Murrell left something behind."

"I wish we could go now." She felt like getting out of bed, but her body wasn't paying any attention to what she thought.

"You know, Molly, staying up all night and talking about it isn't going to help things."

"You can't expect me to sleep after everything you told me."

"Just rest then. You'll need your rest tomorrow. It's a long ride to Nacogdoches, and I can't have you falling out of your saddle."

Moments later he began his nighttime log sawing occupation. Waiting patiently for morning, Molly dozed occasionally. Then, abruptly Boots was standing over her, and the sun was up.

"You got some sleep," he said. "That's good."

She jolted awake.

"Sun's been up for over an hour," he added. "We need to go."

Pushing herself up, she swung her feet over the side of the rope bed to the floor, realizing then that her body had transformed into something heavy and inflexible during the night. "I guess I was more tired than I thought," she said.

He handed her a biscuit and a slice of jerky. "This will get your blood moving. We don't have time to make coffee."

When they had saddled their horses, they rode out of Fort Teran and crossed the Neches. Swatting mosquitoes, Boots rode up out of the river and east on the Alabama Trace, saying, "That camp should be right over here." Before long he found a clearing and dismounted.

Molly also dismounted, and noticed that the camp lay along the banks of Shawnee Creek. The central part was barren. She could see sprigs of grass springing up between flat rocks, and the banks were littered with dry, lumpy horse manure.

"This must be it," Boots said. "There was a fire here, and there's water and grazing over there. It can't be more than a couple hundred paces down the creek to where we found that body last night. Look at this." Kneeling by a cold fire pit, he pointed to a stick laid purposely over a shorter stick in the ashes. "Someone left a message here. This is telling someone they went down the Coushatta Trace to Bevil."

Lifting the longer stick, he used it to sift through the ashes. "Looks like there's some slag here." From the ashes he flicked out a hard piece of porous matter. "They've been making rifle ball here. And there's some bones here, too, probably venison by the size of them." With the stick he lifted a snatch of charred threads. "This was someone's clothing, maybe the man we found last night."

Walking along the creek bank, Molly searched the grass and examined the trees. "I think I found something over here," she said. "There's marks on this tree, like there was rope or chains around it. Probably chains, because there's chunks missing from the bark."

Boots joined her, and he also examined the tree. "I think you're right. Nice job. And look at this over here. That isn't horse manure, it's human. There were slaves here." He stood back and folded his arms.

Glancing around Molly asked, "So this is how the freebooters smuggled slaves into Texas? They'd bring them in through here?"

"It would seem so, but like Sam said last night, the floodgates are open since we defeated Santa Anna. What makes this place strange is the slave traders are bringing slaves in on the main roads now. They don't have to hide it anymore. Anyone coming in this way doesn't want to be seen. They come this way because they've got something to hide."

"Like that body we found last night?" Molly asked.

"Yes. I think that body might be a stolen slave, not one being transported by traders or a runaway. He was stolen. That's the only thing that explains why he was laying in the bottom of that creek. Someone was trying to cover up what they did, until we found that body."

"So, what are we going to do about it?"

"It's not a question of what we do. It's a question of what they do when they find out that we know about the body."

"How will they know? Do you think Sam will tell them?"

"You can bet he'll be telling folks about it, and we don't know who to trust." Mounting up, he added, "Let's move on away from here. There's too much trouble here, and that's not what we came for."

Climbing up on Angel, she trotted along with Boots. Looking back she noticed a deer in the thicket across Shawnee Creek and asked, "Are you getting tired of eating those stale biscuits and rock hard jerky? Would you like some fresh meat?"

"I saw it, too," Boots replied, pulled back his reins, and from the scabbard on his saddle he pulled his rifle.

The deer stood in the thicket watching them. Molly looked closer and reached over to Boots saying, "Don't shoot. It's not a deer. I think there's a little Negro boy hiding over there."

NOMUSHA

BOOTS SHOVED HIS rifle back into its scabbard and said, "Just leave him, Molly."

"No!" she demurred. "He's just a little boy. He doesn't know anything. We can't just leave him there like that. Look at him. Can you see him?"

"Yes."

"He knows we see him. He's not running away. It's almost like he wants to come out to us." She lifted her hand and motioned to the youngster.

"Someone will find him, Molly. Most likely there's clansmen looking for him. He belongs to somebody."

"That's right, Boots. He probably belongs to the ones who put that body in Shawnee Creek."

"We don't know that, but you can be sure that he's someone's property."

"Then we should find his rightful owner and return him, like you were saying."

"I also said that capturing slaves and returning them is not our job."

Toward Shawnee Creek she turned Angel and said, "I'm going over there."

The little boy also turned and disappeared deep into the thicket. Down to the creek and up the other side, Angel picked a sure footed way among the flat rocks. She seemed to understand what Molly wanted to do and took her to the thicket where the boy had been standing.

Dismounting, Molly noticed an opening in the weeds, a game trail large enough for a person or a hog, and knew that the little boy had gone that way. She was not unfamiliar with the thicket, pulled on her gloves, laid down her hat and her repeaters and dropped to her hands and knees. Crawling in, she found the grasses parched and the briars dry. She was glad that she had her jacket to protect her, but could feel the scabrous ground through the holes in the fingers of her gloves. The boy didn't have a shirt. She noticed that he was bare to the waist and hoped that the thorns weren't cutting him. The thicket was not a hospitable place for a small boy.

Ten or twelve paces in, she could see him scrambling ahead of her, maybe nine or ten-years-old. Increasing her pace, she was thankful that her leather riding trousers were protecting her knees. Again she could see him. His arms and legs were pumping like a rabbit, and she couldn't help but smile at him. When he saw her he screamed, and he sounded to her like a frightened girl. His scream made her think of Amy, and his fear gave Molly a surge of energy, which enabled her to overtake him.

She grabbed him by his heel, and he wouldn't stop screaming at her. Thrashing and kicking his free leg, he connected with her arms, so she grabbed that one, too. He writhed, twisting back and forth, and screamed like a wild animal caught in a trap. "Shush!" she said. "It's all right! I won't hurt you."

"Peez, don keel me, mista! Don keel me."

"I'm not going to kill you," she replied and dragged him closer to her by his feet.

When he was within reach, he pummeled her with his little fists, striking with stinging speed and accuracy. She tucked her chin to protect her face and yanked him under her. Laying over him, she encircled his arms, and held him tight, all but his head. Swinging his head, he struck it hard against her cheek bone.

"Ouch!" she yelled. "Will you stop?" Pressing her cheek against his, she pinned his head against the ground and said, "It's all right, son. I'm not going to kill you."

He began to weep, sobbing and heaving beneath her. "Don wanna go!" he screamed. "Peez, don wanna go."

His screams broke Molly's heart, and she began to weep, also. "You don't have to go anywhere. We'll just stay right here."

"Y'all keel me!"

"No, I won't kill you. Do you have anything to eat?"

"Eats?" he asked and began to scream again. "Y'all don eats me, peez."

"I'm not going to eat you." She laughed. "I'm your friend. I want to help you."

"Y'all ma fraynd, mista?"

"Yes, and I have food. Would you like to eat some food? What's your name? Do you have a name?"

He was breathing hard, but he'd stopped screaming. "Nomusha," he panted. "I am Nomusha."

"I'm Molly. It's nice to meet you, Nomusha. Have you been here a long time."

"I donno long time," he panted.

"Are you hungry?"

"Yeah, Mista Mally."

"If I let you go, will you come with me and get some food to eat?"

"Yeah, Mista Mally."

Slowly she lifted her face away from his, released his arms and rose up on her hands and knees. Out from under her he shot, like a bolt of lightning. Lunging after him, she thrust herself over him again and surrounded him with her arms. "You're very strong," she said. "You run like a deer, jump like a rabbit, and kick like a mule."

He was panting again.

"Do you ever see big bore hogs in here?"

"Bik bo hawgs?" he asked.

"Yes, big bore hogs. Do you ever see them? Do you hear them at night?"

"Yeah, Mista Mally."

"Did you know they eat little boys?"

"No, Mista Mally," he squealed. "No wanna eat me."

"I think I hear one right over there. Y'all should get out of here before he finds you. I can keep you safe, you know. Do you want to go back with me where it's safe?"

"Yeah, Mista Mally."

Releasing him again, she turned him around and pushed him out ahead of her and chased after him. Mere seconds later he emerged from the thicket, and he was promptly scooped up by Boots.

"Whoa," he said, as he swung the bundle of thrashing arms and legs into the air, entrapping him in his arms.

"Don wanna eats, peez," the boy screamed.

"Y'all don't want nothing to eat?" Boots asked.

Molly crawled out from the thicket, and explained, "He thinks you're going to eat him."

"I'm not going to eat you." Boots laughed long and hard. "If y'all stop kicking me, I'll put you down."

The boy's feet stopped thrashing, and he began weeping again. Boots set him down, and Molly held her arms out to him. "Come on," she said. "I'll protect you."

The boy's eyes were big as saucers and white as egg shells set in a gaunt ebony face. He leapt at her and clung to her, turning his cheek against her. Around him she reached her arms and smiled. "There, you see. We're friends. We'll protect you."

"What did he do to you in there?" Boots asked.

"What?" she asked in return.

"Your face, you've got a big lump on your cheek bone and your eye is turning black and blue." Reaching out, he turned her face to look at the other side. "You've got another one on your jaw over here, and your neck is bruised."

"I've got one on top of my head too," she added. "He's quite a fighter for a little guy, and we were wedged into a close space in there."

Boots shook his head. "I wouldn't have been able to move around in there like you did. Now that you got him, what do you want to do with him?"

"Let's give him something to eat first." Molly practically dragged the boy, clinging to her waist, over to Angel where she took out a helping of jerky and biscuits for him.

Ravenously, the boy consumed the morsels, barely chewing them and then choking and coughing. She gave him her water gourd and offered more food. "Do you think we should get him out of here before someone sees us?" she asked Boots.

"You know I'm against this, Molly. But, now that you have him, let's head on up the Coushatta Trace and put some distance between us and Fort Teran. We can decide what to do later."

Gathering her hat and repeaters, Molly mounted Angel. Boots lifted the boy up behind her. Then he mounted up, and led them down the rocky bank to Shawnee Creek. Angel stepped into the water, and Molly looked both ways. Her heart stopped when she noticed Sam Pallet's son with his two little friends, standing in the middle of the next bend, waist deep. They were holding their frog spears up above the water, and silently watching her and Nomusha.

Boots turned in his saddle and said, "So much for not being seen. Let's keep moving."

At the Coushatta Trace they turned north and kicked their horses into a canter and kept up the pace for a couple hours. All the while Nomusha clung tightly to Molly's waist and pressed his cheek against her back.

"Do you know where we're going?" she asked Nomusha.

"I donno whar we gowen."

"We're going to Nacogdoches. Have you been there before?"

"Yeah, Mista Mally. We be sailed dare."

"You were sold there?"

"Yeah, Mista Mally."

"Is he calling you Mister Molly?" Boots asked.

"He doesn't know any better," she replied.

"I axe my pawpaw whar we gowen," Nomusha continued. "My pawpaw sait Na-coe-doe-ches. He sait, 'one mo tie, an we be freet.'"

"One more time and your family would be free?"

"Yeah, Mista Mally. He sait, 'one mo tie.'"

Molly was afraid to ask about his family, afraid that she already knew the answer. "Where's your papa?"

"He dait, Mista Mally."

"And, your mama?"

"She dait too, Mista Mally."

"Do you have any brothers or sisters, Nomusha?"

"Dey aw dait, Mista Mally. Da mens dey comes an keelt dem. Dey sait, 'dey rack-no-eyes y'all.'"

"They recognize you?"

"Yeah, Mista Mally. Dey rack-no-eyes my pawpaw, an dey rack-no-eyes my mawmaw, an my brobbers, and my sissas, an dey sait we cain't sail y'all no mo, an da mens dey keelt dem."

"Is he saying what I think he's saying?" Boots asked. "I can't understand a word he's saying."

"He says that the men can't sell his family anymore because they recognize them."

"They must have been stolen slaves," Boots surmised, "a whole family. They were trying to sell a whole family of stolen slaves, probably selling them and then stealing them back again."

"Yes," Molly added. "And, someone recognized them."

"Yeah," Nomusha said. "Dey rack-no-eyes dem, an dey cain't sail dem no mo."

"So, they killed his whole family," Boots concluded.

"They sold you in Nacogdoches?" Molly asked.

"Yeah, Mista Mally."

"And then what did they do."

"Dey sait, y'all weet an we come an git y'all."

"Who came to get you?"

"Da mens."

"The ones who sold you came to get you?"

"Yeah, Mista Mally. My pawpaw sait, 'come on, dey git us. So, we gowen weet fo da mens.'"

"Where did you wait?"

"In da ticket. We weet aw night, an dey git us, an my pawpaw sait, 'one mo tie an we be freet.'"

Molly reiterated, "He said one more time and they'd be free."

"I understood that part," Boots replied. "The traders must have been promising to free his family in exchange for their cooperation. That would make them easier to steal again, wouldn't it?"

Molly added. "It would until the prospective buyers recognized them, then they wouldn't be worth anything to the traders anymore."

Boots nodded his agreement. "That means there's a lot more bodies that we didn't find back at Fort Teran."

Molly asked Nomusha, "How did you get away?"

"I poe my hay-ands rat tru dem tangs."

"Shackles?" Molly asked.

"Yeah, Mista Mally." With his arms yet around her, he encircled his wrist with his index finger and thumb and drew his hand out between them. "I poe my hay-ands rat tru dem cackles, an I runned awee. I runned awee in da ticket."

"You ran into the thicket?"

"Yeah, Mista Mally."

"That's a pretty good place to hide, isn't it?"

"Yeah, Mista Mally."

"What did you eat while you were hiding in the thicket? You were hiding in there for a long time, weren't you?"

"I kitch dem mut buds, an eat dem."

"Mud bugs? You mean crawdads? You were eating crawdads?"

"Yeah, Mista Mally. I eat dem mut buds. Dey be lots o dem in dare … Can I half summo dat eat thangs?"

"You want some more jerky? Yes, go ahead. Just reach inside that saddle bag you're sitting on and get some."

His hands were gone from her sides for a moment, and then one of them returned with jerky in it. "Y'all wan sum o dat?" he asked.

"No, you go on ahead and eat it."

Boots was looking over at them and smiling. "He is cute," he admitted.

Entering a land of low oak and walnut covered hills, Molly noticed an occasional loblolly pine. Beneath them the trail was made of quartz-like sand and clay, dark red in color, and giving their horse's hooves a solid thudding sound against it.

Early in the afternoon they reached the Angelina River, and its low wooded banks of sugar trees and Magnolia, and swarms of mosquitoes.

They stopped for water, but didn't tarry long, swatting and scratching, and then riding on.

Cantering to escape the insects, they passed a native village nestled against the banks of the Angelina. The natives' field ran to a cluster of sugar trees at one end and to a cluster of small thatched huts at the other end. Behind the huts a corral made of stacked deadwood enclosed a number of horses.

"Do you know these people?" Molly asked.

"Nacodochitos," Boots replied. "Not many of them left anymore. The bigger tribes are coming down from the states and driving these people out."

"They look so poor," Molly observed.

"All they have is hunting," he explained. "They hunt deer, bear, and ducks, for meat. They keep the feathers and sell the hides. They put in a few crops, but the soil here won't grow much."

Molly watched the women out in the field, as they watered their meager crop of corn. Standing about shoulder high the stalks were topped out and pale. The women drudged slowly along dry, dusty rows, lugging heavy wooden water buckets, which they had filled from the river.

Youngsters ran among the huts, and with them ran very thin looking curs. Around a central pit of small flames, the Nacodochito braves were sitting cross-legged on the ground. One of them took a pull from a long, wooden-stemmed pipe. Duck feathers dangled from the stem, and the end was fitted into a smoldering stone pipe bowl. Allowing the smoke to trickle from his lips, the brave then passed the awkward looking contraption to the next brave.

"Why aren't those men working in the field?" Molly asked.

By this Boots seemed amused and said, "The women do all the work. It's the way of the Nacodochitos. The men hunt and fight. Well, they don't exactly fight anymore. There aren't enough of them left to put together a war party. They just hunt, and the women do all the work. That seems fair, doesn't it?"

"It does, if you're a man," Molly retorted. "Should we stop and greet them? They're all watching us."

"Are you a smoker? They'll want you to smoke with them."

The thought of sucking smoke from a stick, which everyone else was sucking from, disgusted her. "No, I guess …"

"Look at that," he said, and he smiled at her. "They're waiving us in. Guess it's too late to back down. They must've seen you looking at them."

"You were looking at them, too," she protested.

Leading them off the trail a few paces, he dismounted and suggested, "We should take a couple handfuls of that jerky to share with them. It's all we got, and it's their custom to share something. It shows respect, and you never know when their friendship might come in handy."

Dismounting, Molly slipped Nomusha to the ground, opened her saddlebag, and gasped. "Nomusha, how much of this did you eat?"

His eyes became big saucers again, as they had when she first found him. Looking down, he folded his hands and said nothing.

"Half of this jerky is gone. Did you eat all this?"

He confessed, "Y'all sait fo me to git some. So, I git some, Mista Mally."

Around the back of his head she reached her hand and laughed as she pulled him close to her. "It's okay, son. You need it more than I do."

"Is there enough left to give to the Nacodochitos?" Boots asked.

"Just enough." Molly divided the remains between them and Nomusha. "This is for those people over there," she explained to him. "They're hungry, too. So, don't eat this. You give it to those people, okay? Will you give it to them?"

"Yeah, Mista Mally."

The Nacodochitos rose to their feet as the three of them approached, and their youngsters ran up eagerly to see who they were. From the field the women watched Boots and Molly distribute their jerky, and watched Nomusha distribute his portion to the youngsters. The Nacodochito braves seemed to be pleased. As they consumed their gift, Molly noted that their hair was braided and tied with strips of leather and decorated with duck feathers. Their skin was shiny and deeply brown. They wore whitish-tan leather shirts, which were pulled down over their loose fitting trousers. Resuming their seats they crossed their legs, and motioned for Boots and Molly to join them. When Boots, Molly, and Nomusha had seated themselves, an elder seated himself between them, and in his hands he held the long, smoking pipe.

"You have returned to us," the elder announced, as he happily gummed a piece of jerky.

"We are traveling to Nacogdoches," Boots replied.

"They know you?" Molly asked.

"Yes, I've been here twice before. These are important folks, Molly. They know what's going on in these parts. You can learn a lot of things from them, things you won't learn from other folks."

The elder's eyes and cheeks crinkled as he smiled, and he nodded to the others in the circle. Then from the fire he withdrew a branch with a flaming end and relit the pipe. Sucking on it vigorously, he produced puffs of heavy smoke and said, "Today you have black child. I have seen this child." Then he passed the long pipe to Boots.

He took a pull, not a short one and not too long, and then he let the smoke trickle out from his lips, and did so without coughing. This surprised Molly, but she sincerely hoped she would not also have to do it, although the musty-sweet pungency it left in the air was not altogether unpleasant.

"How do you know him?" Boots asked the elder as he passed the pipe to the next brave.

"I see him with others who have black skin. Men with white skin tie them together like dogs. We see them on road."

"The men with white skin, have you seen them before? Do you know who they are?"

"I have seen their chief. He has face like wood that worms have eaten."

"Pock marks." Boots added.

"I think I see his teeth in these holes in his face."

Amused by his remark the braves around the fire began to laugh enthusiastically. Molly smiled with them as the brave who now held the pipe laughed until he spilled the contents of the stone bowl, which brought even more laughter from the other braves. A pouch was quickly passed to him, and he refilled the pipe. Another brave lit it from the fire. Sucking hard and deep several times, he puffed until it was working again.

The elder continued, "He has shirt of fine cloth this chief with white skin. His shirt looks like flower petals here." He encircled his neck with his finger, and then extended his finger down the front of his chest. "I tell him I like to have this fine shirt. He say no. He like it very much. He says he has gold at Fort Teran, and he wants to buy from us."

About halfway around the circle the pipe was now in the hands of a brave across from Molly, and he was passing it to the brave next to him. She wanted the elder to talk faster, to conclude his discourse before the pipe got all the way around to her.

"What did he want to buy from you?" Boots asked.

"We have skin from deer." The elder held up both hands with one finger folded down. "And beaver." He lowered one hand.

"Nine deer hides and four beaver." Boots said.

"Hunting no good. Deer and beaver they are no more."

"Did you sell your hides to the chief with white skin?"

"He say twenty dollar. It is good price. He has gold at Fort Teran. So, I send best brave with him to bring back gold. He take skin from deer and skin from beaver to Fort Teran, but brave does not return to us."

"How long ago?"

The elder held up both hands with two fingers folded down.

"Eight days." Boots announced.

The pipe was in the hands of the brave next to Nomusha. He sucked his lungs full, rocked back, and blew a plume into the air. Then he handed the pipe to Nomusha.

NACOGDOCHES

"THE CHIEF WITH white skin, he did not return to you?" Boots asked the Nacodochito elder.

"He does not return," the elder replied.

In both of his hands Nomusha took the stem of the pipe from the brave next to him; he lowered the smoldering stone bowl to the ground where he watched it curiously.

The elder raised the backs of his fists to his mouth, extended his index fingers straight out together toward Boots, and flipped his index fingers alternately up and down as he explained, "The chief with white skin he speaks with two tongues. His skin is white, but inside he is filled with things the deer and the beaver leave on ground behind them."

The braves were again given to hearty laughter.

Nomusha lifted the stem of the pipe to his lips, and Molly snatched it away from him as everyone around the fire watched her intensely.

"Have you ever seen the chief with white skin before this?" Boots asked.

"Others have seen him," the elder replied.

Molly examined the images of deer and bear carved into the sides of the sandstone bowl. She admired the scrollwork on the stem and the way it tapered cleverly to the end. Duck feathers dangled from it on leather strands. Glancing over at the elder, she intended to pass the pipe on to him since she was not interested in smoking it. Boots was talking to him and looking at her over the elder's shoulder at the same time. To the elder's back she lifted the pipe, but Boots narrowed his eyes, stopping her. His eyes told her that she should do what she was expected to do, and she was expected to smoke the pipe. The thought quickly became a knot in her stomach.

The elder continued to explain, "His pistols bite like snake that rattles. I have been told these things."

Molly lifted the tapered end about half way to her lips, and then stopped. The glare that Boots gave her intensified, and she understood that refusing the pipe would insult the Nacodochitos, and Boots might not get the information he wanted. A tendril of smoke twisted up from the tapered end, and its pungency constricted her stomach even further. Swallowing helped keep the sensation from rising up.

"Do you know his name?" Boots asked. "What do they call the chief with white skin?"

"I know what he is called by others," the elder replied.

Holding her breath Molly raised the tapered end to her lips and lifted the pipe up in front of her, maybe, a little too high. From it she pulled a mouthful of smoke and a mouthful of liquid residue, which flowed from the stem. Acrid and bitter, the residue tasted worse than raw current, which she had tasted only once as a youngster. Lowering the pipe, she hacked and spit the smoke and residue out of her. Blinking tears from her eyes, she could see that the braves had found this quite amusing, and they were laughing at her. Even the elder was laughing, but Boots watched her soberly.

Reaching up behind her, Nomusha patted her back and said, "Y'all be aw-wite, Mista Mally. Y'all be aw-wite."

She cleared her throat and whispered, "Obliged, Nomusha."

The elder took the pipe from her, and he was still laughing as he said, "Earl, that is the name others have called the chief with white skin. He is called Earl."

At this Boots became unusually intense. "Do you mean Murrell? Are you sure they don't call him Murrell?"

The elder lifted his chin. "I am not sure of this. They might call him Murrell. I hear them say Earl." He glanced around at the braves and asked. "Do they say Earl?"

The braves were still laughing at Molly, and now they were also nodding in agreement with the elder.

"It is Earl," the elder concluded.

Molly was dizzy and her ears were ringing. "I'm not feeling so good," she said and stood up. The knotting in her stomach had worsened.

"Drink some water," Boots suggested. "Nomusha, go get her water gourd."

Nomusha sprang to his feet, but Molly held out her hand to stop him, saying, "I'll get it. I need to walk around a little anyway." Toward Angel she took Nomusha by the hand. Then, when she reached her horse, she placed one hand on her pommel and her other hand in Nomusha's hand, and hung her head. From the pommel she slipped her water gourd and drank. The water seemed to quench the fire in her stomach, and her dizziness gradually subsided.

Boots stood behind her and asked, "You alright?"

"Yes, I'm fine."

"You handled that just right back there. They might have been laughing, but they respected you. That's important."

"I understand." She mounted Angel and Nomusha scrambled up behind her, clinging to her sides. "Can we go now?" she asked.

Boots mounted and turned to the Nacodochitos, raising his hand to them. The braves stood, and they also raised their hands.

Once again Angel's hooves were thudding up the Coushatta Trace toward Nacogdoches. Side by side with Molly, Boots said, "I'm sure it was Murrell, and I'm surprised he's selling stolen slaves. He thinks he can get away with it because he's here in Texas where the states can't go after him."

"Yes," Molly added. "And, not only did he murder Nomusha's family, but he murdered an innocent Nacodochito brave."

Boots shook his head. "And all for twenty dollars worth of hides. By the way, I gave the elder twenty dollars."

"That was a very kind thing for you to do for those poor people."

"I'll get it back," he said. "I'll get it from Murrell himself."

The sun had peaked and began its descent toward the horizon on Molly's left. They had stopped for water and taking the opportunity, she said, "You know I'll never forgive you."

"For the pipe?" he asked.

"Yes, for the pipe. That was the most disgusting thing I've ever had to do. I can still taste that horrible thing."

"It's an acquired taste," he contended.

"Well, you acquired it so from now on you can keep it, okay?"

"My apologies, I should have had you and Nomusha stay with the horses. I thought you might enjoy meeting the Nacodochitos. Didn't you find them interesting?"

"Can you see that over there?" Molly pointed into the forest.

Low hills east of the road were littered with broad stumps and felled trees, most of them over a hundred feet in length, and wider than Molly could reach around. The thump of axes echoed in the distance, telling her that tree felling was yet in progress. "There must be a lot of homes going up in Nacogdoches," she guessed.

"They've cut a lot of trees," Boots observed. "But, they're leaving them lay. They didn't even limb them out. It looks like a waste of good timber to me."

Between the felled trees wound a trail connecting to the Coushatta Trace and then turning north toward Nacogdoches. A team of horses pulling a farm wagon was about to pull out in front of them. Boots was first to catch up, trotting alongside and then slowing down next to a bearded driver, who wore a sombrero. Boots doffed his hat and said, "Afternoon."

The driver rose with a start and reached for the rifle propped against the seat-board next to him.

"You won't be needing that," Boots warned him. "If I was robbing you, you'd already be dead."

The man twisted his head to look at Molly, alarm yet in his eyes. He didn't pick up his rifle, but kept his hand on it and said, "Twixt the border ruffians and them Injuns, a man ain't safe no more here abouts."

"I think I know you," Boots said. "You're Dugan Hoxie, from Hoxie's General Mercantile?"

"Yes, sir, who might y'all be?"

"I'm Captain Boots Williams of the Texas Rangers, San Antonio. This here," he pointed to Molly, "is Ranger McCracken. I was up in these parts a month ago putting on a recruiting festival for the Ranger Service. As I recall, you had a sizable part in that."

"Glory be," he squawked. His upper lip was shaved clean, and the rest of his beard stood straight out from his chin, bouncing as he said, "I remember you. You was the one holding them hoss races, and them shooting contests. We ain't had that much fun in Nacogdoches since the war. What brings y'all back here?"

"We're on our way to Fort Casey. When I saw your wagon I was expecting to see it piled with logs. It looks like you've got nothing but Spanish moss back there."

Dugan Hoxie pushed his sombrero back and replied, "It's Spanish moss alright, Captain Williams. I'm selling it faster than I can haul it in. I got a couple day laborers back there working for me. They're Castilians from town. I've got them cutting trees, stripping the moss, and stacking it. Hard to get them to do much of anything. Mostly, they like to just sit around, smoke cigars, and drink all day, so I pay them by the wagon load. The more they do, the more they get paid. The trees are too big to pull the moss down, so I have them cut the trees down. I'm hauling five loads a day, sometimes six when they get enough of it on the ground."

"How much farther is it to town from here?" Boots asked.

"Four miles, more or less."

"Why are folks buying all that Spanish moss?" Boots laughed. "Did they start smoking it or something?"

"Heavens no," Dugan Hoxie chuckled, as he took his hand away from his rifle. "For ten cents you can stuff a mattress with it. Folks like it, because it fluffs itself up when you're not laying on it. It stays alive in there for a long time, and when it loses its liveliness you just get some more and stuff it in again. And they use it to plaster the outsides of their houses and chimneys, too. They use a lot of it. It's a good binder when y'all mix it with clay. Heaven knows we got plenty of clay around here. They mix it together and use it to seal things up against the cold. I even plastered the outside of my mercantile with it, and stopped all the drafts in winter, but it gets a might too warm in the summer now, ain't bad this time of year though."

Boots, Molly and Nomusha clopped alongside the wagon to the end of the clear-cut, where a homestead was nestled behind a stand of loblolly pine. In a state of severe disrepair, the cabin had large areas of thatch missing from the roof. Log rafters and cross ties were exposed to the weather. As they approached, two impoverished youngsters ran out from under a partially collapsed porch, a boy who looked to be seven or eight, and a girl who was about Nomusha's age. Both wore sackcloth, which was cut out at the neck and arms, and both were scratching themselves.

Dugan pulled back his reins, stopped the wagon and said, "How you youngins doing this afternoon? Where was you when I came by this morning?"

"We was fetching berries, Mister Hoxie," the little freckle-faced girl replied.

From under the seat-board he brought up a grain sack about a third full. "Your ma sent this. There's bread and salt pork in here. Your ma says y'all better make it last. She's got no more money until next week."

The girl took the sack from him and thanked him saying, "Obliged, Mister Hoxie." Holding the sack in one hand, she scratched her side with the other.

Molly noticed a rash encircling her wrist and extending up her arm to her elbow. "Come over here and let me have a look at you," she said to the girl.

"Hey!" Dugan Hoxie exclaimed. "There's a woman's voice coming out of you, Ranger McCracken. Y'all didn't tell me she was a woman, Captain Williams."

Nomusha asked, "Y'all's a wooman, Mista Mally?"

"That's right," Molly replied. Dismounting, she held Nomusha back, instructing him, "Stay up here." To the little girl, she asked, "May I see your hands?"

Both youngsters held their hands out to her, and she examined the peculiar scaly burrows, the 'S' shaped tracks, and rows of mosquito-like bites, which had crusted between their fingers, around their wrists, and up their arms. "Does it itch?" she asked.

"We got the itchies real bad, ma'am."

"How long have y'all had this?"

"I don't know. All summer I guess."

"Where is your mama? Does she know you have the itchies?"

"I don't know."

"Her mama don't know nothing," Dugan said from his seat-board. "She lost her husband in the war, and now she went to Nacogdoches. I'm paying her to harvest the moss off this land of hers. Ain't much left though. I'll probably have it all out in a couple weeks."

"Why didn't she take these youngsters to Nacogdoches with her?" Molly asked.

"Ain't no place for youngins where she's staying. Besides no one wants them around. They got the seven-year-itch. Folks are afraid of them. They don't want the whole town getting it."

"Is that what they've got?" Boots asked. "The seven-year-itch?"

"If it's the seven-year-itch, then that means they've got the scabies," Molly informed them. "I've heard of folks having it for seven years, sometimes more."

"What can you do for it?"

"I haven't had to deal with this before, I'm not sure."

The girl began to cry, and so did her little brother as Molly noted, "We can't leave them here like this. They need someone to care for them."

"There's folks in these parts that's a lot worse off than these youngins," Dugan informed her.

"Well, those folks aren't here right now," Molly replied. "And these youngsters need our help."

"I check on them every day," Dugan bickered with her.

Turning back to the little girl she asked, "When was the last time you and your little brother had a bath?"

The girl shrugged. "I don't know."

"Do y'all have soap in there?"

"No, ma'am, we don't got no soap."

"Mister Hoxie, do you have soap in your mercantile?"

"Folks make their own soap," he answered. "I got lye and such in the mercantile, and I'm sure the wife's got soap she made back home."

"If y'all bring them soap, I'll pay for it."

"I can do that. I'll bring it tomorrow. Y'all don't have to pay for it."

"Obliged, Mister Hoxie, and make sure they take a bath."

"I can do that, too."

The youngsters stood at the side of the road and watched as Molly mounted Angel, and as Dugan Hoxie cracked his reins. His wagon rolled forward. Glancing back at them, Molly didn't want to leave them by themselves, but didn't have a choice either. Her mission was to find Amy. Yet something tugged persistently on her heart, and an inexorable small voice commanded that she stop where she was and do something. Closing her eyes, she searched for the right answer. Then Nomusha tugged on her shirt. "What is it, darling?" she asked.

"My mawmaw sait wen y'all gits da itchies, she makes da bacca-po-tice, an it go awee."

"She makes a poultice with tobacco?"

"Yeah, Mista Mally, bacca-po-tice."

"That's a good idea … Mister Hoxie can y'all make a poultice for those youngsters with tobacco?"

"I can get tobacco for them. You'll have to pay for it, and they'll have to make their own poultice."

"You won't make it for them, Mister Hoxie? You can't do a small kindness like that for them?"

"I ain't their mama, and I'm doing enough already."

"Then hold up, Mister Hoxie."

"I ain't stopping neither."

"Nomusha, hold on tight," she said, and she kicked Angel's sides. Her horse leapt past Boots' horse. He watched with evident amusement as she passed, and then caught up with Dugan Hoxie's team, grabbing them by the hames, which fastened together the reins and harnesses. She pulled back, stopping his team. "I said hold up, Mister Hoxie."

"You ain't got no right stopping me," he hollered. "I got things that need doing."

"So do I, Mister Hoxie. I'm helping those youngsters back there. All I ask is that y'all let them ride in the back of your wagon on top of that Spanish moss."

"Y'all are taking them to town?" he asked. "Ain't no place to put them up. Nobody will take them in neither."

"Molly," Boots cautioned her. "You're making it more and more difficult for us to get to Fort Casey. You know that, don't you?"

"I have to do this," she insisted, and motioned for the youngsters to come up the road and get in the wagon.

Clutching the sack of food as she ran, the girl climbed in, followed by her little brother. Their cheeks were damp and glistening, but they were smiling as they took places atop the moss.

"What are your names?" Molly asked.

"I'm Callie Owen and this here is my little brother, Toby."

The boy lifted his palm to her, wagged it back and forth, and said, "Hi," in a raspy, little boy voice.

Molly released the reins. "Obliged, Mister Hoxie, these youngsters shouldn't be living out here by themselves anyway. They're too little. You should have brought them to town a long time ago."

"Maybe so," he replied. "But I still don't know where y'all are going to put them up … Haw," he yelled, and again cracked his reins.

"Come on, Mister Hoxie. You must know Nacogdoches better than anyone else. There must be some place you can think of where we can put them."

"Don't include me with no scheme of yours, ma'am. I ain't got time for it. Y'all want to take them to town? Fine! I'll take them. Then y'all can put them up. Not me!"

Boots was shaking his head and smiling.

"What?" Molly asked.

"Nothing," he said.

Callie and Toby sampled the food in their sack as they clopped closer to town. Molly counted five more homesteads and noticed that the cabins looked as if they'd been built from dirt. She realized they'd been plastered with the clay and moss mixture Mister Hoxie had told them about.

The sun was setting on the horizon and casting long shadows from the trees. Teams and wagons crowded the road, and she assumed they were closing in on Nacogdoches. Others rode past on horseback, traveling in both directions.

Crossing a creek and then across the shallow La Nana River, a town of a hundred and fifty or so dirt buildings stood before them. Continuing north into town they came upon the first commercial structure, an imposing, two-story building on their left, built of sparkly, dark brown stone, and lined with windows around each of both stories.

The structure stood at the corner of a crossroad and the crossroad was marked 'Camino Real.' Below the sign and nailed to the post which held it was an arrow pointing southwest marked 'San Antonio.' The structure faced the Camino Real, about twenty paces long, and butted up to the Coushatta Trace, about eight paces wide. Molly could see that, by far, the structure was the tallest in Nacogdoches except for a steeple in the distance, which poked up among a cluster of thatched and shake roofs.

A porch extended from the sparkly, dark stone structure, a two-story porch held up by posts and covered with a shake roof. Above the main structure stood dual masonry chimneys that gave the building a look that reminded her of New Orleans.

"That's La Casa Piedra," Boots informed her.

Inside there were no lights. The building appeared vacant, but the porch held stacks of milled lumber and adobe materials, and the exterior walls were lined with work tables.

Dugan Hoxie explained, "Juan Mora and Vicente Córdova bought La Casa Piedra a couple years back. They're having it renovated into a courthouse."

Continuing north, the Coushatta Trace became La Calle del Norte through Nacogdoches, and when they crossed Main Street, Molly glanced down the street and saw that it was crowded with smaller commercial buildings. Law offices were located on the corner, and Hoxie's Mercantile was sandwiched between two crowded taverns. Hoxie's was one of a few buildings with an attached and covered boardwalk facing the street. Across the street Molly could see a bordello and beyond that a barber shop. Further down were other shops and businesses. She couldn't make out what they were, but they interested her. Nacogdoches was a real town with more than just taverns and bordellos. She wanted to explore every store-front and see what they had to offer.

Turning his wagon, Dugan Hoxie entered a parallel alley behind the commercial buildings lining the north side of Main Street. Callie and Toby Owen grabbed the sideboards as the wagon rocked and lurched through ruts and potholes. A hundred paces down the alley, the wagon stopped in front of a double door warehouse. Across the alley from the warehouse, the rear door of the Hoxie's General Mercantile stood open, and a woman came to the doorway waving to Dugan.

He waved back, and turned to address the youngsters. "End of the line," he announced. "You folks can take these youngins and go. There's a livery around the block. Y'all might try the hostel over on La Calle del Norte for the night. You'll ride right past it. Or, y'all can go to the old Spanish Garrison. We kicked Santa Anna's army out of there. It's ours now."

Callie climbed down to the alley clutching yet her sack of food, and Toby climbed down after her.

"The Garrison's probably full," Dugan Hoxie continued. "Lot of folks living there now, mostly Injuns and freebooters. I suppose y'all should stay away from there with womenfolk and youngins. Over at the hostel the keeper is American. That's your best bet."

"That's where I stayed during the festival," Boots said. "The food is good." Dismounting, he tied his horse to a nearby rail and went toward the Mercantile. "I'll be right back."

"Are you getting food?" Molly asked, we're all hungry.

"Cigars, field tobacco for a poultice, and soap. That is, if I can talk Missis Hoxie into selling me some of her soap."

"So, you're taking up cigar smoking?" Molly asked.

"You'll see."

"I want to go in with you," she said.

Callie jumped up and down, squealing, "Can we go?" Toby and Nomusha began jumping up and down also.

Molly extended her hand to them, saying, "Come on."

Hoxie's General Mercantile was growing dim with twilight when they walked in. Only two customers remained in the store and stood at a counter paying for their goods. Molly assumed the woman behind the counter was Missis Hoxie, who glanced over at Molly and said, "We usually close at sunset."

"We won't be long," Molly assured her. "We've been traveling all day. Is it all right?"

"Okay."

A young man lit a lantern and set it up on the counter, as the patrons left the store with their goods. Boots extended his hand to Missis Hoxie. "I'm Captain Williams of the Texas Rangers, San Antonio. I just need a couple things."

She embraced his hand saying, "I remember you, Captain Williams. What can I get for you?"

Molly walked around barrels stacked in the corner and examined rows of shelves stocked with bins and crocks up to the ceiling. The containers were filled with flour, lard, salt, rice, a few vegetables, sugar, corn, beans, and other hard to find goods. Across from her, Missis Hoxie stood behind a long, oak counter lined with stools. Behind her were shelves stocked with wine and whiskey, rows of glass jugs filled with hard candy, and a display case filled with rifles, pistols, and hunting knives. Boots paid for the goods she had fetched for him, as the youngsters climbed up on the stools next to him.

Missis Hoxie asked them, "Would y'all like a sarsaparilla?"

"Yes," they cheered.

Molly nodded in agreement, and Missis Hoxie dipped three mugs into a crock, and slid the foamy beverages over to the youngsters. "I recognize these two," she said. "They're the Owen's youngins. This boy here is he your slave?" she asked Molly.

"He's in our custody," Molly explained as she took coins from her pocket. "How much for three sarsaparillas?" she asked.

"Three cents." Missis Hoxie shook her head as she watched Callie and Toby sip foam from the tops of their mugs. "Why are you youngins wearing sack cloth?" she asked them. "Don't you have clothes? Your mama doesn't make you clothes?"

The youngsters shook their heads, and Nomusha was also shaking his head, bare to the waist and sipping foam.

"Jeffery!" she called out to the young man working in the store. "That's my son, Jeffery," she pointed out to them. "Why don't y'all watch the store while I'm gone for a moment?"

The youngster's drinks were half gone when she returned with an armload of clothing. "These are too small for my youngins," she explained.

"They're too good to throw away. I've been saving them for quite some time now. I always knew someone would use them sooner or later. So, why don't y'all take them in the corner behind them barrels over there and pick out what you want."

The boys returned to finish their sarsaparillas wearing baggy cotton shirts and trousers with the cuffs rolled up, clothing which appeared to provide them with plenty of space for growing and enough room to bring a smile from Molly and Missis Hoxie. Callie had found a pink cotton dress, which tied at the waist, and she seemed quite pleased to have it.

"That's much better," Missis Hoxie said as she examined them and smiled.

"Obliged," Molly thanked her.

At the front of the mercantile Molly noticed needles, several colors of thread, a selection of buttons, and every kind of linen she could imagine for clothing. One of the fabrics caught her fancy. She felt it and then felt the next one. "This is really nice," she said. "I wish we had cloth like this in Liberty."

When they left the mercantile, Molly noticed Dugan Hoxie across the alley at the warehouse. He had unlocked a heavy brass padlock and opened the double doors, lit a lamp, and was pitching moss into a stack on the plank floor inside.

Boots looked in and told him, "We'll be going now." Stuffing his goods into his saddlebags, he also stuffed a handful of cigars into his shirt pocket.

Dugan Hoxie apologized as they prepared to leave, "Sorry I don't have a place to put y'all up for the night. I'm full up with hides. I'll be shipping them out when the teamsters get here in a few days. Y'all can stay here after that, if you want."

"We won't be here that long," Boots responded. "Obliged."

Molly stood outside with the youngsters, and marveled at the hides stacked to the rafters from the back of the warehouse all the way up to the double doors. "How many hides do you think you have in there?" she asked.

Dugan Hoxie stabbed his pitchfork into the ground, folded his arms over the end of the handle and smiled at her as he explained, "This here is just a smidgeon of what I take in every year. A lot of backwoodsmen trade with me because I pay good prices. The Injuns like to trade here, too, because I have goods they can't get nowhere else. When I'm full up, I ship my hides to New Orleans. Before this year's over I'll ship over forty thousand deerskins, fifteen hundred bearskins, about twelve hundred otter pelts, and probably six hundred beaver pelts."

"You are a busy man," Molly confessed.

"Sometimes I have to go without sleep to keep up," he admitted.

Boots lifted Nomusha behind Molly's saddle and lifted Callie up behind him. Then he lifted Toby behind his own saddle and mounted up. "I'm not going to get scabies, am I," he asked Molly.

"I don't know," she replied. "If you do, maybe, you can smoke them out with those cigars you bought."

From the alley they rode up La Calle del Norte past the hostel and around the corner to the livery. From there they carried their belongings back to the hostel where a sign hung from the porch roof, which read 'BRODY'S HOSTEL' in large letters.

"There's a big loft above the kitchen," Boots explained. "And there's a ladder around the side. They've got twelve beds up there, but they're usually full."

"We all have to sleep together?" Molly asked. "Men and women in the same room?"

"Men-folk on one end and womenfolk on the other," Boots replied. "There's never any womenfolk up there though."

The door and windows into the kitchen were standing open since the evening had not yet begun to cool down. Molly could see men inside sitting at a bench-like table, three of them. Then a Negro man came out to greet them.

Over his bare torso hung a grease stained apron, which was fastened around his neck and at his waist. On a crumpled cloth he wiped his hands and said, "Eve'nin Cap'in Williams, wekkome back. Y'all be wantin' suppa?"

"Obliged, Tito. Do you have beds available tonight? We need three beds."

"Yessar, we got's bads. Com-mon in." Back inside he went.

Molly stepped up to the doorway and saw a white man with his back to her. Across from him sat two natives. Tito ladled supper into their dishes from a kettle, which he held with a rag wrapped around a wire hoop handle.

From the natives nostrils hung silver rings, and rings within rings. Intrigued by them, Molly proceeded through the doorway, but Boots grabbed her arm, drew her back and whispered, "They're friendlies, Molly. Don't be afraid of them, they're Cados."

"I'm not afraid of them," she replied.

The lobes of the Cados' ears were stretched around wooden medallions, which were intricately carved and decorated and almost a handbreadth in diameter. Tiny bones and colorful feathers were also cut into the cartilage along the edges of their ears. They'd shaved and painted the sides of their heads, and braided long strands of hair on top, which dangled to their shoulders. Their faces were painted bright red. They ate their supper by leaning their faces over their dishes and fed themselves with their fingers, smacking their lips loudly as they did so, even though tableware had been provided for them.

Boots was holding Molly yet outside, and he leaned toward the youngsters. "They like folks to call them red men," he whispered. "Not white or black. That's why they paint their faces red. So don't be afraid of them. They make a lot of noise when they eat so folks will know they like their food. It's their custom." He took them in, and as he did he and Molly stashed their belongings on the floor beside the door.

Molly noticed the sour stench of whiskey inside, and saw two bottles on the table, one at each end. The Cados filled their mugs and laughed as they drank from them. Molly scooted Nomusha along the bench next to the white man, and then seated Callie and Toby alongside. The man seemed uneasy, side glancing at them as he lifted a spoon to his lips. Next to the youngsters she took a seat.

The white man's hair was long, parted and combed back into a ducktail. Again he glanced at her, his beard was scruffy and black, and he wore a handlebar moustache. A pink scar notched the bridge of his bulbous nose. Glancing again at her he said, "Y'all don't be feeding no slave boy at this table."

Tito brought in a stack of shaky dishes and a trembling kettle, and he appeared to be quite nervous. Boots took a seat across from Molly as Tito distributed the dishes and ladled them full.

"You got bugs in your ears, Tito," the man said, and slammed his fist on the table. "Can't y'all hear me? Stop serving your slop to that slave boy, and take him out back or wherever you people eat your supper."

As the white man with the pink scar reached for Nomusha's dish, Molly reached over Callie and Toby like lightening, and stabbed her boot knife into the tabletop between Nomusha's dish and the man's hand. He stopped abruptly, and from the other side of the table the Cados turned their faces toward her.

"You don't have to make nothing out of this," the man with the pink scar added. "Just take him outside."

"He's staying in here, at this table with us," she demanded.

Twisting to face her, the man lifted his eyebrows as if surprised by what he'd just heard. "I can see y'all are wearing men's clothes," he remarked, "but you ain't no man."

Molly narrowed her eyes and straightened her mouth. "I can see that you're wearing men's clothes, too, but you ain't no man either."

EPILOGUE: LOST IN TIME

MOM LOOKED UP from Molly's diary, across the table at me and asked, "What time is it anyway?"

Pulling out my smart phone I punched it on and replied, "I think we got lost in time listening to you read, Mom. It's five-thirteen." It seemed as if only a few minutes had passed. I couldn't believe we had been sitting in the restaurant all afternoon, so I reminded Mom and my wife what our purpose was today, saying, "We need to get moving if we're going to have enough time to pack up the rest of Grandma's things."

"We can't leave right now," my wife objected. "We have to find out what happens to Molly at Brody's Hostel."

"It's an hour's drive to Gonzales," I reminded her. "By the time we get out of here and then drive all the way over there it will be six-thirty or seven. Maybe Mom would like to read while we drive."

Closing the diary, Mom slipped it into her handbag and said, "You folks might be able to go over there and work this time of night, but I'm getting too old for that kind of thing."

"This time of night?" I asked her. "It's still daylight."

"Nine o'clock is it for me," Mom replied. "How are we supposed to do everything we have to do in Gonzales, and drive me back by nine? There's three or four hours of packing left when we get there, and we still have to carry everything down from the attic."

"It won't take as long as you think, Mom. I can have you back here by …" I had to think about it for a moment and the best case scenario I could come up with was midnight, so I acquiesced and told her, "I guess you're right. But what about the moving van? It's due back today."

"We'll rent it again next weekend," Mom suggested. "I'll pay for it. I'll pay for everything. It's just too late for me to start any work today. I think I'm worn out from all the packing we did yesterday."

"You don't have to pay for anything, Mom," I countered. Turning to my wife, I asked, "How about you, honey? You up to making a run over to Gonzales with me to finish up? I think the two of us can handle it without Mom. I don't want to rent the truck again if I don't have to."

"You mean one of us," she answered. "You'll have to go by yourself. I don't like to work after nine either, remember?"

"That's right." I lowered my chin against my fist, lifted my eyes to her and gave up. "Alright, next week it is, bright and early Saturday morning."

"And I'll pay for the truck," Mom reiterated.

"I'd like you to pay off our mortgage too, Mom, but you don't have to do that either. I'll take care of everything."

"You're a good son."

"And you're my favorite mom."

She turned to my wife, smiled and said, "I love it when he says that."

~~~~

Here ends Tuck's Landing, Volume 2 of the Black Dress Trilogy. I hope you enjoyed it. If so, please visit the retailer where you purchased it and kindly leave a review. Thank you. KT.
~~~~

SELECTIONS FROM
Call Of The Grackle
BLACK DRESS TRILOGY VOLUME 3

THEY RODE OUT to the corner of La Calle del Norte and paused. Boots glanced to his right. "I don't think they went north," he presumed. "Not a big enough market for slaves up there, not unless they know someone, and I doubt they do. They won't go back to Louisiana. Most likely they're wanted by the law there. I figure they're going down to the lower settlements here in Texas, down to the plantations."

Molly glanced left and said, "I'm glad you want to get Nomusha back."

"What I really want is to get those freebooters," Boots explained. "I might even get a chance at Murrell himself."

"Would you go after them if they didn't have Nomusha?"

He looked at her and smiled. "You went and got yourself attached to him, didn't you?"

"And you haven't?" she asked.

"Suppose I have," he admitted. "I told you awhile back that chasing slaves wasn't our job, and now that's just what we're about to do. Somehow though, I don't think of Nomusha as a slave, and I haven't figured that one out yet."

"You fell in love with him."

"Well, I … Molly, you have a part in this, too. It has to do with how you wanted to help Nomusha, and the way you're always helping folks who are down on their luck. It gives you a certain kind of charm that I'm growing fond of."

"You love him. Why don't you admit it?"

"Suppose I do." Reining his horse left, he smiled at her and nudged his horse south on La Calle del Norte adding, "But, I can't bring you back to town after we get him."

"Can't bring me back to town?" she asked. "What do you mean? I have to come back to town. I'm not finished with Margie and her youngsters yet."

"A man can get himself killed bringing you to town," he continued. "It almost got me killed today." Then he kicked his horse, smiling yet as he galloped away.

Molly galloped after him, past Brody's and across Main Street. Galloping south, they continued until they reached La Casa Piedra, the sparkly brown-stone commercial building, which was being renovated into a courthouse. A crew of carpenters worked outside on the porch decks, hammering and sawing on their work tables all at the same time and making the jobsite sound like a banging battlefield. Boots pulled up and whistled at them. The hammering and sawing stopped as they turned their faces to him.

Around his mouth Boots cupped his hands and hollered, "Did y'all see a bunch of freebooters ride past here, six or eight of them with a little slave boy?"

"Sí!" One of the workers nodded. Another agreed, and both pointed down the Coushatta Trace.

Molly drew a quick breath and said, "That means they're going to Fort Teran."

"Not what I expected either," Boots added. To the carpenters he raised his hand, and hollered, "Obliged." Then the hammering and sawing began again.

Cantering across the La Nana, and then past the few homesteads at the outskirts of town, he motioned for Molly to ride up beside him. "This could get real dangerous," he said. "I think you got the fight in you, but I want to make sure you know what you're getting into first. I want to be sure you still want to do this."

"I do," she testified. "It's the right thing to do. I feel it in my heart. You couldn't stop me from going."

"You could get killed. Both of us could get killed. Aren't you afraid?"

"A little." She nodded. "Okay, a lot. I'm a lot afraid, but that hasn't stopped me yet."

"You said just the right thing, Molly. You admit your fear, and that's what will keep you alive."

"But, I've always heard that the Texas Rangers have no fear. They say that folks who show fear can't serve."

"Well, that's right," Boots explained. "Showing fear is just plain cowardice. We won't let folks like that in the service, but I'll let you in on what folks aren't saying. What they aren't saying is that fear is what keeps us from getting stupid. Courage is what makes us successful. I won't ride with someone who has no fear. Folks like that get reckless, and they can get other folks killed. I'm used to riding with experienced Rangers when I do something like what we're about to do. I'm used to riding with courageous Rangers, who are afraid of being stupid, and there's usually a lot more than just two of us."

"Would it be better if we go back? Do you want to get more help?"

"No, not if we want to catch them. Any delay we give them will just be that much harder to make up for. And Molly, I believe in you. You've shown your courage. You have it in you, just like me. If I didn't think we could do this, I wouldn't be here with you now. We're both sanctioned Rangers of the Republic of Texas. That means we are the law. There isn't anyone else to do this job except us. We are the judge, jury, and executioner until a judicial system can be established in the land. We are the only protection folks have. Like it or not, you've been appointed, and no one can stand in your way, except me, Colonel Karnes, and General Houston himself."

"I'm overwhelmed."

"That's understandable. These aren't the sort of things womenfolk usually have to deal with. They're not expected to take to fighting the way you have. You don't hesitate and you're fast. That's your advantage."

She nodded and said, "Aunt Ruthie said the same thing. So, what do we do from here? We're on campaign now, aren't we? I've never done anything like this."

"Yes, we are on campaign, and we're outnumbered almost four to one. Does that mean anything to you?"

"It means we're probably in trouble."

"Good," he said. "That's good. You said the right thing again. Remember the Nacodochito's village?"

"Yes. I can still taste that awful pipe you made me smoke."

"Well," Boots continued. "Come sunset that's about where I figure we'll be. What do you think of Nacogdoches so far?"

"I think the town is too rough for me."

"You seem to be fitting right in." He laughed.

"It's wearing me down."

"Nacogdoches or the Ranger Service?" he asked.

"Both."

"Yes, it does wear you down. It wears me down, too. I haven't seen many recruits stay in it for long. I could hardly get my eyes open when I woke up this morning. But, Molly, I never said it was easy, remember? All I said was that I lived more in a few seconds than most folks live in a lifetime. Sometimes those seconds can turn out to be rewarding, especially when folks are better off for it, like Margie and Hamadi and Adama, and those youngsters, but mostly it's not easy and not very fun."

"It's not just that, Boots. I agree. I think the Service itself is rewarding, but I'm having trouble with more than that. You see, I'm just not angry anymore. I'm tired of being angry."

"You have a right to be angry, Molly, after the suffering you went through. Everyone in Texas has a right to be angry."

"Maybe so," she added. "Maybe that's what's been driving me to do the things I've been doing. Maybe that's what keeps driving me to find Amy. I don't know."

"You love Amy."

"Of course, how can you even say something like that?"

"Love and anger are next of kin, Molly. You wouldn't be angry about the things that happened to you if you didn't love the folks who were hurt by it. That's what I love about you."

For a moment she glanced over at him and lost herself in the depths of his ghost-blue eyes, and then rescued herself from the undertow of his unsuppressed expressions toward her. "I'll be glad when it's over," she replied. "I'll be glad when we can leave here, and I'll be glad when we can go back to Tuck's Landing where it's peaceful and safe."

"With me?" he asked.

She didn't answer.

"Could you love me like that?" he asked. "Could you love me until it makes you angry?"

"You promised not to talk about this," she reminded him.

"It's still Emmet, isn't it? You haven't said much about him."

"I suppose I haven't. I guess I don't like to talk about him. He changed so much after we were married that he wasn't the same man I met. I felt like I didn't know him anymore. The only one who understood was Emily. We used to talk a lot. I suppose I probably should talk about it more considering the likeliness that he's no longer alive, but it makes me uncomfortable to do that. I don't like to say bad things about folks no matter what they did, and everything I have to say about him is bad." Molly sighed. "I'd give anything if I could talk with Emily again, like I used to."

"Do you still love him?" Boots asked. "Do you still love Emmet?"

For a long while she didn't reply, then she said, "I think it was the farm that changed him. The farm wasn't what he thought it would be. It wore him down, and his hard work didn't pay much. He heard stories about folks coming down here and getting rich off the land, and there are a lot of rich plantation owners down here, but he wasn't one of them. We were barely getting by and it made him angry. It turned him into an angry man, Boots, kind of like Dugan Hoxie, but without principles."

"I don't think I'd call Dugan Hoxie a principled man," Boots balked.

"Then you see my point?" Molly added.

"You said you weren't angry anymore. What did that mean?"

Molly thought for a moment and then said, "Something inside me can't stay angry anymore. I've been angry for a long time about Emmet, Emily, Innis and Amy. I thought I hated those men who did all those bad things, but I realized that I didn't really hate them. I just wanted to make them stop doing the things they were doing."

"Then you've changed, Molly, because I remember when the only thing in the world you wanted was vengeance for your suffering."

"You think that's what it was? I was vengeful?"

"It was written all over you."

"I suppose I was, now that you put it that way. I could see that all that hate and anger was changing me into someone I didn't want to be. It changed me into an angry person just like Emmet, and that scared me, Boots. It really scared me."

Looking over at her, he said, "I notice a difference in you. You look softer in the eyes and mouth. You're pretty. Even that shiner you got is pretty, now that it's turned all green instead of purple."

"You're such a flatterer," she said with a laugh and watched him again. "You've got some green on your face, too, from those bruises. At least the swelling went down, so you look like yourself again."

"You never answered my question," he reminded her.

"What question?"

"Do you still love Emmet?"

"I don't want to."

"You don't want to love Emmet, or you don't want to tell me? Is that supposed to be an answer?"

"It has to be for now, Boots."

When they reached the Nacodochito camp, they joined the braves who had gathered around the fire to eat with their youngsters. Their women had cooked a mush-like stew and distributed it in wooden bowls. Boots and Molly traded cigars for their supper and fed themselves with their fingers, in the manner of the braves. The elder had joined them, and as they ate, Boots asked him if the freebooters had ridden through with Nomusha.

"We see men with white skin ride with black child," the elder replied. "They do not come here."

"Do you think they'll ride all night to Fort Teran?" Molly asked Boots.

"I'm not sure what they're up to, Molly. They already did a pretty good job of throwing us off."

"Are we going to Fort Teran?"

"There isn't much else we can do." He held his bowl out to a woman, who offered to refill it with a mixture of corn-mush and meat. Then he continued, "The thing that's bothering me is the freebooters know there isn't anything else we can do."

"They're going to ambush us, aren't they?"

"Most likely."

"So, are we going to Fort Teran, or are we going back to Nacogdoches?"

"What do you want to do, Molly? Do you want to run, or do you want to fight?"

"I guess I don't want either. I just want Nomusha back."

"Is he worth dying for?"

"Yes," Molly replied without hesitation. "Yes, I would die for him, if that's what it comes to."

"You are a rare kind, Molly." Setting his bowl in the dirt beside him, he stood and faced her saying, "I don't know anyone who would die for a slave. I admire that in you. If you want to fight for Nomusha, then I'll fight with you. We'll ride out in the morning. If we die tomorrow, then we'll die together."

Molly spread her bedroll by the fire, but her eagerness to rescue Nomusha had begun to fade with the reality of an ambush and the certainty of death. She began to doubt her ability to survive in such an unfavorable situation. The freebooters would lay in wait and then strike from a cloak of surprise. They were experienced fighters, and their shots would not miss. She would never see it coming. She dozed on and off throughout the night until Boots woke her, saying, "Let's get on with it,"

Saddling their horses they prepared to ride out.

The Nacodochito elder joined them as they mounted up, and his braves joined him as he asked, "Do white men, who ride with black child, go to chief with white skin named Earl?"

Boots paused, turning to face the elder and replied, "They might be going to meet their chief. We don't know for sure. Their chief has a meeting place at Fort Teran. The men might be taking the black child to meet with him there."

The elder pursed his lips, and said, "The chief with white skin has stolen our hides, and he has killed our brave. For this we will repay him. We will ride with you to Fort Teran. You say that today you die. If you die, we will die with you."

"Well." Boots smiled. "I wasn't expecting this. You have no obligation to help us. This is our fight. It's not your fight."

"It is our fight," the elder insisted. "Today we make this our fight."

"Then we shall fight together," Boots agreed. "Do you have rifles?"

"We have three good rifles, and we have bow, arrow, tomahawk, knife, and good horses." The elder turned to the others, and in their language he explained what he wanted to do.

To their huts some of the Nacodochito men ran, others ran to the corral and placed bridals on their horses. Mounting up, they assembled, and Molly counted fourteen armed Nacodochito braves in all.

Boots climbed again up on his horse, turned to Molly, and said, "I think our chances of surviving today and getting Nomusha back just got a lot better. It's good to have friends in places like this, isn't it?"

The elder Nacodochito rode up and joined Boots and Molly, and motioned his braves into two columns as they clopped down the Coushatta Trace. On his head the elder had placed a war bonnet, a colorful, beaded headband circled with duck feathers, like a king's crown. From the rear of the bonnet dangled a train of feathers down his back, and in his hand he carried a spear decorated with tassels and feathers.

Underway south toward Fort Teran, Molly asked Boots, "What do we do next?"

"We need to find out where they are. And, we have to do it without giving ourselves away. They could be at Fort Teran, or they might be at that campsite we were looking at the other day, or they might have left and went somewhere else, Bevil maybe."

The sun had peaked and began its downward slope toward the western treetops when they approached Fort Teran. The elder raised his spear and everyone halted. After he instructed one of his braves, he turned to Boots and said, "This one will go to Fort Teran to buy whiskey. They will expect this from him, because his is Nacodochito. He will look for white men who ride with black child. When he returns, he will tell us what he sees. We will wait for him." Into a nearby thicket the elder led them.

When she had dismounted, Molly leaned against a tree exhausted and had just dozed off when the brave returned. At length the elder talked with him and then to Boots he said, "Brave says white men buy food and whisky for camp. I know this camp. It is not far from here."

"We could wade up Shawnee Creek and take them by surprise," Molly suggested.

"I know this Shawnee Creek," the elder recalled. "This is good plan." Nodding, he glanced around and spoke with his braves in their language. Then to Molly and Boots he said, "We go to Shawnee Creek. I will send some braves on road and we will wait for them." The elder made a circular gesture with his spear, explaining, "We will surround the white man's camp. When you hear the call of the grackle, braves will come from the road. Then we kill the white men. We kill white chief named Earl, who steal our hides and kill our brave. Black child, he is for you."

In a single line they walked out from the thicket, spread about ten paces apart, and quiet as mice. Five or six hundred paces took them to the Neches River, where they waded downstream to Shawnee Creek, then up the creek toward the freebooter's camp. The banks hid them, and the trickle of shallow water on exposed stones masked the sound of their approach. Twilight had settled over the forest as the campsite came into view. The elder raised his spear. Everyone spread out into the woods and waited for the call of the grackle.

From where she hid Molly could see many more freebooters than she expected. Two of them stood in the road beyond the campfire with rifles, and beyond them she could see a wagon beside the road. Around the campfire most of the freebooters were seated. Some were standing. In their hands they held mugs, and they were drinking from them and laughing. The fire gleamed from their faces and glinted from their teeth as the night surrounded them.

Another stood closer to the fire than the others. Tossing back his head he laughed the hardest, and he wore a fine, ruffled white shirt. Shadowy pock scars marked his face. Molly hadn't seen him before but knew who he was. It was John A. Murrell himself, the one the elder mistakenly called Earl, the most nefarious freebooter of them all. Even if the others could manage to escape, he had to be taken. She wanted to shoot him right then, but waited for the call of the grackle. The sound jolted her, such a dreadful sound coming from the elder, like the shucking of corn and the cocking of a rifle both at the same time.

CPSIA information can be obtained at www.ICGtesting.com
Printed in the USA
BVOW03s1104240713

326734BV00002B/3/P

9 781939 927408